ANIMAL ATTRACTION

THE ELLER SERIES

KATHRYN HALBERG

Supervising Editor: Stephanie Marrie
Associate Editors: Alexandria Boykin, Jaret Czajkowski, Erika Skorstad,
Viviana Moreno
Cover Designer: L. Austen Johnson, www.allaboutbookcovers.com

ISBN (ebook): 978-1-952919-35-0
ISBN (paperback): 978-1-952919-36-7

www.GenZPublishing.org | Aberdeen, NJ

CONTENTS

1

———

"*O*live! Put. It. Down!"

Smothering a frustrated grunt, Rachael stalked across the bright bedroom in stealth mode. Easing her outstretched arm toward the miscreant, prepared to lunge, she caught nothing but drifting dust particles as Olive slipped away again at the last second. *What had gotten into her?*

"I do not have time for this!" she vented, glaring at Olive's dancing figure.

His eyes tracking their movements, Martini lounged on the bed with the casual grace of a bored aristocrat.

"You're a good boy, Martini," Rachael crooned. Swiveling his head, he grinned with pure elation, tiny pink tongue lolling out the corner of his mouth.

Turning back to Olive, she threw her hands in the air and seized the emergency stash from the bookshelf. "Olive. Want a yum yum?"

Interest piqued, Olive froze with her head cocked to the side.

"That's right," Rachael purred. "Come get your treatsie."

The little minx inched closer until she determined it was the real deal. She sat down and whipped her short tail back and forth, finally dropping the shoe. Rachael snagged it and tossed Olive the treat simultaneously, one of the least thrilling ransom swaps of all time.

"Spoiled girl," she muttered, tossing another treat to Olive's brother Martini before assessing the leather pump to make sure it wasn't damaged. Rachael could just imagine attempting a massive pitch while tiny punctured leather bites tickled her heel.

Other people Rachael's age were getting married and having kids. Yet here she was, squatting in the guest bedroom of her parents' house—as temporarily as possible —and raising a recently adopted pair of rambunctious furballs. Nary a man in sight, let alone a dream of the pitter-patter of chubby feet. Which was fine. She had other things to focus on.

Like nailing this client.

"Okay you two," she snapped them to attention. "Out!"

They chased each other through the open door, leaving her remarkably short on time to finish getting ready.

"Rachael!"

Seriously?! What could they possibly be doing already?

Five more minutes. That's all she needed. Her face was done; she just had to pull out these curlers. Rachael ignored her dad's increasingly agitated expletives and focused on her hair. Four minutes.

"Rachael Eller!"

Damn. The next curler was tangled in her hair. Cursing

as she ripped a few strands clear, she stuck her head out the door. "Yes?" she shouted innocently before racing back to the mirror to assess the damage and pull out the next curler.

"Your dogs!"

Three minutes. Her eyes watered as she yanked out the last two and flipped her head over, spraying and fluffing the golden-blonde tresses. Upright, she reviewed and primped, correcting the flowing fall of curls over her dark fitted jacket. There! And with two minutes to spare.

Pulling the door closed behind her—no sense leaving temptation available to Olive—Rachael stomped down the stairs. "What about them?"

Dad pointed to the kitchen.

Oh.

Milk was puddled on the ceramic tiles, and both dogs lapped at it excitedly. Martini's head nudged the now-empty cup as he stretched to reach a fresh patch of white.

"How did that happen?"

"They knocked over the side table."

She ran into the kitchen, shooing them out the door to the fenced yard. At least they could go wreak havoc in peace.

"Who the hell was drinking milk?"

Silence greeted her.

"Sorry," she muttered.

Dad watched her dab at the mess before shaking his head and reaching into the pantry for the mop. "We're out of coffee creamer. And now we're out of milk." He spritzed some cleaner and removed the last traces of dairy.

Shit. "Thanks," Rachael mumbled.

3

As he settled down with his coffee and wall of newspaper, he bent the pages over and eyed her tailored outfit and glossy heels. "You have McAllister today, right?"

Nodding, she washed her hands and tossed away the mess of paper towels. "At nine o'clock."

"You've studied the dossier, the decision-makers?"

"Mhm."

"Which line are you planning?"

She didn't even hesitate. "The digital comms package and the content management system."

He looked through her and she could practically hear the wheels whirling. Their family business had become a billion-dollar global leader in marketing, communications, and innovative technology because of those wheels of his. He was known around the world as "The Great Charles Eller." But to Rachael, he was just her attentive and inventive dad. Resisting the urge to tap her foot, she waited.

"Focus on their growing overseas markets and how this will help them launch faster and with fewer barriers," Charles said.

"I will."

He still didn't look satisfied. "And don't forget about the early access to the segmentation platform your sister is building."

"I won't. Please stop worrying; I've got this." Rachael smiled at his nervous expression.

"I know you do. You'll knock 'em dead."

"You keep cranking out the goods and I'll get the buyers lined up," she teased. She checked the time. If she left now, she'd have time to grab some caffeine on the way. "Will you let them in before you leave?"

He eyed the back door with a grimace. "Of course."

Pressing a quick kiss to his cheek, she grabbed her leather shoulder bag with the EHL Global embossed logo and ran out to the car. "See you at dinner!"

Now to deal with Gabe.

～

"Rachael Eller, EHL Global," she greeted the receptionist. "I have a nine o'clock."

The young brunette eyed her over the sleek computer screen. "Please have a seat."

Rachael nodded to the faintly smiling woman, glad to step away from the overly perfumed desk area. Like Charlie Brown and Snoopy's cartoon friend who was perpetually surrounded by a cloud of dust and dirt, this receptionist wore a swirling, invisible ball of fragrance. Crossing her ankles beneath her seat on the low sofa in the waiting room, Rachael inhaled fresh air and mentally reviewed her presentation.

Calm down, girl. This should be easy. You've sold this product line hundreds of times.

But not with him in the room.

She had booked this meeting two weeks ago when everything was still normal. He was just another prospective client, albeit a rather famous headline maker. She was a polite and perfectly persistent rep. No history. Nothing to be embarrassed about. Nothing to wonder about.

"Ms. Eller? Right this way, please."

Pasting on her sugar-sweet smile, Rachael stepped into the woman's perfumed wake. Rachael wore four-inch heels, while the receptionist wore kitten heels but still towered over her. Rachael admired tall women who wore heels. She kept telling her sister to give them a whirl, but Carlie only pulled out the pumps when attending unavoidable business functions. What Rachael wouldn't give to have that height, those forever legs. Instead, she was genetically hand-me-downed Mom's petite stature. Not that she had anything to complain about, but it sure would be nice to not have to look up at everyone all the time. In the business world, people equated height with power. Sadly, she didn't have that tool in her arsenal, so she had to rely on her wit, prowess, and charm.

The gatekeeper led her down a blindingly bright hallway, her shoes and Rachael's echoing on the sterile white tile floor. *Click-click, clack-clack, click-click, clack-clack.* They passed several occupied offices with frosted glass walls before the receptionist opened a heavy glass door, ushering her in. After the receptionist closed the conference room door, a muffled, solitary set of *click-clacks* resumed and faded away.

The three men in the room rose to their feet and she marched forward, exchanging a firm handshake with each before urging them to sit. Rachael turned to the other woman in the room and smiled, offering her hand. She shook it as well, watching Rachael with open interest.

The woman was Calista McAllister, sister of Gabe. Both were strikingly tall and frequently graced magazine and tabloid covers, the public never tiring of their long black hair, pale blue eyes, and string of celebrity romances. While Gabe had a reputation to make fathers hide their daughters, Calista was an unknown quotient. The two siblings flanked the other gentlemen, the core of McAllister Corp.

Rachael addressed the CEO, Bruce McAllister, looking

straight into his blue eyes, so similar to those of his children. His was the only opinion that would drive this negotiation. "Good morning and thank you for agreeing to see me."

"Ms. Eller, this is purely preliminary," came a dry voice, raspy with condescension.

Ah, yes. Ivan Stoneworth, Esquire.

He tapped his slightly long, manicured fingernails on the table, one at a time, before leaning forward to scan the other two gentlemen in the room.

"I have yet to see why this meeting is necessary," he continued, looking down his nose at Gabe.

Smiling pleasantly at the archaic, sour-faced lawyer, Rachael nodded in ready agreement. "I agree, Mr. Stoneworth. This is absolutely just an introduction. I wouldn't dare come in here and presume to know about your current business models and practices, including your existing outdated model of client and prospect management. Nor would I come prepared with plans to help you double your nineteen percent yield and smooth the way for your tactical forays into Germany and Sweden."

She caught Gabe's smirk and Calista coughed lightly into her hand, but Rachael's gaze remained focused on the lawyer and CEO.

"Let her speak, Ivan," grumbled Bruce, eyes narrowed as he seized on the audacious projections.

Smothering her smug reaction, Rachael appropriated the floor and settled into executive pitch mode, smiling and cajoling, parrying in time to their questions; two steps forward, then one strategical step backward. She kept the dancing duel moving toward the ultimate goal.

They felt it was their own decision.

They never had a chance.

Leaving a folder with an outline of EHL Global's services and a customized plan for their corporate implementation and rollout, Rachael smiled warmly at each of them, even the curmudgeon.

"Thank you again for your time today," she closed. "I look forward to partnering with you on this transition."

"I'll escort you out." Gabe rose, gliding around the table to hold the door open.

"Thank you," she said calmly while her heartbeat accelerated.

They didn't speak while traversing the cold white hallway and continuing out the front door. "Which one?" he asked, gesturing to the cars.

She pointed to her black Lexus, and he leaned casually against the driver door.

"You didn't call," Gabe stated.

His tall, powerful body lounged deceptively at ease against the car, long muscular arms crossed across his chest. Rachael couldn't read his guarded expression. His lips were pressed together, his gaze hooded. She knew if she asked, he would stand aside and let her escape. Yet, her curiosity reared its head.

"Were you expecting me to?"

Gabe's brow furrowed and he dropped his arms, hooking his thumbs into the pockets of his Armani pants. "Well, after we . . ."

Swallowing, she waved away his words and shook her head. "Stop. We were both drunk and I sincerely doubt you were looking for a relationship."

"Maybe I wasn't expecting to want one."

Oh, brother.

"You think one fun, messed up romp in the private room of a bar is the start of something? Something the headlines repeatedly scream that you don't want?"

He shook his head, long black hair sliding off his broad shoulders.

No wonder they call him The Playboy.

Her face heated as she recalled how well he played.

His pale blue eyes traveled over her from head to toe, and he smiled seductively at her marked discomfort. "Have dinner with me."

It wasn't even a question. So arrogant.

Stay cool, Rach.

Until the ink was dry on the contract, she couldn't mess this up.

"When were you thinking?"

Grinning broadly, his perfect white teeth sparkled in the sunlight over the dimple in his chin. "Tonight?"

Rachael made a show of pretending to think it over. "Oh, shoot. I can't. Have a family thing."

"Friday?"

"Busy."

"Saturday," he deadpanned, sensing the trend.

"Plans with my sister."

"Tell you what." He smirked. "You tell me when you're free."

"Lunch tomorrow?" Lunch was good; lunch was safe. It rarely involved drinking or inappropriate behavior. Like hooking up with your prospective client. Yeesh.

"Tomorrow then. I'll pick you up at the EHL entrance."

Gabe raised to his full height and pressed a kiss to her cheek. "Until tomorrow," he added with a delicious smile before strolling back to the building's entrance. As much as she didn't want to, she couldn't help but stare after him. Lord, she could eat him up. Again.

"You did good in there, Miss Eller," he said over his shoulder as he disappeared into the steel-and-glass tower.

2

*J*une was Rachael's favorite time of year in Cincinnati. The trees were full, the grass green, the Reds were hitting homers at Great American, and festivals frequently lined the riverfront. So often, their coastal clients and international bigwigs teased her parents about their choice to remain in Ohio. They didn't get it. They couldn't understand. The communities, microbreweries, restaurants, parks, museums, zoo. So much to do. The only thing she wasn't wild about was sitting in traffic. But she'd still take the traffic here over that of most other cities.

As she idled on the interstate waiting for the cars to start moving again, Rachael considered Gabe. He was unbelievably dazzling, with a strong, chiseled face full of sharp angles, straight black brows, and that decadent silky black hair. And when he looked at you with those all-too-knowing ice-blue eyes . . . She shook the shiver away. Those eyes were what got her in trouble in the first place. They met at a networking event last month and he was receptive to arranging this meeting—a huge get for Rachael. When they bumped into each other a little over a week ago at the bar, he bought her a drink to further discuss things. And that started a crazy evening that she wished she could forget, but still haunted her at night.

Surely another notch in his decorated belt. Ugh.

And now he wanted to wine and dine her? Rachael congratulated herself on coming up with the lunch plan. She simply needed to figure out how to keep things professional. Easy. No problem.

Her phone vibrated and she glanced at the text notification.

Security deposit processed. All the best to you and the dogs, Rachael.

The old landlord. At least he wasn't penalizing her for unexpectedly bringing dogs into the condo. When she found Martini and Olive in the animal shelter, she fell in love. They were too sweet. Smallish, mixed-breed brother and sister, definitely some terrier and maybe Shih Tzu? Since they were well past their puppy days, everyone doubted they would get adopted together. The thought of them being separated was too depressing to consider. Unfortunately, bringing them home meant her zero-pets-allowed residence was in jeopardy. After two volunteer shifts, she decided they mattered more than a rental. Rachael's mother thought she was insane. But it didn't matter. Thankfully, her heretofore empty-nester parents hadn't commented much on having their adult daughter and mischievous dogs move in. Though they would all breathe easier when she found a new pet-friendly place. Especially after this morning's fiasco.

The traffic started chugging along, and she turned

down the exit toward their offices. The big EHL Global logo sat atop the high, shimmering building. Dad's crowning achievement. Around the time Rachael was born, he started Eller Communications. He did all the programming and legwork; Mom did all the contracts in the evenings when she returned home from the court-room. When her sister Carlie came along, they decided to take the leap and grow, committing fully to the next wave of integrated communications, emerging technology, marketing, media, and strategic planning. Dad built it; Mom protected and expanded. Then they brought on partners Brian Henderson, CFO, and Brian Lyles, COO, collectively known as "the Brians," who rounded out the C-suite. Henderson was a quiet financial genius and Lyles was an affable charmer who could motivate anyone to do anything, from working with purpose to taking out the trash. Thus, EHL Global was born. And the rest was busi-ness history.

The security guard waved Rachael into the parking lot. She pulled into her reserved spot and sat for a few moments, rejuvenating herself before heading up to the office. Glancing in the rearview, she brushed at her eyeliner, smudging it a bit around her bright blue eyes. Carlie might have gotten all the height, but Rachael got Mom's elfin California blonde looks. After applying a quick touchup to her lipstick, she closed her eyes and took a deep breath. Big presentations leeched the energy out of her, but the results were worth the effort. She was the top sales executive for EHL, grossing more than the other sales team members combined. Not a bad achievement to hit before thirty.

Dropping her bag on the desk, Rachael slid the McAllister Corp magnet over to the pending column. This was going to move to closed. She would make it happen.

"I thought I heard you come in."

"Mom," she acknowledged, pulling her laptop from the leather bag.

Mary Eller smiled expectantly at the project board. "I knew it would go well."

"It was good. The intel on Stoneworth was on point, and the three McAllisters were very open to the pitch," Rachael confirmed.

She nodded. "I pulled in a few favors to get their backgrounds and profiles compiled in time. Next time, maybe give us a little more of a heads up?"

"Sure. But you know how it is. When the opportunity presents itself . . . irons and fire and all that."

Her mother rolled her eyes and pointed to the desk. "Contracts for the other deals. I need you to review them and compare with the changes the clients requested. You'll also find some additional details on rentals in the area that are dog-friendly."

Smooth, Mom. Guess she was anxious to get rid of the dogs. Rachael was equally as eager to get her own space again. It's not exactly a walk in the park moving in with your parents after more than five years on your own.

"Thanks."

Her mother stood in the doorway for a moment, before adding, "Don't let Gabe McAllister get to you too much."

Rachael was supremely grateful she wasn't facing her when she said that.

How did she do that? She's like a freaking spy.

"I won't."

"Good. See you tonight."

MARTINI LICKED Rachael's nose while Olive climbed over her arm to bury her muzzle under her chin. She snapped a selfie with them for Instagram, then rolled over, hopping up onto her knees. "Okay, you two. Let's go outside."

They slipped into the backyard, thankful for the escape. Dad was cooking up a storm and Mom was lecturing Carlie about her boyfriend Brent, who was once again a no-show for dinner. They were going on four years together, and Carlie had recently finished grad school. "You need a little time to breathe, adjust to living together before you go pushing for a ring."

Classic Mom. Other parents might be concerned about their twenty-three-year-old daughter living in sin. But Mom was pragmatic. Marriage equals contracts, risks. Or maybe she had other reasons. Who knew?

Considering Rachael's longest relationship was all of six weeks, she had nothing to add there. That's the thing with being the daughter of "The Great Charles Eller"—it was awfully hard to find a date. Carlie was lucky she met someone in college. Rachael was not wild about her sister's choice in men, but that was her decision. The men Rachael had met in college, well, she wasn't wild about them either. Every time she met someone with potential, it rapidly devolved into a game of twenty questions within the hour, asking about Dad's career, technology, media holdings, connections, and openings. After enough years of that, Rachael realized relationships weren't worth the effort. Someday she might meet someone who would change her mind, but she wasn't going to hold her breath.

Life was infinitely better since she had decided to put her heart's efforts into her work.

Besides, now that she had Martini and Olive in her life, every day was full of snuggles and kisses. And neither of them pressed her for introductions to her dad. Rachael ran around in the grass with the dogs chasing her. *Definitely need a place with a good-sized yard*, she added to her mental checklist.

"Rach! Come eat!"

Nodding at her sister, Rachael threw two tennis balls in different directions, sending the dogs off to their own playtime.

"Tell me about the McAllisters," Carlie demanded as soon as Rachael crossed the patio door's threshold into the kitchen. The rich scents of fajita night assailed their nostrils. Rachael's stomach growled with hunger.

"What do you want to know?" Rachael asked, pausing by the kitchen counter, not wanting to bring this conversation into the dining room.

"Was *The Playboy* there?"

Laughing at her sister's hopeful expression, Rachael teased her, "Why? Did something happen with you and Brent?"

She blushed. "No, but is he as hot as they say?"

"I guess so."

"You guess so? He is or he isn't."

"I swear to God, Car, if you start talking like Yoda, this conversation is over."

She grinned down at Rachael, her fingers curled up into claws next to her shoulders. "There is no try."

"*That* is your Yoda impression? Sounds more like Kermit the Frog," she laughed.

Carlie cracked up and they joined their parents in the dining room.

"I told him I'd meet him for lunch tomorrow," Rachael said under her breath.

"You what?!" Carlie screeched.

Mom and Dad froze and everyone stared at her. Rachael counted to ten before continuing. "I'm meeting Gabe McAllister for lunch tomorrow."

Dad raised a brow at Mom, and she shook her head subtly. Carlie was working her jaw, and Rachael braced herself, waiting for the fireworks.

"Rach, this guy . . . he's got a reputation," she stammered.

Rachael didn't respond.

"Like, a *real* reputation," Carlie emphasized.

Silently, Rachael waited.

Frustrated, Carlie grunted and waved her hands in the air. "He's the personification of a dine and dash, Rach. Bad news."

Dad shushed her sister. "Carlie-Q, that's enough. We can't always trust the stories in the tabloids, most are fabricated. But Rachael, please be careful. Some reputations are deserved."

Mom said nothing, watching her daughter with a carefully neutral expression.

Sliding her chair in, Rachael rolled her eyes and tried to reassure them. "It's just lunch, you guys."

They didn't need to know that she and Gabe had already . . . dined. And as for dashing, Rachael was coming to believe that reputation was not one hundred percent accurate. Maybe.

The conversation blissfully dropped, and Carlie and Dad started into shoptalk as they loaded up their tortillas. Rachael smiled fondly at their bent heads, probably solving complex algorithms. Those two were so much alike, both tech nerds of the highest magnitude. Mom was picking at the grilled onions and peppers on her plate, eyes repeatedly drawn toward her office, obviously itching to get back to work. Rachael could relate.

Isolation at a family dinner, she thought to herself. Rachael didn't mind being alone. At least the food was better than the takeout she had been living on at the condo.

3

———

*S*taring at her closet, Rachael stressed over what to wear. How to dress for a lunch date with someone you've already been intimate with, but also knew very little about? She closed her eyes and indulged in a moment of memories from that evening. Their conversation—and the liquor—had flowed freely. When Gabe intercepted her outside the restroom and invited her to a quiet back room, she didn't even hesitate. It was extremely out of character for her, but the pleasure was also extreme. Sighing, she resumed contemplating the wardrobe conundrum.

Settling on a cream skirt and matching silk top with a lightweight dark-red blazer, she examined her reflection. The red and cream did great things for her warm complexion and blonde hair. Working in sales, you quickly learned to identify the items that made you look stronger, more powerful, more appealing. She took stock of her shoes and snagged a tall pair of cream pumps that would allow her to get a few inches closer in height. One last look in the mirror and she adjusted her curls, smudged her eyeliner. Perfect. Her wide, blue eyes stared back and she took a deep breath, smiling to make sure she didn't have any lipstick on her teeth. Nodding in satisfaction, Rachael finished her morning routine and went to work.

The hours crept by at the office, and she found herself re-reading the same contracts multiple times. At eleven thirty, she gave up the pretense and flipped open her web browser, snooping on the life of Gabe McAllister. By thirty-one years of age, he had accumulated a mass of horsepower, a drool-worthy collection of luxury sports cars. Gabe was also known for his love of high fashion, good drinks, and attractive women. The lengthy list of models and A-listers he had been associated with was more than a little intimidating. Almost as an afterthought, a singular listing referenced his work for his dad's company, excelling in business acquisitions and product expansion. At least they had that last part in common, working for the family business. Though her work was more than an afterthought.

"Knock, knock," said a deep voice. Rachael jumped and quickly closed her laptop. Gabe stood in the doorway, lounging against the frame.

"Hi," she chirped, startled.

"Hope you don't mind, but that nice young woman out front agreed that I could surprise you," he said, blinking his cool-blue eyes.

I'll bet she did.

"May I?" he asked, gesturing to her office.

"Sure. Come in." She gave her most polite smile. Perhaps she could pretend this was nothing more than a business meeting. No problem. Drawing on her years of salesmanship and managing people and opportunities, Rachael blanked her expression and put on her big-girl panties.

He remained standing, trailing his palm along the back of the chair across from her. Rachael watched those long fingers slide back and forth. Fascinated, she recalled what else Gabe could do with those fingers. And about those panties . . .

Stop it, Rachael!

She tore her eyes from his hands and let her gaze travel to his face. His long, dark hair was pulled back in a low ponytail, and his smile was downright scandalous. Gabe knew exactly what he was doing. And he did it well.

Giving herself a mental shake, Rachael rose and collected her purse. "Shall we?"

He looked her up and down, male appreciation lighting his face. He nodded and stepped back. "After you."

They walked to the elevator and Rachael tried to ignore the stares coming from the neighboring offices and cubicles. She also tried to ignore the nervous energy coursing through her. Clearing her throat, she asked, "Any trouble finding us?"

He chuckled, the rich sound tickling her insides. "No. Anyone around here knows how to find the EHL building."

Mental facepalm. Of course. They waited for the elevator and Rachael was reminded of just how large he was. The top of her head barely reached his shoulder. In heels. Thank God she wore the heels.

"Where are we going?"

"You'll see," he said cryptically.

On the ground floor, he waved to the receptionist, who

was literally drooling at the sight of him. Tempted to hand the woman a tissue, Rachael stalked past her, annoyed that she went completely unseen as they exited into the sunshine.

"Here we are," he said, opening the door of a sleek black Audi. Sliding into the creamy leather seat, she examined the interior. Pure elegant luxury.

"Nice car."

"Thanks. She's one of my favorites."

She. Why do men always call their cars "she" and give them female names? Rachael smirked as she debated what he named this car. Lolita? Marilyn? The engine purred as they pulled into the street. Rachael glanced at his profile, but he didn't look her way. Turning her attention to the passing city blocks, she reevaluated the decision to meet for lunch. Admittedly, he was dreamy to look at and he was unquestionably deserving of his reputation with women. Was she interested in him romantically? Stealing another peek at him from the corner of her eye, Rachael measured his appeal. Sex? Yes. Emotional connection? She couldn't see that happening. She sighed and reminded herself of the contract.

They stopped outside a swanky sushi bar. She hadn't been there yet but had heard good things about it. Not a total loss of a lunch meeting.

"Ah, Mr. McAllister, welcome back," the host groveled. He not-so-discreetly looked her up and down before turning back to Gabe. "Table for two? The usual?"

Rachael's pride pushed her eyebrows sky-high, but she refrained from commenting.

Gabe nodded and they were shown to a curved booth in the back of the restaurant. The tabletop was a high-gloss white, unmarked by scars or stains. The black floors, black booths, and other black accents made the white that much more jarring. It created the illusion that the tables were floating in space. No other diners were nearby, at least none she could see.

The waiter delivered a bottle of wine and Gabe poured generous portions.

Guess it's going to be that kind of lunch.

"Tell me more about you, Rachael," he said, picking up his glass by the stem, watching her with a lazy, half-lidded gaze.

"What do you want to know?"

"What do you do outside of work?"

She took a sip of the aromatic wine. "My work is pretty all-consuming. I adopted two dogs not long ago, so they occupy much of my time of late."

"What else?"

She pursed her lips. "I'm close with my family, especially my sister, Carlie, and our friend Kim. And when they're not tied up with their kids or work stuff, I enjoy an occasional night out with some of my girlfriends."

Gabe cringed. "Everyone seems to be popping out kids left and right these days."

Unimpressed by his reaction, she turned the tables. "And you?"

"I don't have kids," he said, displaying a charming half-smile and teasing a laugh from her.

"What do you do outside of work?"

He considered the question and took a drink of his wine. "I enjoy life."

"What does that mean?"

He set down his glass and picked up her hand, turning

it over in his own. He trailed a fingertip along her palm and she suppressed an echoing shiver. "I mean I enjoy the touch of life." Gabe lifted her hand to his face and inhaled. "The smell of life." He pressed his mouth to her hand and traced his tongue along the faint lines there. "The taste of life."

Rachael picked up her glass and took a fortifying drink. *Contract, contract, contract . . .*

He smiled seductively and released her hand. "You like sushi?"

Another rapid change, but she went with it. "Sushi? Sure."

They picked their way through lunch, enjoying a variety of fresh rolls on beautiful geometric plates, also glowingly white. She nursed her wine, attempting to keep her thoughts clear.

"Are you afraid of me?" he asked.

The question came out of nowhere. Puzzled, Rachael put down her chopsticks. His gaze was steady and intent.

"Am *I* afraid of *you*?"

He nodded.

That's absurd. "I don't think so. Should I be?"

He hummed. "No. But you seem to withdraw every time I ask you a personal question."

"Do I?" She was puzzled by this observation.

He nodded again. "You have been slowly inching away from me."

"Have I?"

He reached across her lap, hooking a hand around her hip to slide her closer to his side.

"Enough that I worry that if I try to do this," he placed a soft kiss on her lips, "you might push me away."

Rachael stared, baffled at this . . . this . . . game. She recalled how much more relaxed and conversational he had been that night at the bar. He was charming and seductive, but also unfailingly polite, respectful, and direct. This college-boy behavior was a whole different Gabe.

"I'm not afraid of you, Gabe," she glared, placing her palms flat on the white tabletop. "But I don't trust you. Why are you here? With me? And please, drop the pathetic schmoozing act."

He blinked, sitting upright.

"For God's sake," she continued. "If you had behaved this way the last time we met, there's not a chance in hell we would have continued beyond the first line. What do you want? Why are we here?"

Contract, Rachael. Damn. But she couldn't sit there and listen to this any longer.

Frowning, he toyed with the stem of his glass. "I want to get to know you better. I'm intrigued by you."

Ha!

Her lips twitched. "Really. I don't believe that's what *this* is," she gestured around them. "If I *had* called you, you'd have moved on already to the next girl. You're not used to someone not falling head over heels for you, are you? And it's *eating. You. Up.*"

If she wasn't the object of his desire, if this was happening to someone else, the whole situation would have been laughable.

He gazed into her eyes, trying again. "I don't know what you're talking about."

Rachael laughed, rolling her eyes at the act. "Oh, please. Stop batting those gorgeous blue eyes at me, hoping I'll drop my panties for you." Again. "No wonder they call you The Playboy. Grow up."

Frustration flickered across his face. "Is that all you think I'm after?"

"Put yourself in my position. What would you think?"

He stared at her dumbly, then tilted his head back and roared with laughter. A waiter froze midstep, astonished, before he remembered his place and fled the scene.

Rachael glared at Gabe. *He's lost his damn mind.*

Not one to tolerate foolishness or play the wilting flower, she slid away, scooting across the booth's curved leather seat to leave. He held up his hand. "Wait! Wait, please," he gasped, trying to catch his breath. "I'm sorry. I really am," he squeezed out between his laughter. "Please, I'm not laughing at you. This is—this is entirely self-directed," he continued, pressing a hand to his chest and trying to regain control of himself. "I'm such an ass. Can we start over? Please?"

At least we could agree on that.

She pushed the wine glass away and faced him. "What, exactly, is happening here?"

He was quiet for a moment before slumping against the seat. "Look, I know you think I'm crazy, and I probably am. But the truth is, I was nervous. This was me trying to impress you. It backfired."

"And now?"

"And now, let's start over." He held his hand out for a handshake, of all things. "Please?"

Sighing, she slid back into the booth and eyeballed his hand before shaking it. "I must be nuts to stay here. You'd better be worth this."

"I am." He smiled.

Rachael quirked a brow at him. "You sound pretty confident for a guy who just struck out over sushi and wine."

"You can't blame me. I don't do this often."

"Do what?"

"Go on a date. With someone I might actually like."

"Who said this was a date?" she murmured, watching him squirm.

"Touché." He lifted his chin, an appreciative grin curving his mouth, then waved a hand dismissively. "Lunch, a date, call it what you will."

She took a sip of water and weighed the risk she was assuming, both to herself and to her career. "If you can show me the real you and not some crazy, pawing creature, I'm willing to give this one shot. One. I'm serious. One more cringeworthy line or juvenile prank and I'm out. Deal?"

"Deal."

Turned out he was a pretty normal guy when he wasn't being an egotistical frat boy. They shared the last of the sushi while he talked about how his family ended up in Cincinnati.

"You don't miss California?"

"Of course I do. I still travel a lot, but now that we've been here a couple of years, the area's grown on me."

"Soon you'll be cheering for the Buckeyes and telling everyone the Wright brothers did it here first."

"The Wright brothers?"

"Never mind, you'll eventually get it. Or not," she shrugged.

He laughed and turned his phone face up, bringing them back to reality. "This has been fun, Rachael."

Shockingly, she couldn't disagree. "I have to get back to my office," she replied.

He nodded. "Me too."

Rachael made him let her pay for part of the check before they returned to the car. "I hear you have quite the collection."

Petting the top of his Audi, Gabe smiled fondly at the black coupe. "I confess: I like pretty, fast things."

Hold up. Was he referring to more than cars? Did he think she made a habit of one-night stands?

He held open the car door and she slid in, trying to decide if she should address it. After the awkwardness at the start of lunch, she wasn't eager to return to it. Yet . . .

Damn it. Might as well get it out of the way. "About the other night," Rachael started, watching him buckle up. "I don't normally do that. I mean, like, I *never* do that."

He grinned, a dimple returning to his chin. "I know."

Huh? "You know? What do you know?"

He started the car and stared ahead. "You're not the only one who knows how to research a prospect, Miss Eller."

Crossing her arms over her chest, she leaned back into her seat and mulled that over. "And what did you learn about me?"

"For starters, you can sell anything to anyone. Your record is unparalleled. You're a natural. I wasn't lying when I said you did a good job in the presentation. Man, I'd pay to watch you put Stoneworth in his place again."

Laughing, Rachael nodded and shrugged. "What else?"

"Aside from your family, work, a small circle of friends, and a few very short-lived relationships, you're pretty isolated. Though I do know, ahem, that you're passionate and not opposed to physical connections."

Her face must have been as red as her jacket. "You found that through your research?"

"Some of it took a little personal research. Very personal." Gabe had the decency to not look at her as he won that point.

Flustered, she remained quiet as they pulled up in front of EHL, her home away from home. When she had her own home, that was.

"But I also recently discovered something else."

"What's that?"

"You're as boldly fascinating as you are beautiful, and a person I'd very much like to know better."

She searched his clear eyes, speechless, not seeing anything to make her believe he wasn't being truthful.

Gabe leaned over and kissed her cheek. "Can I call you?"

Rachael slowly nodded and exited the car, wondering if it was a mistake to let this go on, but how could she say no? Leaning over, she rapped on the window until he unrolled it. She flashed him a genuine smile. "Thanks for a surprising afternoon, Gabe."

He grinned hugely and drove off.

She stared after him for several minutes, replaying his last comments. This all went much worse and much better than she thought it would. But she wasn't sure if allowing him to be closer was better or worse.

4

$\mathcal{W}$orking through her contracts, Rachael kept picturing those eyes and that incredible smile. That dimple. Oddly enough, she was actually looking forward to seeing him again. She groaned as she recalled her embarrassment at his "research."

The sun was well into its downward arc in the sky when she wrapped up her work to head home. Along the way, she swung by the store and bought a bottle of wine. A glass of wine on the patio with the dogs would be the perfect way to end the day.

A note on the table said Mom and Dad were out at dinner, so she dug through the fridge for some leftovers, grabbed a corkscrew and glass, and went out to the deck. Olive was sitting on the top step, watching Martini run through the freshly cut grass. The lawn company must have come out today. She poured a glass of wine and picked at her cold plate. Both dogs ran to her feet, looking up with giant, hopeful eyes. Tearing off a bit of turkey for each, she secured their love and devotion for another day.

Rachael sipped the wine, watching the dogs lick their muzzles, happy and content. Relaxing in the chair, she thought about the lunch with Gabe. She still couldn't believe she sat through those first few minutes. That was asinine, with a capital ass. But she was glad she called him out on it. Once he shed the nauseating veneer, he went back to the charming and casual man she had met at the bar.

Could she see something coming from their spending time together? He was certainly attractive and given his family, she didn't need to worry about him being infatuated with her dad. But with that reputation, she doubted she could trust him enough to be in a real romantic relationship. God, she was being so judgmental. But this was one area where an individual had every right to be, right?

Martini sat by her foot and whined.

"Where's your ball, buddy?"

Both dogs perked up at the magic words, taking off down the stairs. They came flying back in record time with their fuzzy, well-loved tennis balls. She played tug-of-war with Martini and threw his ball out to the right side of the yard. When he scampered off, she repeated with Olive, throwing hers out to the left. Rachael watched her fluffy form fly down the stairs and around the side of the deck while Martini ran back, dropping his beloved ball at her feet.

She scratched behind his ears and simultaneously stole the ball, throwing it out to his side again. Rachael glanced over to the other side, searching for Olive. Where was she? Martini came back, and she patted his head absently, throwing the ball once more.

"Olive?" She peered over the edge of the deck and

groaned. The fence gate was open. Crap. The lawn company didn't close it before leaving. Making a mental note to tell her parents, Rachael grabbed her phone then started off into the gathering dusk to hunt for Olive, pulling the gate shut behind her.

"Where are you, girl?" She flicked on the phone's flashlight and kept walking, careful not to trip in the dark shadows. The deck extended just past the edge of the house, casting a dim light into the side yard, but not enough to avoid the tree roots and landscaping rocks. She peered into the shadows around the trees, hoping Olive was tucked in between some of the foliage.

The quiet rumble of a vehicle coming nearer reached her ears, and her eyes flew toward the road, where a pair of eyes reflected the streetlight. "Olive? Olive!" She stopped and looked toward Rachael, but didn't move.

Racing down the long driveway, Rachael saw the headlights grow brighter between the tall trees on the street as the car progressed toward them. "Olive! Come!"

Ignoring the commands, Olive remained still as a statue in the street, motionless in the face of the oncoming car.

Rachael wasn't going to make it to her in time.

Oh, God. No, no, no!

Her mind raced as her feet flew faster. What could she do to get her to move? "Olive! Come here, girl! Come! Want a treat? Come here!"

At the last second, the little dog scuttled toward her, but it was too late. It happened in slow motion. The driver didn't see her. It was too dark. She was too small. The car clipped her. Olive disappeared from view, and Rachael imagined she could hear the sound of Olive's whimper, of her tiny body being crushed by the rubber and steel. She was going to be sick.

"Olive!" Rachael gasped, running into the street. "No!"

The car continued down the road, the driver unaware of the unfolding tragedy.

No, no, no, no, no!

"Olive?" she whispered, dropping to her knees on the asphalt. "Please be okay."

Her dog didn't move. Olive was breathing, but not moving. Rachael looked in horror at the blood coming from a gash on her side and gagged.

Oh my God, oh my God, oh my God.

"Just hold tight," Rachael cried. "You're going to be just fine."

She peeled off her jacket and gingerly wrapped Olive in it, trying to press the fabric against the gaping wound. Clutching her firmly but gently, she raced back to the house to snag her car keys. "Hold on, Olive," she begged, the tears falling faster.

In the car, Rachael asked Siri for the nearest emergency vet and let her navigation dictate the way. She babbled nonsense the entire trip, softly stroking Olive's coat peeking out from the bundle in the passenger seat. The dog was warm but remained immobile. Rachael made two wrong turns and sobbed harder, convinced she was not going to get there in time.

After an eternity, she turned into the well-lit parking lot. Her elbow hit the horn as she swept Olive off the seat and ran out the door. Rachael carried her as quickly and steadily as she could, tears running unchecked down her face.

I just adopted her, how could she be dying?

This could not be happening.

Nudging the door open, Rachael rushed to the counter. "Please help! My dog got hit by a car."

The matronly woman at the desk looked up with sympathy. "Sure, honey. Just take a seat right there and I'll see if the doctor is available."

Rachael stared at her in disbelief. "Take a seat? Take a seat! My dog is dying, and you want me to take a fucking seat?!"

"Now, now, there's no need for that kind of language, young lady. Why don't you take a seat and I'll be right back with you."

Fuming, Rachael paced around the cool waiting room and felt her fear escalate into a near panic. What should she do? She peeled back the jacket from her wound, and saw the pool of blood soaked into the fabric. Olive whimpered weakly and Rachael's heart stuttered.

"Right this way." The evil receptionist had returned.

Rachael glared at the woman and stormed through the door, clutching Olive to her breast.

The veterinarian was bent over, typing notes at his computer station.

"Please, Doctor. She got hit by a car. I didn't know what to do, she's not moving," Rachael babbled on, not entirely sure what she was saying after that. Her tears increased and she swiped at her face with her shoulder, trying to clear her vision.

He turned toward her, his warm eyes full of concern. "May I take her from you? Or if you prefer, you can lay her down here." He patted the steel tabletop.

Trembling, Rachael laid Olive down and continued to

stroke her small head, touching her here and there. "You'll be all right," she whispered.

"Her name?"

"Olive," Rachael sobbed.

"How old is she?"

"Six or seven. I rescued her and her brother from the shelter a few weeks ago."

He gently unwrapped Olive, murmuring soothingly as he pulled the red jacket away from her wounds. The vet glanced at Rachael. "There's a sink in the corner there, and a sweater on the back of the door if you're cold."

She glanced down and realized all she had on was the cream skirt and somewhat sheer cream camisole. Spots of blood marred the shirt, and she had blood on her hands. Rachael shrugged his comment away, not wanting to leave Olive's side. "Is she . . . ?" She couldn't bring herself to finish the question.

"She has a couple of deep lacerations and at least one broken bone. We'll need to run a few tests and sedate her for her own comfort. Are you able to fill out some paperwork?"

Rachael nodded absently, and turned to the sink. A stack of forms on a clipboard appeared at her side as she scrubbed the blood from her knuckles and nails, the soap bubbles tinged with pink.

When she finished drying her hands, the vet took her elbow and led her to a chair in the corner.

"Thank you, Doctor . . . ?"

"Thomas. Richard Thomas. But please, call me Rick." He smiled and gave her shoulder a small squeeze before returning to Olive.

Working through the papers, she reached the end and

scrawled her signature across it, allowing the chained pen to dangle from the clipboard. The woman from the front stepped in to collect it. Remembering her outburst, Rachael flushed as she handed over the paperwork. "I'm sorry. I was out of line."

She gave her a grandmotherly smile and patted the back of Rachael's hand. "It's fine. Sometimes fear and worry make us do funny things."

The sympathetic response got her tears going again, and Rachael hunched over, weeping.

"There, there, honey," she said, wrapping an arm around Rachael. "Rick, get this young lady a tissue."

He looked up at her, perplexed. "A little busy over here, Nancy."

"Oh, pish," Nancy said, then waddled over and returned with a box of tissues and the sweater from the door. She placed the box on Rachael's lap and draped the sweater around her bare shoulders. "This sweater is going to swallow you whole, dear, but it's the only thing we've got right now."

She left and Rachael sniffed into the tissue, shuddering as she tried to catch her breath. Recalling Carlie's frequent childhood panic attacks, Rachael thought of how they had helped her deal with them over the years. Feet firmly on the floor, she closed her eyes and focused on breathing, in and out. In and out. She felt her pulse begin to calm. The warmth of the sweater was comforting, and she noted a hint of cologne. It smelled good. Soothing.

Finally coming back to herself, Rachael returned to the steel table where Olive was quiet and unmoving. She gasped, thinking the worst. Dr. Thomas—Rick—heard and quickly reassured her. "She's sleeping," he explained.

"Can I?" she stretched her shaking hand toward Olive's head and he nodded.

"Gentle," he cautioned. "We still need to clean these wounds, and she has a broken leg that will need to be set. I can patch her up, but we will need to watch for infection and see how she responds to the treatment. She'll stay here until she's stable enough to go home."

Another tear leaked out of Rachael's eye, and she felt a burst of affection for her broken girl. "You're going to be fine, Olive. I'll make sure of it."

An assistant came in and conferred with Rick. He turned and introduced her to Rachael. "This is Cora Willis, an intern and a pre-veterinary medicine senior from UC. With your permission, I'd like to allow her to clean and treat Olive's lacerations. Cora has extensive experience in this area already. I'll review her sutures and address the fractures once that is complete."

Rachael nodded and greeted Cora, a bespectacled young Black woman. "That's fine."

The future veterinarian glowed with pleasure and began cleaning and assessing Olive, talking to her patient in a low voice. Rick turned his attention to Rachael, taking in her state. "Now, Ms. . . . ?"

"Eller. Rachael Eller."

"Ms. Eller," Rick nodded, "is there someone I can call to come pick you up? I'm not certain you should be driving right now."

She shook her head. "No, I'm okay. I'm not far from here."

"I think it would be best if—"

"I said I'm okay," Rachael lashed out, unexpectedly angry.

Cora glanced their way and quickly returned her attention to Olive.

He looked like he wanted to argue, but held up his hands placatingly. "Can I at least convince you to stay for a few minutes until you are more at ease? Perhaps a snack?"

Glancing at Olive, she realized she was not ready to leave her yet. "That would be nice," she murmured. While Cora turned to collect supplies, Rachael ran her finger across the bridge of Olive's little nose, smoothing the soft and damp hairs down on either side. It was jarring to know how quickly these two little balls of fur had lodged themselves in her heart. She thought about the first time Olive had leapt up into her arms at the shelter, and how Rachael knew they would be coming home with her. To see that spritely dog now crumpled before her was heartbreaking and devastating.

Rick returned to the exam room with small bags of pretzels and cold sodas. "Vending machine snacks. I hope you don't mind."

"Not at all," she replied, plucking a can of pop and a snack out of his hands.

They settled on the chairs in the corner. Rachael angled herself so she could keep an eye on her sleeping dog while Cora tended to her.

He followed her gaze. "No need to worry. She is in excellent care. You said you adopted her recently?"

"Mhm. I volunteer at the shelter downtown when I have time. Olive and Martini—her brother—were so sweet and lovely. Everyone doubted they would get adopted together, so I had to take them home."

"It happens," he nodded, "but not nearly enough. A lot of pets out there need homes."

Rachael frowned and popped a pretzel in her mouth, chewing slowly. So many Olives and Martinis left abandoned and afraid. It made her sad.

"They are lucky you found them," he said, trying to lift her mood.

She smiled, noting his light-brown hair and wide, warm brown eyes, his classic features reminding her of Barbie's mate, Ken. A light scruff of five o'clock shadow lined his square jaw. He was younger than she originally thought— maybe mid-to-late thirties. Tall, long-limbed, and fit. He was a sight for sore eyes. Groaning inwardly, Rachael wondered what her eyes must look like now.

"Thank you for letting me use your sweater," she said, holding up her arm. They both laughed at the extra length of knitted cloth dangling from her hand.

"You're welcome." He glanced over to the countertop where her bloody blazer was balled up. "Would you like your jacket to take home?"

Cringing, she shook her head. "Please dispose of it." Rachael couldn't imagine ever wanting to wear that again. Even if the blood came out, it would be permanently stained with the pain of this evening.

He watched her for a moment then picked up a notepad and pen. "Here's the office number and my personal cell. You can call me any time you want an update on Olive."

"Thank you," she said, taking the paper and tucking it into her pocket.

"Eller . . . Any relation to Charles Eller?"

Here it comes.

"Yes, he's my dad."

Rachael glanced to see if Cora was listening, but she was engrossed in her work.

"Oh, what's that like?" Rick asked.

"Aside from our lives revolving around EHL, I suppose it's like any other family. A little more exposed to the world, I guess. Always something going on somewhere."

"I imagine you get a lot of recognition."

"A bit, but not as much as you might expect," Rachael tilted her head, lost in thought. "My parents never tried to push us onto their stage, the spotlight. While I enjoy the work, the thrill of closing the sale, I prefer a quiet, more private life, and they have always respected that."

"That's admirable."

"I think so. They never demanded that we go into the family business. Instead, they always encouraged us to be independent and self-sufficient, to pursue what we love, what we found interesting." It was true. The Ellers lived simply and worked hard. Rachael and Carlie attended public schools, went to public universities, and each made the conscious decision to join EHL. "We've put in long hours and a lot of elbow grease to get where we are today."

"Quite an accomplishment. A lot of parents could learn from that kind of philosophy."

"We're lucky. I love my life, my family, my work. I wouldn't trade it for anything."

"That is lucky," Rick agreed. "And increasingly rare today."

Rachael bit her lip, realizing she had been babbling. She was such a mess. But at least the vet didn't seem to mind. Or he was used to people falling apart in here.

They finished their pretzels and he returned to

monitor Cora's progress, complimenting her excellent work.

"I'll see you back here tomorrow?" He glanced back at Rachael. "I assume you'll want to check on her?"

She nodded and joined him, giving her sleeping Olive a quick kiss on her head. "Yes, you'll be seeing a lot of me, I imagine."

He smiled. "Until tomorrow then."

5

---

*T*he house felt oddly quiet the next morning without the second half of the Martini and Olive duo. Rachael kept her eye on the single fur baby while she pressed her phone to her ear, relaying the evening's horrible events to her sister.

"I think Martini is depressed, but I'm doing a little better."

Carlie was quiet, and Rachael knew she was managing her own worries for Olive. "I'm so sorry, Rach."

Rachael smiled at the softie that was her sister. "Thanks."

"Still on for tonight?" Carlie inquired.

"Yes, and tell Kim to be on time." Carlie's best friend was notorious for arriving late.

Carlie's laughter filled the line. "She'll be there when she gets there. See you tonight, Rach. Give the pups some love from Auntie Carlie."

Rachael ended the call and stared at Martini, lying

morosely on her foot. "My poor boy. You miss your sister, don't you?"

He lifted his head from his paws and tilted it this way and that, then lay down again with a pathetic huff. Rachael scratched the fluffy fur between his ears and planted a kiss on his head as she got up to leave her room. "You're a good boy," she whispered.

Dad was making a quiet racket, puttering about in the kitchen. She could smell coffee brewing. There were definite perks to living at home again.

"Morning, Dad," she said, grabbing a large mug. "Vanilla creamer?"

He nodded toward the fridge. "In there."

Charles Eller, the conversationalist. Rachael smiled while doctoring her coffee. Mom totally disapproved of her daughter's sweet and creamy addiction, but Rachael told her it was that or smoking. Her mother never pressed again after that. She was such a rotten daughter.

Martini scampered down from upstairs and danced at the back door. She let him out and blew on her coffee. Dad called it his morning medicine. Rachael couldn't disagree.

"Sorry to hear about Olive," he said over his coffee and newspaper.

"Thanks. I still can't believe it. But at least the people at the animal hospital seem like they know what they're doing. I'm going to go check on her later. Want to come?"

His confused eyes met hers over the paper, attempting to ferret out if she was serious. He returned his gaze to the story without answering.

Guess that's a no.

Rachael slipped out the back door and sat on a deck

chair, watching the sun dry the morning dew. Martini ran up the stairs and jumped, his paws leaving little wet marks on her gray leggings.

"Down, boy," she murmured, trying to be patient with him. *He's probably worried. What must that be like, being an animal whose partner in crime suddenly disappeared?* It's not like she could explain it to him. She tickled under his jawline, hoping it wouldn't be too long until Olive could return home.

Her phone vibrated and she checked the screen. It was Kim. *Sorry about Olive. Car told me. Need anything?*

Kim drove her batshit crazy, but she was her little sister in all but blood. A loud, annoying, perpetually late sister, but she cared. She and Carlie had been best friends since they started elementary school together, and Kim was more often at the Eller house than her own dysfunctional family home.

You're sweet for asking. I'm good for now. See you tonight?

You know it, girlfriend.

It would be good to spend some time with Carlie and Kim. It had been strange not seeing them when they were busy with college, but now that they were both settled into their new routines, they were rekindling the tight trio. Rachael did not have a big circle of friends, but those in it were critical to her life. And Carlie and Kim were at the core of the tight circle.

Removing the slip of paper from her pocket, she tapped out a new text message. *Hi. This is Rachael Eller— the nut job who accompanied the sweet dog last night. How did Olive do overnight?*

She absently wondered if he was still asleep. How late did he work? After confirming the gate was closed, she threw the ball for Martini, and mumbled to the now-inattentive pup, "Hope we didn't wake him up."

Her phone vibrated and she glanced down, expecting a response from Rick. Instead she was greeted by a sweet text from Gabe. *Thinking about you this morning. Dinner tomorrow?*

Dinner tomorrow? With Gabe? She tapped her finger on the side of the phone, wondering if it would be better to put this off until after Olive was better. And after the contracts were settled. She was prepared to push it off, when her traitorous fingers typed their own message.

Sounds good. 7?

I'll pick you up.

What was she doing? Groaning, she set the phone down and considered Mr. McAllister. Gabe was a showboat, for sure, but he was also surprisingly forthcoming and willing to admit to his faults. That was appealing. They were doing everything backward, but she had to admit she was intrigued. She still couldn't see him as a romantic partner, but he was fun and easy to talk to.

"Ready to go inside, buddy?"

Martini ran to the door and glanced back at her expectantly. She opened the patio door and followed his racing footsteps. Rachael was more than ready for breakfast and another dose or three of coffee.

"*Another* cup?" her mom asked as she swept into the kitchen, taking in the dirty dishes on the table and stovetop.

"Nerves," Rachael said, sweeping the dirties into the sink, noting her dad had left. "Olive."

Her mom poured a cup of black coffee and sat at the table. "How did it go with Gabe yesterday?"

Rachael turned to the sink and started scrubbing the dishes, careful not to give her mother any ammo. "It went well. He was kind of full of himself until I threatened to leave. Then he chilled and starting being a normal human. Or as normal as he can be."

When her mother didn't say anything, Rachael looked over her shoulder to see what the reaction was. Her bright blue eyes were staring off into space.

"Mom?"

Mary blinked and looked at her daughter. "Sorry, just thinking. He's an interesting kid."

"Mom, he's older than me."

"He's thirty-one. That's still a kid to me, kiddo."

Rachael rolled her eyes and turned back to load the dishwasher.

"Those go on the top rack, Rachael. You know that."

Immediately flashing back to being a gawky twelve-year-old, she grumbled about being an adult and needing her own place again.

Laughter came from the table. "I agree. But as long as you're here, it's still my rules."

After correcting the dishes, Rachael dropped into a chair next to her. "Mom?"

"Hmm?"

"Do you think I can trust him?"

Mary Eller tapped her fingernails on the wooden kitchen table a few times before looking up. "I know Bruce, his dad. We've known each other for years. He's decent enough, but very imposing. I don't know much about his kids, but I think as long as you are careful, there's nothing wrong with pursuing a friendship with him."

She emphasized the word friendship. Heavily.

"And if it were to ever become something more than friends?"

She stared down at her coffee before meeting her daughter's eyes. "Rachael, you are aware of his reputation. It's not flattering, especially to the women he chooses to spend time with. I believe a century or two ago, they would have called him a rake." She smirked. "The more time you spend with him, the more speculation will arise, and the more you're opening yourself up to being in the headlines. Make sure it's something you're prepared for and willing to put up with."

Rachael frowned and considered this. She didn't mind being the center of attention for brief bursts of time, but she also didn't want continual focus and for the wrong things to be said, marring her professional reputation. That would be disastrous for her career. Was that an acceptable level of risk?

Her phone vibrated from the kitchen counter. *Olive is stable. I'll be back in to check on her around 2.*

Relieved, Rachael grinned at Martini. "Your sister is stable!"

Mom rolled her eyes and left.

"Don't let her get to you. Her bark is worse than her bite," Rachael murmured to Martini, looking after her mom's retreating form.

"I heard that," she shouted.

"You were supposed to," Rachael teased back.

Thank you so much. And sorry I took off with your sweater. I'll bring it back.

No problem.

Her curiosity got the better of her. *How late do you work?*

Last night I was there til 11. I usually work day shift, but covered last night.

And you'll be back there again today?

Of course. I need to check on Olive and a couple other patients.

Won't another vet be there?

Yes, but my job isn't something I can easily walk away from. Especially when they have humans as concerned as you.

She smiled at the phone, touched to see he was going above and beyond for her little Olive. *Thank you. See you at 2?*

I'll be the tall guy in the white coat.

She laughed at his description. *Guess that makes me the short girl in the borrowed sweater.*

You wear it better than me.

Laughing again, she put the phone down. A vet with a sense of humor. Who knew?

6

⎯⎯⎯⎯

*T*he same matronly woman was behind the desk. Rachael recalled the last time she entered the building and blushed as she approached the desk. What was her name? She scanned the reception area for clues. No nameplate, no business cards, nothing to help. Well, that was frustrating. She was usually so good with names.

"Ma'am?" she finally landed on.

"No need to ma'am me. Please, dear, call me Nancy," she said, welcoming Rachael as though nothing had happened.

"Nancy." Rachael smiled. "I want to apologize again for my behavior yesterday. I am appalled that I was so rude."

She stood and gestured for Rachael to follow. "No need to keep apologizing. Completely understandable. I would have been flustered, too. Say no more about it. It's behind us now." Nancy nodded emphatically. "Now then, I think you'll be happy to see how well our little patient is doing today."

They entered a different area of the building and

Rachael saw Olive asleep on a light pad in a large, clean crate. Rachael rushed over, skimming the top of Olive's silky head with two fingertips, while noting the white cast around her dog's broken rear leg.

"She's doing well this morning," came a voice behind her.

She turned to see the handsome vet. "Dr. Thomas, I'm so glad to see you here."

"Rick," he gently corrected. He set his laptop aside and joined her at Olive's side. The dog cracked her eye open and lifted her paw halfheartedly into the air, then dropped it back on the pad and resumed her sleep.

"She's still lightly sedated," Rick explained.

"The cast?"

"We'll check it every ten days and assess. It'll be at least two weeks, could be up to six. It depends on how she heals."

Rachael watched Olive doze, reliving those horrible moments. "I'm so sorry I couldn't get to you in time," she whispered, fighting a lump in her throat.

"Miss Eller? Rachael?" he interjected quietly. "You can't hold yourself responsible for this. Accidents happen."

"That's right, honey," Nancy patted the top of her hand. "It can happen to anyone at any time. You should be pleased by how quickly you pulled yourself together and got her the help she needed."

Sniffing, Rachael gave her a smile. "My nerves have been completely on edge since then. I still can't believe this happened."

Nancy's speculative gaze measured her then turned back to Rick. "What are you planning to do the rest of the day?"

"Hmm? Today?" He set down his pen and glanced at Nancy in confusion.

She nodded to Rachael and back at him.

A flush creeped up his neck and he shook his head subtly. The older woman's giddy grin grew at his clear discomfort.

Oh, Lord.

A meddling, matchmaking receptionist?

Clad in a familiar white coat, another man entered the room. "We're all set, Rick. Get out of here and enjoy the afternoon."

"Rachael, this is Dr. Gil Brennan," Rick said. "He'll be keeping an eye on Olive for the rest of the day."

Gil shook Rachael's hand as he ushered her out to the waiting area, Rick following close behind. "Nancy, please call me if anything changes," Rick requested.

"Will do, Rick. Now, you go take that young lady out for a stiff drink. I suspect she could use one after all this stress."

Smothering her amused smile, Rachael waved goodbye and walked out to the parking lot.

"Sorry about that," he mumbled. "She's a bit of a busybody. You probably have a million other things to do today anyways."

Chuckling, she grinned up at him. "That was mildly entertaining, and no, I actually don't have anything going on today."

Shrugging, he half turned back to the door before continuing. "She's probably watching us now. Nancy is a wonderful woman, but she's pushier than a mother hen."

"And you're her chick?"

"In this case, probably." He laughed. "Until someone is

down the aisle and has said 'I do,' she views it as a personal mission. It's the first time she's been quite so blatant about it, though. I wonder what's gotten into her."

"Is it even allowed? I mean, can doctors date their patients?"

"No," he said, a twinkle in his eye. "Human and animal relations are severely frowned upon."

Choking on her laugh, she shook her head at him. "Oh my God. You know what I mean."

"We don't have any rules about it, per se, though I've never crossed that line myself. And Olive is my patient. But," he shrugged and coughed nervously, "what do you think? Have time for a quick drink? I'd hate to disappoint Nancy. Completely your call, and it won't affect Olive's care at all. I promise."

As she took in his warm, genuine smile, light flush, and comforting presence, she felt a flutter in her stomach. "Why not? For Nancy."

Driving slowly, she followed into the parking lot behind him. The butterflies were still fluttering. Rachael counseled herself to calm down.

He's being polite, Rach. Just trying to mollify Nancy. You would have done the same thing. Besides, he probably thinks you're a nut job after yesterday.

He stood by the door and waited, allowing her to enter before him. They slid onto adjacent stools at the bar and he flagged the bartender. "Basil Hayden's, neat. And whatever this lovely lady would like."

Lovely? "Chardonnay, please."

The bartender nodded and walked away, returning with their glasses.

"To Olive and Nancy," Rick said.

"To Olive and Nancy," she agreed, clinking his glass.

Rachael settled into her seat, feeling the alcohol warm her system. "She was right," she decided, sighing in satisfaction. "This was needed."

"Agreed."

A tray dropped in the back of the bar. The sound of dishes clattering filled the air. A few patrons laughed and applauded. Rachael frowned over her shoulder, annoyed at the rudeness. Turning back to the bar, she fiddled with the stem of her wine glass, trying to figure out what to say.

"How did you get involved with the animal shelter?" Rick asked, breaking the silence.

Rachael grinned at the memory. "It began as a punishment. My parents caught me sneaking out of the house in high school. They decided I must have too much free time and that I needed more activity during the day so I would be too exhausted to go out."

"Did it work?"

"Not at first. I was a terribly typical sulky teen. You know, my life was *so* unfair," she grimaced at the melodramatics of her life back then. "But after a few weeks, the animals started to grow on me. It became less like work and more like fun. The animals—and even the other volunteers—became important to me."

She paused to take a sip of wine and he echoed with his bourbon, nodding for her to continue.

"I became a bit obsessive then, to the point where I started dreaming about the pets and worrying about them. My anxiety started to peak, and my parents made me cut down to two visits a week. I doubt anyone saw that coming!"

"Addiction is a serious affliction." He nodded dramatically. "One minute Fido is a nuisance, and the next he's all you think about."

"Right? After high school, my life became more hectic with college then work, but I've always tried to find time to volunteer when I could. You know, help walk and wash the dogs, clean their little habitats, and whatever else they need done. Without that, I wouldn't have found Martini and Olive."

"Did you name them?"

She giggled. "No, they came with the names. I kept them, even though I don't like martinis or olives. Now I love a Martini and an Olive. Irony at its finest."

He chuckled and saluted her with his drink.

"Did you always want to be a vet?"

He nodded. "Except for those years when I was elementally torn between being Spiderman or Superman. Once I figured out there weren't any radioactive spiders nearby and my parents assured me—much to my disappointment—that we weren't, in fact, aliens, I dedicated my energies toward the next best thing: animals. Considering most of the time I'm more comfortable talking to the dogs, cats, and other assorted pets than I am to the people who come in, I probably wouldn't have been such a great crime fighter."

For the next hour, they talked animatedly about their love of animals and he told her about becoming a veterinarian. She laughed at the gross stories from his training, and he at her parents' reactions to the dogs. They ordered another round of drinks and she felt her stress melt away, enjoying talking to a fellow animal lover. And not just animals, but the conversation flowed seamlessly from topic to topic. Everything seemed to click.

"You're living at your parents' house?" Rick asked.

Wrinkling her nose, she grimaced. "Yes, until I find a pet-friendly place."

"Where are you looking?"

"I'd like to stay somewhat close, north of the city." They discussed the pros and cons of the various neighborhoods in the area.

"And your boyfriend? Significant other? Is he in the area too?"

Rachael shook her head, hoping she wasn't flushed. She certainly felt warm. "No. No boyfriend. And you?"

"No, just me."

She had assumed that would be the response, given Nancy's pressuring, but it was good to get that confirmation. They both took another synchronized sip of their drinks and Rachael watched him from the corner of her eye. While he didn't have the model looks of Gabe, he was very handsome, fascinating, and exuded that easygoing boy-next-door charm. Rick was interesting, funny, and loved animals. He was independent and chill. He somehow managed to nonchalantly captivate her. And he was single. What were the odds?

"Tell me, how is it possible that you are single?" he asked, his thoughts running parallel to her own.

Staring down at the grain lines in the smooth wooden bar, she took a deep breath and tried to control what she had little doubt was becoming a fierce blush. Trusting her as-yet infallible instincts, she turned to look straight into his eyes. "I guess I've never met the right person."

He glanced down and swirled the amber liquor in his glass before meeting her direct gaze with a speculative smile. "Neither have I. Much to Nancy's perpetual disappointment."

A smile tugged at her lips. Fortunately, she rarely had to worry about meddling matchmakers. Most people quit trying several years ago, when she made it abundantly clear she did not have the time or the desire to start a relationship.

"Let's say you were interested in meeting a man," he murmured. "You know, hypothetically. What would you look for?"

"Hypothetically, *if* I were looking, I suppose the first thing would be that he saw me for me, and not as a connection to my family." She couldn't count on all her digits the men who had tried to start something with her as a way to ingratiate themselves with EHL Global.

"I could see where that could be a problem."

"Mhm. You wouldn't believe the stories, the lines."

"What else?"

"Obviously there'd have to be real attraction, chemistry, compatibility. Someone I could connect with beyond the physical."

"Obviously."

"Other than that, I guess it's the same stuff most people would say. A sense of humor is a must. Someone who's caring and respectful. He'd have to be independent and understand my need to be independent too. He'd have to respect my family and my job, knowing those were very important to me."

Rick studied her thoughtfully.

"What about you?"

Taking another drink of his bourbon, Rick set the glass down and took a deep breath. "She'd have to have a pulse."

He nodded sagely, a hint of a smile dancing around his lips.

"Oh, my gosh," she laughed. "Did you really just say that?"

"I did. That is very much a legitimate requirement."

Rolling her eyes and conceding the point, she circled her hand for more.

"She would need to love animals and be understanding of my unpredictable work schedule."

"That would be important, considering."

"Like you said, there would have to be chemistry and mutual respect. She'd have to be intelligent and honest. Be willing to commit. I'm very much a one-woman kind of man, and I'd expect the same in return."

They both fell quiet, considering each other, this turn of events. Rachael was confused. She'd spent so much time and energy pushing people away to advance her career and reputation, but now there was this . . . she didn't even know what to call it. Things were changing, and she wasn't sure she could deal with it.

"I'm sorry about Olive's accident, but I am glad I met you, Rachael."

Heat flooded her, and it wasn't from the wine. The unexpected pleasure she felt from his statement was surprising. What do you say to that? She took another sip before working up the courage to look at him.

"Me too," she reached out to squeeze his hand, smiling at the improbability of finding someone so inexplicably in sync with her.

He kept hold of her hand, and the butterflies fluttered anew.

"I don't know if you'd be interested, but I am going to

a fundraiser tonight. Business casual. It's for the pet adoption center up in Centerville. Would you like to join me?"

Yes was on the tip of her tongue, until she recalled her previous engagement. "Oh, I wish I could, but I have plans with my sister," she said, wondering if he thought she was blowing him off. At another time, that would have been a good excuse to brush off an unwanted date. Her phone vibrated and she glanced down to see a text from her dad. That was unusual. He hated texting. She looked closer. *Come get your damn dog.*

Rachael laughed out loud and set down her glass. "I'm so sorry, but it seems our afternoon is getting cut short by Martini."

He looked puzzled and she showed him the text. He broke out into a self-deprecating grin. "Story of my life—the four-legged friends get all the love and attention."

She giggled and stood, stretching her legs. "Thank you, Rick. This was nice. Really nice. And thank Nancy for me too, I suppose."

"Hang on a sec, I'll walk you out," he said, holding out his card to the bartender.

They stepped into the afternoon sunshine and she turned her face up, soaking in the rays. Rick stuffed his hands in his pockets, following along to her car.

"I'll be by to check on Olive again tomorrow. Think she'll get to come home then?"

He shook his head. "I can't say yet, but I doubt it. She'll probably need another day."

"Oh." She frowned and leaned against her car, mentally rearranging her schedule for Monday.

"What's wrong?"

"Just thinking." She shook her head. "But it'll all work out."

Rick hesitated and stepped closer, taking her hand. "I hope I'm not being too forward, but I meant what I said. I'm glad we met."

She squeezed his hand. "Not at all. And I meant what I said. I really wish I could go tonight."

He leaned closer and grazed her cheek with a light kiss; the soft brush of lips shot a flare of awareness through her body. "I'll see you tomorrow. What time do you plan to come by?"

"Around noon?" she proposed.

Rick squinted into the sunlight and nodded, apparently having made some kind of decision. "Would you like to get lunch together afterward?"

"Is this coming from you or Nancy?" Rachael teased.

"Me," he said, his lips curved into a tempting half-smile. "All me this time."

Deep breath, Rach.

"Tomorrow sounds wonderful. I'll see you then," she agreed, sliding her hand out of his warm grasp, noting the interest in his chocolate eyes.

That sounded very nice.

7

$\mathcal{W}$hen Rachael walked in the front door, her father's mutinous expression spoke volumes. He said nothing but pointed toward the living room. Even from where she stood, she could see—and worse, smell—the mess.

Scrubbing the carpet, Rachael glared at Martini. "What did you eat?!"

He slunk down onto his belly and army-crawled behind the chair leg.

"Good thing you're cute," she grumbled.

At last satisfied that her mother wouldn't notice the accident, she put the supplies away and washed up. Martini inched out and cautiously eyed her. Rachael sighed. "I know you miss your Olive. It's okay, Martini." He eased out and gave her ankle a little apologetic lick. "Silly boy," she laughed, reaching down to scratch his ears.

One certifiable mess cleaned up. She grabbed a water and sat on the patio chair to consider another potentially messy situation brewing. After a veritable desert of potential dates, she now found herself with two men to consider within a couple of days. They were both appealing but vastly different.

She pictured Rick's easy charm and melted. He seemed so sweet and she was attracted to him. Even more surprising was how much they had in common, which she would never have guessed, given her business-driven life. But was he too easygoing? As dominant as she tended to be, she wanted to know she wouldn't have to be that way all the time. The very few short-lived relationships she'd had were all with alpha-male types. Rachael needed someone who would keep her on her toes and not cave to her whims. Would she end up walking all over him? That would never work out.

Twisting the water bottle's top, she pegged what the other real problem might be there. It was unlike her to be attracted to someone who gave off the monogamous, relationship-seeking vibe. She was more than a little intimidated by it. Hell, she was scared witless by it. She had never really done the whole girlfriend thing. Where would she even begin? Truthfully, she didn't think she was prepared for something that serious. Not now, not when her career was running at full throttle.

Changing channels, her mind pulled up Gabe's dark angel look. So hot. Too damn hot. But different from what she expected. Humming, she closed her eyes and recalled his mouth, his hands sliding up and down her flesh that night, his decadent domination of her. Yummy. She wanted more of that. But he also was out of her comfort zone. Too well known, smack dab in the middle of the media spotlight. With a womanizing reputation to boot. She giggled at her mom's word for him, a rake.

Two men. Polar opposites. But she was drawn to both.

"What to do, what to do?" she mused aloud. Martini cocked his head, ready to listen. "Months without a single interesting conversation with a man—not one—and bam! Two of them appear at the same time. Life isn't fair, Martini."

He yawned and laid his head down, preferring a nap to her conversation. "Traitor," she muttered.

Passing the day organizing the moving boxes in her bedroom and going through the latest list of available properties, she happily put aside all thoughts of the boys. She glanced in the mirror and admired her perfect blonde waves with a smile. Marie, Rachael's lifelong hairstylist, always got it right, both the cut and the words of wisdom. *Time will tell*, she heard in Marie's voice. She had always been like a second mom to Rachael and Carlie. And right now, Rachael could use some words of wisdom.

PARKING OUTSIDE THE SALON, she waved to the small group of women gathered, mostly regulars. A treasure like Marie was always in demand. Rachael entered the building that would always smell of hair dye and shampoo, smiling at one of her most favorite people in the world, a mama who would fit in perfectly with the *My Big Fat Greek Wedding* cast.

"Rachael!" Marie's surprise was accompanied by her swishing and spinning Mrs. Parker around in her seat. In classic Marie fashion, her apron was not tied well and had shifted to the side. She was stirring a cup of hair dye and chatting animatedly with her current customer. She tapped her client's shoulder with her elbow. "You just sit right there. I have to go say hello."

"Hello, Mrs. Parker," Rachael greeted the seated woman watching her from the mirror, hair matted down on one side, heavy with product.

"Hello, Rachael! Did your mother come with you?"

"No, it's just me."

"Oh. Well do tell Mary I said hello."

Marie shushed Mrs. Parker and pulled Rachael to the side by the trio of vacant hair-washing sinks. "I don't have you on my book today, my little bluebird. Everything okay?"

Rachael shrugged. "I know. Just wanted to pop in and say hi."

Marie eyed her suspiciously. "I don't know that I believe that whopper, but I'll take it. How's my girl doing today? You know, Junior is in town," she hinted.

Rachael groaned dramatically. "Marie, you know he's like a brother to me. Not going to happen."

A smile danced about her lips. "A mother can dream."

Tugging at the askew apron, Rachael straightened and retied it. "Marie?"

"Yes?"

"Did you ever have to choose between more than one person? I mean, I know you and Rob have been together forever, but before that?"

She tilted her head and studied Rachael. "Is that what this is about? Sorry to disappoint, dear, but it was always Robbie for me." Marie paused and looked around the salon, making sure no one was paying attention to them. "But at your age, with your vigor and the times today? I say you take advantage and see what's what. Safely, of course. Nothing wrong with experiencing a little *amour*. Especially for one so serious such as yourself."

Cupid had never fired a bow her way. Maybe Rachael was the kind of person who was better off alone. While other little girls were dreaming of weddings and families and playing house, she had pretended she was being named to the Supreme Court or becoming the next CEO of the family business. Her focus was always on achieving more, getting the next win.

"*That's* your advice?" Rachael teased, raising her eyebrows to ridiculous heights.

She looked smug, but Marie had the grace to blush. "Well, how else are you to determine if it's meant to be? Live a little, my birdie. Spread those wings and let the wind carry you a bit. You'll figure it out."

She could *never* have had this conversation with her own mother. She hugged Marie's plump middle, knowing how special she was. "Love you, Marie."

"And I you, bluebird. Now you go fly away and let me finish my work. You and Carlie come for dinner soon, yes? And, of course, my favorite little anarchist is welcome too!"

Chuckling at what Kim's reaction would have been to that description, she pushed open the door, the dangling bells jingling. "We will," she promised.

RACHAEL CHECKED HER PHONE AGAIN. The anarchist was now thirty-five minutes late. From her seat on Carlie's sofa, she thought about the stack of work she could have made a dent in if she'd had her laptop with her. She twitched and slapped her phone back down on the coffee table.

Carlie smirked. "Give it up, girl. You know she operates in her own time zone. No sense stressing about it."

"I don't know how you can stand it," she grumbled, refilling her wine glass.

"To know Kim is to love Kim, faults and all."

"Where's Brent? I thought he was joining us."

Carlie tossed a hand in the air, twirling her fingers. "Out."

Smothering her frown, Rachael glanced back at the phone. Her sister loved him, but sometimes she wondered if they were actually good for each other. "To you and Brent," she teased. "Carlie and Brent forever!"

Carlie laughed, her dark blue eyes mischievous as they clinked glasses. "So, what about you? Anything going with Gabe?"

She lifted a shoulder. "Dinner tomorrow though, so we'll see."

"Tell me more about this vet."

Rachael sat back and kicked up her feet onto the coffee table. "Not much to tell. He's super sweet and saved Olive's life. He's tall, almost as tall as Gabe. And cute—like a Ken Doll." Hopefully his anatomy was a little more . . . more. Clearing her throat, she added, "We had a couple of drinks earlier."

"You what?!"

"He was off and Nancy—that's his receptionist, sweet older lady—pretty much strong-armed us into grabbing a drink together. Once we got past the initial weirdness, it was," Rachael spun her hand in the air, searching for the right way to describe it, "nice. We had a couple of drinks and we talked about all kinds of stuff, including animals, of course. He told me about veterinary school and how he wants to offer services at prices that make it impossible for people to not take proper care of their pets." Rachael sighed at the selflessness of his work.

"Mhm. And?"

"And what?"

"Rach, you're blushing. Spill!"

Shaking away her nervous smile, she took a deep breath. "After I told him I had plans tonight, he asked me to lunch tomorrow."

Carlie's nose wrinkled and her brow lifted. "That's what's making you blush? You need to get out more often, Rach."

"And he gave me a smooch."

"A smooch? Like a good kiss or a peck?"

"A smooch, Car. On the cheek."

"Who's smooching who?" called Kim from the front door.

Groaning, Rachael took another drag of her wine.

"Rach. She's kissing everyone these days," Carlie shouted with glee.

"Sure, sure," Kim said, laughing as she entered the sitting area.

Rachael glowered at the newcomer. "Am I that unkissable?"

Kim blinked. "Holy shit, you're serious?"

"Kim!"

"Hold up and back the fuck up," Kim said, tossing her jet-black hair over her shoulder. "Who are you kissing?"

"As far as I can tell," Carlie filled in her BFF, "she's making out with a handsome Ken-Doll doctor—"

"A vet," Rachael murmured.

"—and, none other than Gabe freaking McAllister!"

Kim whistled low and long, her gray eyes wide. "Boy, do you know how to pick 'em. Tell me, is McAllister as yummy as he looks?"

"How are things going with Owen, Kim?" Rachael volleyed back to her, referring to her on-again, off-again boyfriend.

She waved off the question. "O's old news. I need details, Rach!"

Carlie handed Kim a glass of wine and together they scrutinized Rachael, fascination pouring off them in waves.

"Well, you may as well help me figure this out," she relented, then proceeded to tell them about Rick and Gabe. Not everything, but enough.

Kim cracked open a new bottle and refreshed their glasses. "Now *that* is a good problem to have," she swooned, a dramatic effect fit for a drawing room in *Gone with the Wind*.

Nodding, Rachael stared at the red wine as it clung gently to the side of the glass. "This is good. Really good."

"It is. Now what are you going to do?" asked Carlie. "And can I come meet the doctor?"

"I'll see Rick tomorrow for lunch and meet Gabe for dinner. Based on my track record, that's about as far as it'll go. And no, I'm not introducing you."

Carlie threw a pillow at her and Rachael swerved to catch it. "Remember," Rachael laughed, launching it back at her younger sister and tilting her glass in her direction, "if this spills, it's *your* sofa that gets ruined!"

Carlie laughed and tucked the pillow under her arm. "It

will just match the rest of the couch then. Maybe I'll paint more spots and we'll call it the wine-leopard seat. Start a trend."

"That's my girl," Kim winked. "Agility is a hot skill right now. We can add that to your resume. You know, in case that whole family business thing doesn't work out."

WAKING the next morning on Carlie's sofa, Rachael groaned at the multiple empty wine bottles on the coffee table. Getting together with the girls was never something Rachael regretted, even with the headaches. Hangovers, Kim, and Carlie just all went together. She thought back to all of their teenage hijinks, and how she and Kim would push and prod Carlie out the door—but then Carlie would be the one who made sure everything went perfectly. Kim was the sassy sister, Carlie the caretaker sister, and Rachael the leader of the sister pack. She rather liked it that way. Their femme pack.

"Morning, sunshine," said Kim, perched on the side chair to tie her shoes, sleek black hair gathered neatly behind her head. Rachael knew Kim's mother had been an Asian American stunner. The apple didn't fall far from the tree. "Carlie has the Keurig set to repeat and Brent's got some scrambled eggs going," Kim informed her.

Rachael's head was pounding and her stomach rebelled. The last thing she wanted right now was eggs. "Good of him to show up," she muttered, a bit disgruntled at his absence of late.

Kim glanced at the kitchen and back at Rachael. "Right?" she whispered. "I don't know what's going on with them, but something's off. Hope they work through whatever it is."

Nodding slowly, Rachael dug back through the previous night's flyover comment. "Did you say you and Owen are done?"

Kim paused while tying the second sneaker and pursed her lips, considering. "Yeah. It isn't meant to be. I think we're done for good this time."

Rachael remained mute on that topic. She knew Kim and Carlie had some knock-down, drag-out fights over this in the past. "Sorry, girl." And she was. For as tough as Kim liked to appear, she was fiercely loyal and deserved more than Owen was willing or able to offer. Even before she knew about Kim's shitty home life and understood just how big of a wanker her dad was, Rachael had always felt protective of her surrogate sister.

Kim finished with her laces and popped up. "All good things come to an end, right?"

"Who knows? I sure as hell don't," Rachael teased, happy to see the bright smile reach Kim's almond-shaped eyes. "You out?"

"Yeah. Gotta go burn off those vino calories. I want updates about your two-timing ways. Good to see you, Alice."

Rachael made a face at the old *Alice in Wonderland* reference and dangled her bait. "Whatevs, bitch. Remind me to tell you what Marie called you."

She scowled at Rachael. "Now you have to say it. You know I won't leave till you do."

"The anarchist," she grinned.

Kim cackled with delighted laughter. "Only Marie! Could you imagine my father's reaction if I changed my signature to Kim Hill, Product Designer and Anarchist?!" She leaned down and hugged her, then disappeared to the kitchen before heading out the door, still laughing.

Carlie wandered into the living room. "She said you were up. Can't believe you slept in this late."

"What time is it?"

"Almost eleven."

"Shit, shit, shit! I've got to be at the animal hospital in an hour!"

Carlie held out a travel mug and a couple of Motrin. "I figured. Take this. I want a full report later."

"You're the best, CarCar. Love ya."

She flew out of the door and zipped home.

8

_____

With a few minutes to spare, Rachael sat on the patio to throw the ball to Martini. "Have to get your exercise in, too, pup," she said, scratching his ears and snagging the toy from him. Her hangover was nearly gone, and she delighted in the sunshine-filled late morning air. The summer-green lawn stretched before her, and she smiled at the bounding dog. "One more!"

He dashed off and was back in moments.

"Ready to go inside?"

He ran ahead and sat at the door, his little puffy tail swishing behind him.

"Here you go," she topped off his water and gave him a treat. "I'm going to go see Olive. You be a good boy!"

He shuffled down onto a cool patch of floor and chased his tail in endless circles before collapsing into a sleepy heap, dismissing her. Such a cutie.

Rick for lunch, Gabe for dinner. Maneater much?

"Oh, here she comes, watch out boys, she'll chew you

up!" she sang as she jogged out to the car. Laughing, she glanced in the rearview mirror, willing herself to decide. She felt a little guilty about seeing both, but it's not like she was in an actual relationship with either of them. No harm, no foul, right?

Sure, right up until they found out about each other.

But that stuff only happened in bad movies.

This was real life, which meant she needed to review what the hell she was doing, and how she was going to juggle this new terrain and her job. She frowned, thinking about her client board, contracts, prospects, and all the work that she needed to do. But Olive came first. And whatever happened at lunch, she would make sure Rick— and Gabe later—understood it was family and dogs, then work, then everything else. Including men, or the lack thereof, which had never bothered her before.

Satisfied with her decision to lay things out and keep her priorities straight, she hummed along to the radio the rest of the short drive. Turning into the small parking lot, she noted the absence of cars. Not much happening on a Sunday. She walked up to the door and discovered it was locked. She double-checked the time and tapped on the glass door a few times, relieved to see a white coat approaching the door.

"Sorry about that." Rick gestured to the door. "We don't typically unlock the doors until two on Sundays."

"Oh. You should have said something. I could have come by later."

"No, this is fine. Now I have an excuse to have a good lunch today."

"How is she this morning?"

"Good. Better." He detailed her progress and Rachael

was thrilled to see she was awake. Olive gave a slight "Yip!" when she saw her human had arrived.

"Hi, girl!" Rachael crooned. "My sweet Olive. You gave me quite the scare." The dog toddled around her crate, the cast looking like more of a nuisance than anything. "You'll be home soon," she murmured, rubbing behind her ears.

Gil joined them and nodded at Olive. "She's a good little patient. She's left her stitches alone and, so far, has managed to avoid the cone of shame."

Imagining a miniature satellite dish around her furry neck, Rachael giggled in relief. "Good to hear. I still feel terrible, but I'm glad she's got an excellent team to nurse her back to health."

Gil smiled. "She should be ready to go home tomorrow."

"Hear that, Olive? I'll be taking you home in just one more day!" She kissed the top of her sweet girl's head. Rachael's brow furrowed and she bit her lip as Olive settled down into her blanket drowsily. The lethargy was concerning.

"She's going to be pretty tired for the next few days, but she'll eventually perk back up," said Rick, noting her worry.

Nodding, Rachael continued to stroke Olive's head until her eyes drooped closed. A moment later, she eased her hand away and watched her Olive doze.

"Ready to go?" Rick asked.

She gave Olive's head one last little stroke then collected her bag.

Relief washed through her as they left the building, a weight lifted, knowing Olive was going to recover. It was one thing to be told that, but another altogether to see the progress and feel the change.

Stepping into the brilliant sunlight, Rick tossed his white jacket into his SUV, adding over his shoulder, "Want to take a walk first? There's a nice little park about five minutes from here."

"That would be great," she agreed, working out the knot in her purse strap so she could sling it over her shoulder.

He gestured to the right, so she began walking, a trickle of nerves tickling her insides. Rick joined her on the sidewalk, placing himself between her and the traffic.

"Which park is it?" she asked.

"It's a little community bark park, a dog park we take some of the recovering animals to when they need some gentle exercise beyond our enclosed play area."

She glanced up at him, shading her eyes from the sun. "Do you come here often?"

He chuckled. "I do believe that's the first time that line has been used on me."

Blushing, she swatted his arm. "You know what I mean."

"I try to come over at least once a week. Check on the upkeep, that kind of thing."

That was a strange thing to say, but she supposed it was important if he was sending recovering dogs there. A light breeze tickled her hair around her shoulders, and she admired the maintained yards along the short walk. Martini and Olive would love something like this—a nice yard close to a dog park.

"Here we are," he said, passing a man-sized faux fire hydrant. She chuckled at the absurdly large structure. "We didn't want there to be any chance a fire truck would ever mistake this for the real thing, but the dogs love it."

"We?"

He nodded. "Me and a couple of buddies built this. When the lot became available, it seemed like a no brainer. One of my favorite investments."

Oh. A full-sized poodle raced up and down a track of smooth green grass, a mutt of some kind matching the fluffy dog, length for length, on the other side of a fence. The pets' owners chatted over the chain-link divider, heads bobbing back and forth as they watched each other and the animals.

"Bev, Georgio! How are Sam and Popcorn today?" he hollered, and the bobbing heads swiveled toward them.

"Rick!" squealed the older woman, her cheeks pink and full. "It's been too long! Oh, my Sam is as good as new. You'd never even know he'd been through so much."

"Now she and Sam keep us on edge." The man Rachael assumed must be Georgio smiled warmly. "Popcorn is good. She's loving life and eating us out of house and home."

"How are you dear?" the woman asked Rick as they drew nearer, stealing a quick hug from him.

"I'm well. Rachael, this is Beverly, Nancy's sister."

Now that he'd said it, she could see the resemblance. "Pleased to meet you." She smiled.

"Rachael? I believe I've heard about you." Her eyes twinkled. "But I'll leave you two be. Georgio, you and Popcorn can take us home now."

"Yes, ma'am." He saluted. "Always good to see you, Rick. Nice to meet you too, young lady. You kids have a good day."

Leashes attached, Sam and Popcorn made their sloppy greetings before they and their humans departed. Rachael smiled after them. "They seem nice. But really—Popcorn the poodle?"

Rick smirked. "Says the mom of Martini and Olive."

They walked the perimeter of the park, and Rick paused at one of the conveniently placed dispensers to get a bag, scooping up the droppings left by previous pets. While they walked, Rachael quizzed him about his other interests and random tidbits. Rick challenged her to the same, and they soon were playing the world's longest game of fifty questions.

When they returned to the veterinary hospital's parking lot, Rachael hopped into her car to follow him to the restaurant, amused that she'd had a delightful time picking up dog poop with Rick. "He's kind of the shit," she told her reflection, laughing.

TRANQUIL ITALIAN MUSIC filled the air, and the smell of pasta made her stomach rumble. After a night of drinking and an afternoon of stool collecting, she was famished.

"Right this way," said the hostess, leading them to a small table off to the side.

Rick walked beside her, his hand settling into place at her lower back. She was surprised and enjoyed his lightly possessive touch. Rachael smiled up at him as he held the chair out for her before taking his own seat. He ordered a chardonnay for her and a bourbon for him, and they relaxed in the cozy, family-friendly atmosphere, perusing the menu.

"I haven't been here before. What's good?"

"Everything. The chicken parmesan is my favorite. The grilled zucchini is great."

They ordered lunch and listened to the soothing music. The dark-green fabric table linen was marked with a wet ring where her water glass had rested. While she gulped down the water, she surveyed the room, seeing families in their post-church Sunday best and groups of every size enjoying the rich Italian fare. Immediate thirst quenched, she dove into the tempting basket of warm bread.

"What made you decide to go into sales?" Rick asked.

Rachael took a bite of the buttery breadstick and considered. "You know how some people are good at building things? Others are great healers," she said, pointing at him with the breadstick. "I'm a good reader. Of people. I like to read the room and find out what they want, what they need, and get them to see that what I offer is a good fit."

"My favorite," she continued, dipping the other end of the breadstick into the creamy alfredo sauce, "is when someone is convinced they don't want our latest product. I love the challenge. I enjoy piecing together the evidence, and showing them how our work can help simplify what they do, work smarter."

"Do you like working for your dad?"

Rachael chewed and debated how to answer. "I don't really consider what I do as working for my dad. I see myself as an ambassador who's helping advance industries and corporations to the next generation. Dad may be the big man on campus, but I don't often deal directly with the R&D division. I actually work more with my mom.

She oversees the legal work, like the contracts and negotiations. That kind of stuff."

"You have a sister, too, right?"

"Mhm. Carlie. She's so much like my dad—quiet, shy, and smart as hell. She's already working on a new system of organizing audience market segments to produce better results. Once it launches, she's going to be a rockstar. Like Dad. And I'll sell it," she grinned, taking a voracious bite of the dripping breadstick.

Picking up a breadstick with a crimp in the end, Rick toyed with it between his fingers, eyes filled with a faraway memory. "Must be nice having such a close family."

Rachael nodded, taking a sip of wine to clear the breadstick. "For the most part, absolutely. What about you? Family? Siblings?"

He shrugged and put the breadstick on his plate, tearing it into bite-size chunks. "My parents are back home in St. Louis. I see them a few times a year. I'm an only child. Probably why I was so drawn to animals. My dogs, our cat, they became my siblings."

Rachael couldn't imagine not having her sister. And now that she had her fur babies, she could see why he gravitated toward the animals. "We had a cat when we were growing up, Pixie. But she was more Car's cat than mine. I'd put me squarely in the dog-person category."

"I've noticed," he said, saluting her with his drink.

Lunch arrived, and they spoke about their families, past jobs, future hopes. She was struck by how laid back this was, how easy it was to be with him. Lulls in the conversation were not awkward; they were companionable. And the conversation was fascinating, not boring or slow. Rachael kept waiting for the bottom to fall out. But so far it was smooth sailing. Smooth enough to be unnerving.

After lunch, they were not ready to go their separate ways. Relocating to the bar they visited yesterday, they reclaimed their former seats. Rachael was a little giddy when he scooted his seat closer to her own. And when he rested an arm across the back of her stool, she sighed contentedly and leaned back into him. This was good. Really good.

"Think you'll ever move back to St. Louis?" she asked.

Rick shook his head. "No. My practice, my future is here. I'm happier here than I ever was there. This just feels like home."

She crossed one worry off her list. "Any pets?"

"As much as I'd love to, my work schedule and living alone wouldn't be fair to them." His mouth twisted with regret. "They deserve more than I can give right now."

"I work a lot, but the dogs have each other when I'm out. And my dad's been helping. He tends to go in later than the rest of us. As much as he complains about them, I think they're winning him over."

"How's Martini handling the solitary life?"

"Remember the text I got yesterday?"

Rick nodded.

"Let's just say he's showing his concern through bodily functions." Rachael grimaced, and he laughed. "You laugh, but you didn't have to clean up after those particular functions. Gag!"

"That's not uncommon."

She chuckled. "This is totally a dating first for me to start the day with a pooper scooper and top it off with disgusting details over drinks."

"Would you believe it's a first for me, too?"

Rachael took a sip of her drink. "It's not your standard MO?"

Rick shook his head, amused.

They listened to the soft music and swayed in their seats, drinking and chatting. The bar lighting was dim, and the bright outside world felt miles away.

"This is nice," she said, setting down her empty wine glass.

He slid his hand up to the top of her shoulder and caressed the back of her neck. A shiver worked its way up her spine.

"Very nice," he said, leaning down and kissing her temple, awakening the butterflies.

"Can I ask you something?" she asked.

Leaning back, he looked down at her, his face serious. "Anything."

"What are you looking for? I mean, I know what we talked about yesterday, but are you just wanting a fling? Or . . . ?" she blushed, knowing that didn't come out very well.

He measured the confusion in her eyes before answering. "I'm definitely more of the 'Or.'"

Now I've confused myself.

"You know you're beautiful," Rick grinned and poked the tip of her nose with his index finger, "but it's more than that. I don't know what I'm looking for, per se, but I do like talking with you, spending time with you. This seems like something that has the potential to go somewhere."

"And where is that?"

"You tell me." He shrugged helplessly. "But I like it. And I like you."

Replaying his words, Rachael debated how to respond. Glancing at him from the corner of her eye, she saw that he was watching, waiting for her to say something.

"I have to be honest," she blew out her breath, hoping her revelation wasn't going to blow things with him. But better for him to know upfront. "I'm a borderline workaholic. I am my job. I love it."

"In case you missed it, so far you've seen me at work in the evening and on the weekend. I get it."

Well, then. She moved on.

"And, I don't really *do* relationships. Or at least I haven't. They don't work out for me." Rachael bit her lip and looked up at him. "Though I do like you, too."

He took a deep breath, settling his glass on the bar. "What do we do now?"

Isn't that the question of the day?

"Tell me more about you," she prompted, diving into the relationship queries that she'd avoided thus far. "When was your last relationship?"

Raising a brow and nodding slowly, he stared through her, seeing a different person, a different time. "About a year ago."

"How long were you together?"

"Two years. Enough to love, not enough to hold. Emma was great, but she didn't want to get married, didn't want to have kids. At first, I thought she simply wasn't ready, that she'd come around. But toward the end, it became apparent that she didn't want the same things I did." He shook his head, returning to her. "We went our separate ways amicably. She's dating someone new, and I'm happy for her."

Swallowing, Rachael debated if this was a good time to

tell him that she wasn't sure either. Were marriage and kids things she could seriously entertain, given her corporate lifestyle? How would he respond? Would she become another mistake in his life? *Too soon for that conversation*, she chastised herself.

"What about you? Your last relationship?"

"I'm afraid I'm a virgin." She lifted a shoulder, then laughed as he froze. "Not that, you goof. Let's just say I tend to go on a lot of first dates, but rarely agree to more."

"Are you afraid?"

Thinking back to Gabe's question, she deliberated if that's what it was. Was she pushing people away? "Maybe. The relationship side of things freaks me out a little." Rachael was twenty-seven years old and still couldn't say she'd ever been or ever would be ready for something serious. Was that unusual? Was she not normal? She buried her face in her hands, her brain too jumbled to sort that one out right now.

Catching her wrist, he pulled a hand away from her face and spread it flat on the bar, face-up, tracing the shape of her fingers, her palm. "And what about the other side of things?" he murmured.

His gentle touch tickled her palm and she laughed, tugging her hand away. He stopped her retreat, grasping her hand more firmly. "I have a confession to make," he whispered in her ear, his warm breath stirring her insides and sending the butterflies into overdrive.

"Hmm?" Her pulse was racing, her breath caught.

Get a grip, Rachael.

"As much as I do want to pursue things—the 'or'—with you, I'm also exceptionally attracted to you."

"You are?"

"I am." He lifted her hand from the bar and pressed a kiss in her palm, curling her fingers around it. "And, hell, I can't believe I'm going to say this, but I was wondering, hoping, if you might feel the same way?"

A fork in the road. The tines were pulling her in different directions, each leading to a disparate future. Dare she turn toward him? Could she start down this path even if she wasn't sure what she wanted? And what about Gabe? She was supposed to meet him later. Why was this all happening at the same time? This was not fair. Or easy. Shouldn't it be easy?

"Rachael?"

Get a grip, girl. Go with what makes you happy. What did Marie say? See what's what?

"Mhm?" She regarded his melting chocolate eyes, his sensuous lips.

Silent, Rick watched her, his hand clasped around her curled-up fist.

He's leaving it up to me. Do I want this?

It was a risk. She could do nothing, and she knew he would be fine with that. He was probably expecting that.

Or she could take a leap of faith. Something in her urged her to jump. To see. To try. To hope. And she couldn't turn away.

Everything about him, about this moment, felt so right. They might have just met, but she felt she knew him more than anyone else. It was unbelievable—and if she thought too hard on it, it would scare the shit out of her— but it was right.

She took a deep breath and inched forward, watching his eyes watch her.

Curling her free hand around his neck, the fine brown

hairs tickling her palm, Rachael urged him closer and stopped thinking. She paused just before his lips, the barest hesitation, before closing the distance between them. He leaned into her, wrapping a hand into the hair at the side of her face.

Rachael breathed him in, savoring the warmth of the bourbon. He slipped his tongue between her parted lips, sliding against hers, caressing and learning the taste of her mouth. He released her and she felt pleasantly trapped by the heat in his gaze. Rick lifted his eyebrows in question, tilting his head toward the door, and she nodded. He paid the tab and escorted her to the parking lot.

"Want to check out my place?" his deep voice rumbled, a tempting smile on his lips.

She took the leap.

"Yes."

9

----

*R*ick opened the passenger door and Rachael slid into the SUV. The leather seat was hot from the sun. She shifted as the heat permeated her leggings. He drove through the streets, passing her parents' neighborhood and glancing her way periodically, a nervous smile curving his lips.

Parking in the garage, he gripped the steering wheel and took a deep breath. "Are you sure? I don't want to pressure you."

Enveloped in his warm eyes and his concern, she fought the urge to giggle in anticipation as she slipped from the car. "Yes, I'm sure."

They met at the garage door. Rick grasped her hand and they walked up the stairs together.

"How long have you lived here?" she asked.

"Coming up on three years," he said, his keys and wallet clattering to rest on the entryway table. The open kitchen and living room were bright and welcoming. He led her to the kitchen and glanced into the fridge. "Water? Pop? Wine?"

"Whatever you're having."

He poured two glasses of wine and ushered her into the living room. They settled onto the sofa, facing each other. He was nervous and it was freaking adorable, so refreshingly different from the guys she had been with in the past. Rick looked around the room, and she could tell he was trying to see it through her eyes. She followed his path, noting the large picture window, the dark-brown sofa and loveseat, the wooden coffee and accent tables, and the modest entertainment center. Along the walls on either side of the television were simple but sturdy bookshelves peppered with a couple of family photos—he definitely looked like his dad—and endless heavy tomes related to his work. A couple of the shelves were full of novels. Her interest piqued, she left him on the sofa to inspect the titles, fingertips tracing the spines of countless horror and suspense novels, lingering over the more worn spines of Stephen King, Scott Thomas, and Neil Gaiman. She paused as she touched some classics and even romance novels.

"Your ex's?" she asked, picking up a Jane Austen novel.

Chuckling, he shook his head. "Mine. Constant immersion in animal psychology, physiology, and immunology texts can drive you to needing unrelated distractions. Do you enjoy reading?"

"Yes, though I don't have much time for it lately. I have a Goodreads list about a mile long of books I want to read. Someday I'll get through them."

"What do you like to read?"

"Oh, a little of this, a little of that," Rachael said evasively.

"That's not an answer. You saw my collection," he teased. "Tell me."

"Promise you won't laugh?"

He nodded solemnly.

"I've read several of these," she gestured to the shelf of suspense and mysteries, "but what I really enjoy—my guilty pleasure—are the historical romances. The dresses and hair, the debonair men, wild attraction, passion, the patently absurd declarations of love and lifelong commitment . . . all those grandiose romantic gestures that don't really exist."

Head tilted to the side, he looked surprised. "I wouldn't have pegged you as a cynic."

"I'm not. I'm a realist. I adore the escapism of romance, but I keep myself rooted in the here and now."

Under the guise of skimming through the last row of books, she considered what he was offering. Given his nerves and hesitation, she knew it was her decision to make. Rachael pooled her confidence. She was definitely rooted in what was here and now. Exhaling, she set her glass on the coffee table in front of him, slipping between him and the table. Immobile, he held his wine steady, eyes glued to hers. Easing the glass from his hand, she took a long drink before placing it next to her stemware. His throat worked, but he remained transfixed.

"Is this okay?" she asked, unaccustomed to initiating what was to come. What she hoped was to come.

He nodded.

"Are you sure?"

"Yes," he said hoarsely, his eyes twin whirlpools of dark chocolate.

Rachael picked up his hand that had been holding the glass and turned it over in her own. His hand was so much warmer than hers, her own dwarfed by the long, smooth palm she held. His breath caught as she continued examining, her finger tracing the lines of his palm. Rick watched her movements, fascinated, yet still holding himself in check. She wondered what would happen when he let loose.

"Do you read palms?" he asked.

"Oh, yes," she said, raising a single eyebrow. "See this line here?"

He nodded, entranced.

"It means you're a very passionate person."

"It does?"

She laughed and shrugged. "Truthfully? Not a clue. But perhaps there's a better way to find out that answer."

Leaning forward against his chest, one knee on the cushion beside him, she pressed her lips to his, letting the warmth of their breath tickle their gentle kiss. Falling into him more, she ran her tongue along his lower lip and pressed her body against his. He was solid and broad, her weight not causing him to move back. He groaned, yet still exercised more restraint than she cared for.

Maybe she had misread him.

"Rachael?"

"Mhm?" she murmured, bracing herself on her knee, one hand against his chest. His heart was racing, thudding insistently against her palm.

"I don't want to ruin this by going too fast."

Tilting her head to try to read him, her confusion

increased. Was she blowing this? "Am I going too fast for you?"

"No." He shuddered. "But I don't want to scare you away."

She smiled at him, his concern, wondering if this was the same man who professed his attraction to her in the bar. Rachael hesitated, wondering if she should move away, then spoke her truth. "I don't think you will."

He stared at her, his body heating beneath her. "Thank God."

Unshackling his desire, Rick wrapped a firm arm around her waist, bringing them closer. As he rubbed his arm up and down her back in delicious caresses, Rachael groaned, understanding why cats purred. His hand disappeared into her hair and she let her head fall back. Bending down to inhale along her neck, his heated breath warmed her thin skin. So close but not connecting. Anticipation built, her belly tensing. His other arm wrapped around her, fitting her flush against him, and she balanced, straddling his lap, their hearts beating against each other. It was intense and passionate, yet he still hadn't kissed her.

"Come here," he said, tilting her face up to his. His gaze caressed her face, her eyes, her lips. Fractionally, he moved in closer, his mouth hovering a breath away.

"Yes," she whispered, pleading.

It was all the encouragement he needed. His warm lips captured hers. She skated her tongue along his lips, sliding in and out, dancing with his. He skimmed his hands down her sides and gripped the backs of her legs, branding her through the stretch leggings. A sigh escaped her lips as his fingers massaged the lean muscles along her thighs. Leaning against his chest, Rachael deepened the kiss and enjoyed the sensations of being there with him, pressed against his warmth. She looped her arms around his neck, and he moved his lips across her jaw to the side of her neck, nibbling lightly, then back up to tug at the tender earlobe. She pulled him back, reclaiming his mouth.

Rolling them over, Rick's huge body captured her under himself. "What do you want?" he whispered, his voice husky and low. The words reached deep inside, unfurling a need that left her breathless.

What do I want?

"More."

Grinning, he devoted himself to the task at hand. He took the lead and crushed her mouth in a devouring kiss. As his weight pressed against her, she could feel the pressure of his rising need against her thigh. Snuggling against him, Rachael wriggled and lost herself in him.

He ran his hand up her side, his thumb grazing her breast. She dug her fingers into his hair and tugged lightly before tracing the muscles of his shoulders and his back. Slipping her hands under the hem of his shirt, she ran her fingers along the exposed skin. He shuddered and pushed himself up, tugging then tossing the shirt over his head.

Surveying the room, he grinned roguishly before standing and scooping her up in one swift movement. Rachael laughed in surprise as Rick carried her up the stairs to the next level, and turned into a large bedroom with a huge four-poster bed in the middle, covered in piles of pillows and soft blankets. He lowered Rachael to her feet next to the bed, where she leaned against the post, catching her breath.

"Rachael." He said her name like a prayer, his eyes

burning and muscles tensed, coiled with pent-up energy. "Tell me to stop now if you don't want to do this."

Her eyes were even with his chest, his heart, and she looked up at him through her lashes, trailing her fingers along his tight stomach and developed chest, tickling the sprinkling of springy hair. His pecs danced to her touch. He was muscular, but not bulky. "More," she whispered playfully.

A heart-stopping smile burned as he caught her hands and wrapped them around the bedpost behind her. "Do not let go," he commanded.

Rachael laughed at his order but obeyed, surprised by her willingness to hand him the control. "Yes, sir," she replied.

"And no laughing," he admonished with a grin, tapping her nose with his finger. She bit her lower lip and nodded.

Rick slipped down to one knee and unbuttoned her loose shirt from the bottom, one button at a time. His eyes focused on the task. The top of his head and those industrious hands inched closer to her breasts. He was laying a fire, the temperature rising with each additional expanse of skin he revealed, stoking the embers and urging the flames higher. He pressed a warm, wet kiss to her stomach and continued, finally reaching the last button and spreading her shirt open.

Palms itching to caress him, she started to move her hands away from the wooden spindle, but he stopped and shook his head imperiously. "I said do not let go," he growled. Grasping the bedpost again, she was intrigued and more than a little turned on by this dominant side of him.

His hands traveled up her sides and curved over her

shoulders, sending her shirt on a downward slide, trapped where her hands and lower arms crossed against the bedpost. Rick tugged at her leggings, sliding them down, followed by her underwear. She fought the urge to close her eyes. She was not self-conscious of her body, but it was unnerving to be so exposed like this, waiting for his reaction. He wrapped a hand around her foot and lifted, pulling the materials over and off her foot with his other hand. He bent and kissed her ankle, his tongue tracing the groove there before returning her foot to the ground. Impatient, she shifted and kicked the remaining clothing from her other foot. Smirking at her eagerness, he began the return trip up, dropping kisses and caresses across her legs, a hot lingering kiss at the top of her pelvis.

Rachael sucked in her breath, watching his progress. The man was torturing her.

Still on his knee, he slid his warm hands up her flat belly and around her chest before unhooking her bra as she breathed in his scent. He ran a hand down one of her arms, raising goosebumps as he pulled the strap and shirt material down. He pulled her arm away from the post and let the fabric drop, before placing her hand back on the wooden column. After repeating this with her other arm, she was actively squirming, wanting him to touch her, kiss her. Instead, he sat back on his heels, looking but not touching. "You are so beautiful."

In his bottomless brown eyes, she saw tenderness and desire. "I want to see you, too," she whispered. Needing no further encouragement, he rose to his feet and stripped down until they were both bared to each other's gaze.

"Oh," she breathed, taking in his long, fit body, muscles

flexing as he held himself still for her approval. His arousal was evident, rising thickly between them.

"More," she said again, smiling.

Chuckling softly, he came to her and grasped her backside. She gasped as he pulled her against him, bending down to reclaim her mouth, his erection pressed against her belly. He kissed her senseless before dropping back down on a knee.

"Stay," Rick reiterated.

Nearly dizzy from passion, she gripped the bedpost gladly.

His hand caressed the side of her breast before lifting it to his mouth. The heat and sensation caused her breath to catch. He teased with a lick before nipping gently, closing his mouth around the puckered nipple and sucking, licking, and driving her mad. Her sex clinched with need and her back arched. His hand massaged her other breast, and she pressed her head against the rail, a moan escaping her lips. At the sound, he lifted his head and grinned before turning his hunger to the other breast, the fire burning brighter. Oh, yes.

Moving up, he kissed and bit her neck while his hand moved lower, searching. She gasped as his hand cupped her mound. "Oh," she breathed again.

He pulled his head back to watch her, fingers sliding to a stop as they inched closer to where she wanted him. "Rach? Are you sure?"

"Yes," she urged him on, and he shuddered with relief and passion.

Exploring her mouth with his tongue, his fingers slid between her folds. Rachael gripped the wooden post at her back as he increased the pressure on her mouth and moved a finger deep inside her passage, teasing it slowly in and out. She started to sway her hips in time to his finger and his teeth claimed her lower lip, tugging gently.

"Rick!" she gasped. His hand continued to tease and torment, and they both moved to the same rhythm. "More," she pleaded.

"More?"

"I want to touch you."

He withdrew his hand and she felt the loss. "Now you can let go." He grinned.

Lifting her by the waist, he tossed her onto the bed, both laughing at the turn to playfulness. He prowled, chasing and matching her movements as she slid to the center of the huge mattress. Rachael reached for him as he approached and met his lips, relieved to be able to touch him, explore him now. Kissing hungrily, she slid her hand down his chest, skimming her nails along his flat nipples, scratching as they continued down, searching for his imposing manhood. He shuddered when she reached the destination.

"Rachael," he panted.

"More?" she asked against his lips.

Rick nodded. "More."

She traced the head of his erection with the pad of her thumb, teasing out a droplet of moisture. Sliding her fingers down, she spread her palm under the weight of him, before encircling him. She ran her hand up and down, slowly but firmly, pulsing around him. He closed his eyes and his chest rose and fell more rapidly.

Rick moved his hips to thrust in and out of her hand, his arousal turning her on. He continued to thrust as his hand dove down and he slid one then two fingers into her heat, plunging in and out in time to his hips. Her breath grew ragged and they continued stroking and pumping each other. She closed her eyes and focused on the increasing tightness, the tension growing, nearly unbearable.

"Shit, I'm going to come," he grunted, and still he kept his hands moving, his fingers filling her, sliding in and out, finding the right spot and hitting it over and over.

"Just there, keep going . . . like that, yes!" she encouraged, moving closer and closer.

"Christ, Rachael," he groaned as a rush of heat sprayed onto her stomach. At the same time, her tension exploded, and she gasped, her body spasming and gripping his fingers, both lost in the moment, the release.

10

_____

"Wow," he said, pulling her against him.

"Mmhmm," she agreed.

He picked up a corner of the sheet to wipe her stomach, before leaning up on his elbow to gaze down at her, his eyes a buttery brown now, his dark hair damp with sweat at the temples.

"Rachael?"

"Yes?"

He swept her hair back from her face and kissed her. "Thank you."

"Thank *you*," she replied, a lazy, satisfied grin pulling at her lips.

"You look like a cat that got the cream." Rick chuckled before taking her mouth again in a slow and luxurious kiss. She rolled toward him and they snuggled, kissing and petting each other, tasting and exploring at leisure. She wriggled against him, surprised to feel him growing firm again. She arched a brow at him. "Again?"

He smiled wickedly. "You wanted more?"

Rachael laughed and lay back as his hands and mouth discovered all the places that made her gasp and moan. "Rick," she pleaded.

"Hmm?"

"More," she panted. "I want more. I want you."

He groaned then kissed her before pulling away to reach into his nightstand. He held up a condom. She reached for the package and slid out the rubber disc, lining it up and rolling it down his prominent erection.

He closed his eyes when she let her fingers linger and trace him, dancing up and down before cupping and massaging his balls. He shuddered and pulled her hand away, then lay back and pulled her on top. She straddled his hips, sliding her body forward so she could kiss him, before moving lower, licking his neck and collarbone, then lower to lick a circle around his nipple, all the while scooting down his midsection. She rubbed her sex against his throbbing member, sliding back and forth, delighting in the delicious friction. She continued licking and kissing his chest while positioning herself over him and starting to descend, taking him in a little at a time, circling and swaying her hips as she inched him farther in and out of her.

Rick smirked. "Tease."

She pinched his nipple and he gasped, then laughed, his chest rumbling beneath her hands.

She settled against him, deliciously stretched as he filled her. Rachael stilled for a moment to enjoy the sensation, then began to move, gliding and rubbing against him. He pulled at her hips to guide her as they found their rhythm.

"Yes," he groaned.

She hummed her agreement. "This feels so good."

"*You* feel so good," Rick replied. He grasped her hips and bucked upward, and she gasped, his body driving into her even more deeply. She leaned forward to grind against him, her mound growing more sensitive and more demanding.

His thrusts and grunts increased as they moved. She wrapped her legs around his waist when he sat up, and they continued to rock, holding onto each other. Seated on top of him, their faces were nearly aligned, and he devoured her mouth as he possessed her body, gyrating deep inside. So intimately connected in both places, all awareness faded away, lost in the growing wave of passion as it carried them away. Rick shifted to roll her beneath him, his body pressing against her, plunging over and over. Her eyes rolled back and she sucked in her breath. "Oh my God, oh my God," she murmured, teetering at the edge.

Rick kept moving, increasing the pace. He bit off a curse. "I'm sorry. I can't—hold back—anymore," he grunted, clenching his teeth.

She gasped as he surged deep inside, pulsing and throbbing, the continued spasms sending her into oblivion. Shock and pleasure collided as she came apart beneath him, around him, her body milking him as ripples of pleasure coursed through her. He collapsed against her, nuzzling her neck as their chests heaved with effort.

"You certainly know how to deliver on 'more,'" Rachael teased, slapping his damp chest as he rolled over.

"What can I say, you inspire me," he groaned, flinging his arms out spread eagle, one pinning her to the bed.

She snuggled against him, under his arm, and snagged

the sheet. She tossed it over them and closed her eyes to rest for a minute.

~

WARM AND COZY, she didn't particularly feel like moving. Her muscles were the tiniest bit sore, but in a good way. Rachael smiled and stretched, waking as she rolled over.

And . . . she was not home. Or alone.

It all rushed back and she flushed.

Wow.

Rick was sprawled out next to her, still asleep. She watched him, a happy, giddy warmth filling her. She liked him. A lot. Like *really* liked him. Not only was he gorgeous and attentive, but they had so much in common, each dedicated to their jobs and the community. She wanted to see where this went. That in itself, wanting more, was a new sensation. It was more than the sex, though that was great too. This was the desire to let herself be close to someone. She could imagine walking the dogs to the park together, reading on the couch, and ending the days like this.

The only other sex she'd ever had that even compared was with Gabe. Gabe was sexy and fun, but there was no emotion there. He was safe. And dangerous, but not to her heart. He was dangerous to her reputation.

Rick was dangerous in other ways. He made her think of things she'd never imagined before. And that was something she wasn't sure she could afford at this point in her career.

The early evening sunlight slanted through the windows and she frowned, recalling her dinner plans.

What should she do about Gabe? She could text him and cancel, but that would just lead to future asks and might nullify the progress she was making with the contract. She knew what needed to be done. She needed to meet with him face to face, explain they could only be friends, and get back to business. But Rachael just wanted to stay here, soaking up this glorious newness with Rick and learning more about him.

Come on, Rach. Don't be lazy. Do the right thing. Wrap things up with Gabe, then figure out what you'll do with Rick.

Sighing, she sat up and slid to the edge of the bed.

"Where are you going?" he mumbled.

Rachael glanced over her shoulder and her breath caught. There are some images in life that you know you'll remember forever. Her heart memorized the picture he presented. His half-lidded eyes were turned her way. His light-brown hair was messed on top and a crooked smile filled his face. His muscled arm was bent and tucked beneath his head. He was perfect.

"I have to go, Rick. I have a dinner I have to attend."

"That's a lot of 'have to's."

"What I'd really like to do is stay here with you," Rachael confessed, a blush warming her cheeks.

"Then let's do that," he said with a tempting smile.

Rachael shook her head. "I'm sorry, but I do have to go. Want me to call for a ride back to my car?"

"No." He frowned. "I'll take you."

She located her clothes and dressed. He watched for a few moments before breaking the silence. "Rachael, did we go too fast? Did I rush you? Are you running from me?"

Pausing, she weighed his words. If anything, she rushed him. Returning to the edge of the bed, she took his face between her hands and kissed him softly. "No. And no." God, she wished she could just climb back into bed with him.

"Today . . . this is something," he said, staring into her eyes.

"I agree."

Satisfied with whatever he saw in her expression, he joined her in hunting for discarded clothes. She admired his body covertly as he dressed. He was built like a baseball player or a quarterback, long and lean, good hands, strong and capable. Very capable, she amended, turning away as a flush climbed her chest and neck.

Downstairs, she picked up his shirt and collected their wine glasses, trading them for glasses of water. She checked her phone and saw a text from Gabe, confirming for tonight. Dreading the evening, she messaged that she would meet him there.

Rick wrapped his arms around her middle and bent to kiss her neck, a hand splayed across her midsection, pulling her against him.

"Ah, that's not helping," she said, but not wanting him to stop. He worked his way up her neck and she turned in his arms to kiss him, tongues dancing together, his large body curving protectively, possessively, around hers.

She pushed back, leaning away. "Rick," she whispered as his mouth chased hers. "I do have to go. This is *definitely* not helping." She giggled.

"Come back later?"

Rachael shook her head. "I would like to, but I can't tonight. I have this dinner, then I need to go home and spend time with Martini. He's been alone all afternoon."

He exhaled before running a hand through his hair and

taking a long drink of water, looking around his living room. "You could bring him here?" he offered.

She laughed. "I don't think so. Not tonight at any rate. But I'll see you tomorrow?"

Rick nodded. "You will."

"You'll be the one in the white coat?" she teased.

"I will." He laughed, picking up his keys and wallet. "Let's get you to your car."

11

———

*T*he drive to the restaurant was not nearly long enough. Every light was green, not giving her time to sit idly or contemplate turning around. In the blink of an eye, she was handing her car keys to the valet outside the swanky steak house.

"Rachael, you look beautiful," Gabe said, standing as she approached the table.

She allowed him to kiss her cheek before sitting across from him. Unfamiliar sensations made her want to flee— doubt, nerves. Guilt.

"Thank you," she murmured.

A bottle of red and two glasses, one empty, sat on the table. Gabe poured for her then topped off his own. "I'm glad you came."

Play it cool, Rach. Be nice, don't piss him off, don't ruin the contract.

"Sorry I'm a few minutes late. Had some things to take care of."

"It's no problem. I don't mind."

Sipping her wine, Rachael looked around the restaurant. It was fairly crowded for a Sunday evening. Several other couples were near them, one über-romantic pair next to them was slicing into their filets, feeding bits to each other. Gag. A few families peppered the room, the children squirming in their seats. She imagined they wished they were at McDonald's instead.

I feel you, kids.

She stifled a laugh, then turned back to her dinner companion. "Gabe," she began, feeling out the words as she spoke them, "I appreciate you taking an interest in me. I am beyond flattered. But I do want you to know that I'm not looking for anything right now." *With you.*

He was quiet, watching her, his finger tracing the top of his wine glass. "Let's not rush into any decisions, one way or another. I, for one, am just here for the prime rib."

Smiling at his deflection, she was relieved that he wasn't upset or put off by her declaration. "Is it good?"

"The best you can get around here."

They settled into an easy banter, chatting about work and mutual friends. They talked more about EHL and her work there. He told her about his work and growing up in the various cities McAllister Corp had called home over the years.

"Must have been hard to get to know someone when you moved so frequently," she observed.

"I suppose that's why I so rarely get to be myself. I'm always making first impressions. It's almost second nature at this point. The showman has taken over."

Recalling his showboating ways at lunch, she laughed, ticking off on her fingers: "The showman, the clown, the flirt . . . The Playboy?"

Spreading his hands out, he grinned sheepishly. "Yes. To all of the above."

"For what it's worth, I prefer this version of you. The Gabe who can laugh at himself and be honest."

He lifted his glass. "I do too."

"So why the big act?"

He picked up his fork, stabbing a piece of lettuce. "It's part of the job. We all have our role to play in the McAllister Corporation."

"Believe it or not, I understand," she said. Rachael gestured to herself with her fork. "Sales and face *du jour*, right?"

He chewed his salad and watched her thoughtfully. "I believe you do."

"Besides, it gives me an excuse to get all the cool opportunities—like meeting the heads of McAllister," she winked, earning a laugh. "So, tell me," she asked, sotto voce, "is Stoneworth always such a prickly, pompous grump?"

He practically dropped his fork, before releasing a guffawing laugh. "Oh, shit. Yes, Ivan is a legendary tyrant in our company. But the man does know his corporate law." He shrugged and leaned forward. "Your turn. Is your mom as terrifying as they say?"

She burst out laughing, "Oh, yes. Very much so." She wiped a tear from the corner of her eye and laughed harder as the couple next to them openly stared, clearly wondering if they had gone insane.

Go back to feeding each other.

Rachael giggled and made a serious effort to get herself under control. At last able to comment, she added, "Let's just say I wouldn't want to go against her in court. Or chess. My mother is borderline psychic or something. She always knows what's coming before everyone else."

He smirked. "Guess we both have someone like that in our lives."

"To our burdens," she toasted.

He met her glass in mid-air and they dissolved into another fit of laughter.

The rest of the dinner passed in pleasant banter, and she relaxed, feeling their relationship falling neatly into friendship. They knew many of the same people in the business realm and he was very easy to talk to, but he was no Rick.

The waiter took their plates and she groaned, feeling full and sleepy. "That was delicious. Thank you."

He nodded, dropping his napkin on the space in front of him. "More wine?"

"No, thank you."

"What have you got going on this week?"

"I'm hoping to get Olive back home tomorrow."

"Ah, yes. Half of the Martini and Olive combo. Where is she?"

"Animal hospital. She's recovering from a run-in with a Chevy."

"What? When did that happen? Is she okay?"

"It was the other night after we had lunch. She ran out the side gate and into the road before I could get to her. It was awful." Rachael shivered, hoping she never had to feel that helpless again. "But she's going to be okay. They're taking good care of her at the vet." A smile warmed her face as she thought of Rick, Gil, Cora, and Nancy, the matchmaking wonder.

He shook his head. "I could never do that, work with hurt animals."

"It takes a special someone who can," she murmured, thoughts returning to Rick.

"Uh-huh." Gabe watched closely, missing nothing. "And who is this special someone?"

She blushed, realizing she had turned dreamy on him. "What do you mean?"

"I'm used to women looking like that at me. This is a new experience, having someone else get the girl. And while I am disappointed, more than you would imagine, I'm not going to be a dick about it. I can't compete with someone who saved your dog's life. Tell me more about this Mr. Special Someone."

Well, this is unexpected.

"Rick—Dr. Richard Thomas, actually. He's . . . I don't know. He's great."

He leaned back in his chair. "He's a good guy?"

"All signs point to yes, so far."

"And, Magic 8 Ball, do you see something coming from it?"

She fidgeted with the stem of her glass and shrugged. "Maybe. I honestly don't know yet. But I'd like to find out."

"I like you, Rachael. But I also realize you've got me planted squarely in the Friend Zone. Maybe someday I can convince you to give me a shot, but that's probably not going to be possible until after you sort things out with Mr. Special."

"Thank you, Gabe."

"Don't thank me yet. I'm not giving up all hope. But I do enjoy our time together. It's nice to find someone to talk to. Even if you are a tiny thing who, unbelievably, turns me down at every opportunity. All but once, that is," he added wickedly.

"Yes, well, if you don't mind keeping that last part private," she managed behind her flaming red face.

"I don't kiss and tell, love. But I can't control what others make up about me."

She recalled her dad's comment about perceptions versus reality. So true.

"To friendship?" Rachael asked, raising her water goblet.

"To new territories—*friendship* with a *woman*," he groaned.

Laughing at his antics, she pulled her phone out of her bag and checked the time. A new text from Rick. *Looking forward to seeing what tomorrow brings.*

And so was she. Rachael sighed happily. Test the waters with Rick. Be friends with Gabe. Keep work on track. Get Olive back home. It was all going perfectly.

Things were finally going her way.

12

Things were definitely not going her way.

A photo of Gabe and Rachael exiting the restaurant last night, laughing and looking pretty cozy, graced the homepage of a popular entertainment website. "Hot Heartland Power Couple," the headline screamed.

"Oh, my freaking God!" Rachael moaned, staring at the screen.

"I told you it was interesting," Carlie said dryly over the speakerphone. "Care to dish?"

"Fuckity, fuck, fuck, fuck."

"I'm going to take it that's your eloquent way of saying this was not what you were expecting?"

Rachael read aloud the start of the article, unable to believe what she was reading. "America's favorite Playboy may have met his match in one Rachael Eller, as in the EHL Global heiress and eldest daughter of . . ."

She slammed her screen shut and flipped back onto her bed, Martini watching worriedly from his perch. "What am I going to do?"

"First, you're going to tell me what's going on with Mr. Dark and Dreamy, and we'll go from there."

"Nothing! That's the crazy thing, Car. We agreed to be friends. He's a very sweet guy, but my attentions lie elsewhere."

"And would that elsewhere have to do with Olive?"

"Yes . . . what if he sees this?!"

She was quiet for a minute. "Do vets even pay attention to this kind of stuff?"

"How would I know?"

"If he does, tell him you two are just friends. End of story, right?"

Sure. Rachael climbed out of his bed and hours later she was photographed with one of corporate America's favorite players—*The Playboy*—leaving a fancy restaurant together. Who the hell even knew they were at the restaurant?! Who took the photo? God, how could this be happening?

Oh my God. A wave of nausea hit her as another thought occurred. What if people thought that was how she closed her deals?

She slapped an arm over her forehead. "This is a freaking nightmare."

"I'm sure you're overreacting, Rach. I gotta finish getting ready for work, but I wanted to make sure you knew. For better or worse, you're a tabloid celebrity now."

They disconnected and Rachael stared up at the ceiling. What to do, what to do.

She shot off a text. *How's Olive? Still good to come home today?*

And another. This time to Gabe. *Holy crap. Check out the Eyes America website.*

Stomach lurching, she went downstairs to the kitchen, thankful to see a pot of coffee brewing.

"Morning," called Dad, looking over the top of his newspaper.

"Morning," she grumbled, ripping open a packet of sweetener and flinging open the fridge, scouring for the flavored creamer.

"We're out. Use the milk," he said, setting down the paper to watch her more closely. "Everything okay?"

"Fine."

"Uh-huh. Well, I'm here if you want to talk about it."

She shook her head and grabbed the milk, pouring it into the coffee. Not the same, but it would work. "Mom still here?"

"No, she left early."

Rachael debated calling off. Her mom was going to want to talk about it. But no sense putting off the inevitable.

Her phone vibrated, and she leapt to check it.

At least they got my good side. Sorry, love. Like I said, people talk.

I know. It's not your fault. But shit, shit, shit! Talk about terrible timing.

You know we would make a killer couple though. They got that right.

Rolling her eyes at Gabe's comment, she dropped her phone into her bag.

"Heading out. Can you let Martini in when he scratches?"

He nodded. "Will do. Hope you sort out whatever is bothering you. Be careful. Your old man's always here if you need to talk."

"Thanks. Love you, Dad."

"Love you, too," he said as he turned back to whatever headline had his attention this morning.

ON THE DRIVE TO WORK, Rachael replayed the day with Rick, dreaming of how they might top that off. She pictured dinners on the town, drinks at "their" bar, and volunteering together at the shelter. Her smile died on her face as she considered how the conversation would go when she talked to him about the damn photo. Rachael dragged her feet as she approached her office, waiting for her mother to pop up any moment and nag her about said photo.

"Has he communicated with you?" As if on cue.

Out of the fire and into the frying pan, Rachael faced her mother. "Gabe?"

"Who else?"

"He's glad they 'got his good side,'" she made air quotation marks with her fingers, three hundred percent exasperated. Rachael entered her office and sat at the desk, her mother at her heels.

"Did he have anything to do with the photo?"

Rachael considered this. He scheduled the dinner, made the reservations. But what would be the purpose in having a photographer capture them leaving? It didn't make sense. "No."

Mary Eller tapped her finger on Rachael's desk, standing and staring off into space.

The silence stretched on and on, becoming uncomfortable. "Mom?"

She shook her head and held up her hand for continued silence.

Ooookay.

"I've heard nothing from McAllister regarding their contract negotiations, so I think we're secure on that front. Dating Gabe shouldn't impact any of our existing or pending client relationships. This may ultimately be a good strategic move to elevate your standing and help open more doors—assuming you don't date other clients."

"Mother, I'm *not* dating him. It was dinner with a friend. And I have never dated any clients. Gabe was . . . he's different." She threw her hands in the air and spun around in her office chair. No need to explain that one any further. Her frustration level increased again. Just once it would be nice to have her mom ask how she felt about a situation, instead of skipping to future plans. Rachael frowned at the computer, the photo staring back. More than 250 comments on the story. She couldn't bring herself to read them. Internet trolls, probably.

"Whether or not you're dating doesn't truly matter, does it? For now, our best move is to wait and see. Unless there's something more I should be aware of?"

Rachael shook her head. At least there was definitely nothing more she wanted to tell her mom about.

"Very well then. Let's move on. Have you reviewed the contracts for the Clayton account?"

They talked business for a while before her mother left to put out other fires. Rachael was exhausted and it wasn't even lunch yet.

Needing a distraction, she flipped open Instagram and saw she had gained literally thousands of new followers.

"Fantastic," she grumbled. "Hope they like seeing

photos of Olive and Martini. They're not going to see anything about Gabe." She briefly considered making her account private, but they were already following her. Ugh.

Turning to Facebook, the notifications icon glowed with a staggering number of people who tagged her in posts. She closed the app. *Nope, nope, nope. Not dealing with this now.*

She still hadn't heard anything about Olive, so she put in a call to the animal hospital. Her call was forwarded to the vet on duty. "Rachael? Hi, this is Gil."

"Oh, hi! I was expecting Rick. How's Olive today?"

"She's much better, and I believe she's rather hoping you'll be by to take her home soon."

"Aww! I'm planning to leave the office early today. Be there around three?"

"Sounds good. See you then."

She ended the call and drummed her fingers on her desk. Where was Rick? Didn't he normally work days?

Rachael, you're being paranoid. He worked for Gil this week-end, so Gil is probably working for him today.

She repeated that over and over, trying to convince herself it was true. That was the only reason she couldn't talk to him earlier.

And that was the reason why he didn't text her back. *Riiiight.*

The sinking feeling was rapidly expanding, unease tearing up her stomach.

The day inched by and she could barely concentrate, re-reading the same projections and proposals, spending more time checking the clock than anything else.

Unable to tolerate it, she grabbed her cell phone and

messaged Rick again. *Hey! Am I going to see you when I pick up Olive? Planning to be there around 3.*

An hour later, there was still no response.

A desolate feeling settled over her and she knew.

It was over.

13

─────────

*G*il was polite enough, but Nancy scarcely acknowledged her. Rick was nowhere to be found. When Rachael asked Gil about Rick, he became flustered and mumbled that Rick was off today. She considered asking them to tell him that nothing happened, that Gabe was just her friend, but how do you bring that up to people you don't even know?

So here she sat, alone with Olive in the car.

"It's not fair!" she shouted, slamming her steering wheel as she got back in the car with Olive. The dog glanced at her warily from her nest on the side seat.

Frustrated, she threw the car into gear and took off, speeding away from the animal hospital.

What would you think, Rach? You'd be horrified, right?

The melancholy set in. She was equal parts surprised and disturbed by how much this whole thing upset her. Her stomach churned and her heart clenched. It was not possible to be so distraught over someone she had only just started dating, was it? How had she tumbled into this so quickly?

Martini was ecstatic to greet Olive, and they were soon dancing around the yard. Olive's cast didn't slow her down much. Rachael would bring her back to the vet in two weeks for a follow-up. Hopefully, she would heal quickly and get it off then.

"Rachael?" called Carlie from the front door. Rachael remained seated on the back patio, watching the dogs' joyful reunion. Maybe she could absorb some of their happiness.

"Rach?"

"Out here, Car," she finally responded.

Her sister stepped out to the patio and the dogs greeted her, delighted to get extra attention.

"Olive! Martini! Aren't you good dogs! Auntie Carlie is here to spoil you rotten!"

She continued to coo, pulling contraband treats from her pockets. Rachael rolled her eyes but grinned as Carlie and the dogs ran down to the grass to practice simple commands. Once the supply was exhausted, Carlie returned up the stairs, wiping her hands and dropping into the chair next to Rachael's.

"She looks good. That little cast is the saddest thing I've ever seen, but she seems to be dealing with it pretty well."

Rachael kept watching the dogs. They sniffed around the yard, working in tight circles.

"You doing okay, Rach? Mom said you left early."

She stared at the tree line behind the house. "I had to pick up Olive."

Carlie watched her older sister for a minute. "But are *you* okay?"

Rachael turned her gaze to her sister. "What do you mean?"

"You're being very quiet. Very un-Rachael."

"Rick won't talk to me."

"Oh."

They sat quietly, both watching the dogs.

"You like him?"

"Yes."

"Want to talk about it?"

"Not particularly."

They sat for a while longer, until Carlie disappeared into the house, returning with two cups. "Take it," she said, holding one out.

"I don't really feel like drinking right now," Rachael said, staring blankly into the yard.

"It's orange juice, you wackadoodle. Drink it."

Amused, Rachael glanced at her. "OJ?"

Carlie shrugged. "Vitamin C. Sweetness. Orange-y. It always makes me feel better."

They sipped their juice and swam in their own thoughts. Carlie didn't bother trying to fill the quiet. She comforted with her presence, her hushed support. There was something to be said about silence.

"Thanks, Car." Rachael sighed, setting down the empty cup.

"What are you going to do?" she asked.

"I don't know. Try to forget about him?"

"Can I weigh in?"

"Go for it."

"I've never seen you get upset over a guy. *Ever*. You

must really like him. Like, *like* him." She stopped and looked at her sister, waiting for a response.

Rachael huffed at the similar expectant expressions she and her sister had, but twirled her hand, encouraging her sister to continue.

"I'm not sure you should give up on this. And it's not like you actually had something going on with Gabe, right? It's a simple misunderstanding. He's not used to the papers, the photographers. Find him. Talk to him."

If only it were that simple. She and Rick had spent a couple of days getting to know each other, followed by an unbelievable day together, culminating at his place. Then she rolled out of bed to have dinner with another man. What was she thinking?! He was so considerate, so worried about rushing things, moving too fast. And there she went, moving on to another guy when she was still tired and worked over from hours with Rick.

If she were Rick, she wouldn't talk to her either.

"I was just going to meet with Gabe to end things. I didn't want to do that over the phone. We ended up talking about Rick," she whispered, resting her chin on her knee.

Sadness weighed heavily in Carlie's eyes. "Talk to him. Explain it."

Rachael shook her head in frustration. Carlie couldn't understand. It was her own fault. All of it.

"I have to go. Are you going to be okay? I can come back later," said Carlie.

Rachael smiled as brightly as she could fake, swallowing past the gargantuan pile of guilt and fear. "I'm fine. Thanks for the juice and the pep talk, CarCar."

"Liar," she teased gently, nudging Rachael's shoulder. "Call me if you need someone to listen, okay?"

"I will."

14

———

*T*wo weeks later, and still not a peep from Rick.

Thankfully, her job had commanded her attention. After closing the deal with McAllister Corp, she began having regular chats with Gabe to coordinate things, which had turned into a bizarrely unexpected yet comfortable, close friendship. As the paparazzi were now convinced they were an item, they had to conduct most of their business and resulting friendship over the phone, which had the pleasant side effect of reinforcing a platonic relationship.

"The guy is a tool. If he shut you out for something like that, he doesn't deserve your time or attention," Gabe said during one of what had become their twice-daily phone calls. Rachael was on her way home when they started the call.

"I know, but I can't help but feel like this is all a terrible misunderstanding. I want to talk to him. Explain what happened."

"Then call him," he said, as if she hadn't already thought of that.

"I've tried, but he doesn't answer."

"Did you text him?"

"A couple times, but he hasn't responded," she complained.

"If you were my sister, I'd be hauling this guy out of his office and beating the ever-living shit out of him. As it is, I haven't ruled it out yet."

Rachael laughed. "Good thing I'm not your sister—though I doubt Calista has ever had someone ghost on her. And, Gabe, honey, I cannot see you doing that. You're too sweet."

He was quiet for a minute.

"Gabe?"

Clearing his throat, he muttered, "Nothing."

"Anyways, what are you up to this week?"

"Finishing up at the office before flying out to San Antonio tonight. Boston on Thursday. And Rach, I mean it. The guy doesn't deserve you. You're too good for him."

"You're a good friend, Gabe. I appreciate being able to talk to you about this."

"Yeah, yeah, yeah. Don't go ruining my reputation with this good guy stuff."

"Sure, sure, Mr. McAllister. Your sensitive badass reputation is safe with me," she giggled, still amazed at how tight they'd become over the last few weeks.

His warm chuckle filled her ear and she smiled. Who knew that he'd end up being one of her closest friends? She'd never made friends easily, and the way that she and Gabe had clicked so fast was something she tried not to dwell on too much. Of course, Carlie and Kim thought she was nuts, but it was all good. She could control this.

"I have to go," she said, "but I'll talk to you later. Safe travels!"

"Bye, love. Call or text if you need me."

"Will do."

Rachael ended the call as she swung into her parents' long driveway to pick up Olive for her follow up. She didn't expect to see Rick, so she wasn't surprised when Gil walked out to greet her. "Happy Monday! How is my favorite garnish today?"

"She's great, Gil. Glad to see you."

She glanced at the counter where Nancy was studiously ignoring her. Rachael walked past her to the exam room and gave her a small wave. She glared back with ice in her expression. Ouch.

Gil tapped the steel tabletop and she set Olive down. Her paws scraped the metal and she skittered before sitting still.

"Good afternoon, Olive. There's a good girl. How are you today?" He let her sniff his hands before scratching under her chin and behind her ears. Olive was delighted by the attention. "How is her mobility?"

"Good. I think she's completely ignoring the cast. You should see her going up and down the stairs and running after Martini."

He conducted a thorough exam and determined the bones were starting to set. "Everything is looking good. Bring her back in two weeks and this will probably be ready to come off."

Smiling, she toted her healing girl out to the car.

Rachael might not have been over Rick yet, but at least there was some healing happening somewhere.

"Rachael!"

Glancing over her shoulder, she saw Nancy shuffling out the door. Rachael leaned into the car to roll down the windows for Olive, then rushed back across the lot to meet her. "Nancy? What's going on?"

Nancy stared at her, an internal struggle bringing an uncharacteristic frown to her bubbly face.

"Dear, I don't know what happened between you and Rick, but I have to tell you something. Flaunting your relationship with that other man was just cruel. Now I know you didn't set out to hurt him, but I have to say my piece. You are not a nice person."

Tears pricked the backs of Rachael's eyes, and she glanced up at the sky, searching for words that didn't come. When Rachael was able to look back at Nancy, a wet trickle slid down her cheek. "Nancy, that was dinner with a friend. That's all. Gabe and I are friends. I met with him in person that night to make sure he understood that. Nothing more. I swear, I did not mean to hurt Rick. I miss him . . ." she trailed off, unable to continue.

Nancy arched a brow at her, then turned and left.

Wiping the now-twin trails off her cheeks, Rachael returned to the car, reaching in to pet Olive, who licked her hand. "Two more weeks, girl."

Grabbing her phone, she messaged Carlie to let her know about Olive. She stared at her phone for a few minutes, then messaged Rick. *Sorry I missed you again. I miss you.*

Her phone vibrated and her heart raced.

Want to risk dinner with me before I leave tonight?

Gabe. Her smile faded. She could use a friend right now. *Sure. That'd be great.*

Good. Pick you up at your place in a few.

Sounds good. Just come on in when you get there—I'll be out back.

She returned home and caught up on some work, trying to distract herself from what Nancy had said. Closing her laptop, she devoted herself to babying Olive and spending time in the yard with the furry duo. The dogs were loving it here, but she needed to find a place. She had looked at a few rentals when time permitted, but nothing she could see her and the dogs calling home.

"Hey pretty lady," she heard echo through the house. "You here?"

"Out here," she called. "Hey yourself."

Gabe strolled out to the patio and gestured to the dogs. "I thought she would get the cast off today. That's disappointing."

"Two more weeks. Sounds like she'll get it off then."

"Any sign of . . . ?"

Rachael shook her head no.

He wrapped his arms around her in a warm hug, kissing her hair. "I'm sorry, Rach."

"I know I need to accept it and move on, but . . ."

He held her quietly.

"Come on," he said. "Let's go eat."

Gabe took her to a small diner downtown where they ordered classic greasy burgers, fries, and ginormous milk-shakes. Not a photographer in sight. "I know how to put a smile on your face, see?"

Grinning at the mountain of blended strawberry ice

cream, Rachael dug in. "This is so good. And just what I needed. Thank you."

He smiled and scooped out a big spoonful of chocolate milkshake. "You know it's good when you need a spoon."

They munched on their retro food, bantering about work and the tech integrations.

"Seems like the comms platform is working well for McAllister," she said. "How's the content management system going?"

"We've got a team laying the groundwork, and the EHL support team has been very responsive to our needs. Thinking we'll be able to launch the CMS on January first."

While he spoke, a tomato seed slid down his chin. She couldn't help but laugh.

"What?"

"You have something," she paused, grabbing her napkin, "riiiiiight there! Got it." She giggled and pulled her hand back.

He caught her wrist. "Rachael."

"What?"

He didn't say anything, just stared at her, his gaze roaming her face.

"Do I have something on my face?"

He shook his head and remained silent, slowly releasing his hold on her wrist.

"Gabe?" Rachael tossed a fry at him. "Stop it. You're freaking me out."

He grinned and ate the fried missile before calling for the check.

They finished their dinner and shakes and took the conversation outside. It was a nice evening, so they turned toward the riverfront to walk along the banks. While they strolled, she thought longingly of her walk to the dog park with Rick. She wondered if he liked visiting the river. What flavor milkshakes he liked.

Stop it, Rach!

Shaking her head, she returned to the present. "Fourth of July is coming up. It's always been one of my favorite holidays," she mused. "When we were little, Carlie and I would try to write our names in the glow of the sparklers. She always won by saying C-A-R counted."

He chuckled and took her hand as they continued to stroll.

Rachael glanced down at their entwined hands.

Oh.

His thumb brushed the back of her hand, and she looked up at him.

Rachael tried to tug her hand away. "Gabe, I—"

He held tight to her. "Shh. Don't say it. Just hear me out."

Rachael gathered her patience and went along, worrying about his change in demeanor. Hoping, praying he wasn't going to do or say something to change things. The last few weeks of heartbreak had been miserable, and she couldn't handle more stress right now. He stopped at a bench next to the bridge and released her hand. Sitting, he took a deep breath and ran a hand through his long black hair.

"I know you had something going with that guy, the vet. But Rach, he's gone. I've waited and watched. And I don't see him doing anything but causing you more pain. You know how I feel about you. I like you. Hell, I'm halfway to loving you."

Rachael looked into his cool-blue eyes and her heart constricted. He looked so earnest, but he knew how she felt. How could he be saying this? God, why was everything such a cluster?

"Is this a line? Are you messing with me?"

"No. I mean it. I want to try this. You and me. Us."

Frowning, she looked out at the dark Ohio River, watching a rusted barge pass a riverboat. "Gabe, I don't know. I love this, our friendship. Besides Carlie and Kim, you're the only person I can really relax and be myself around. You've come to mean so much to me. Please, I don't want to lose this."

"You don't understand. We don't have to lose it. We could build on it. There's no better foundation for a relationship. This is not a joke, Rachael. I want to be with you. Jesus, I can't believe I'm saying this, but I want to love you. I want you to love me. Choose me."

"Gabe. Please." She raised her hand to stop his words, wishing she could unhear them. "I can't. Not right now. I need more time." And even with time, she didn't think she could be what he wanted. He couldn't be who she wanted.

He sighed and stood, pulling her up next to him. He placed his hand under her chin and looked into her eyes. "I'll wait. For you."

Rachael shook her head and leaned into him, wrapping her arms around his waist. She didn't know what to say, so she simply replied, "Thank you."

"Now cheer up and tell me more about Carlie's matrix platform," he suggested, changing the subject.

Gabe was better than she deserved. But he was also what she needed right now.

15

With Gabe out of town and Kim and Carlie busy, Rachael took to working longer hours at the office. Her client list was growing and the contracts were accumulating. As much as she loved the pitch, the paperwork was a bitch.

"How is it going with the contracts?" Mom asked from the doorway after several days of Rachael sequestering herself in the office.

"It's going. Did you get the signed copies?"

Her mother came in and sat in the chair in front of Rachael's desk.

This is new.

"Uh, Mom? Everything okay?"

"Rachael, I understand you've been under a lot of stress."

She slowly nodded at her mother, watching her warily.

Yes, she was wary of her own mother.

What did she know? Where was this going?

"I'm not the most maternal of mothers," Mary

chuckled nervously and waved a hand through the air. "Nothing like stating the obvious, I know."

She paused and stared over Rachael's shoulder before meeting her daughter's eyes. "I'm sorry that I can't be more than I am. But I want you to know that I see what you're going through, and I am proud of you for pushing through obstacles that would have sidelined others."

Rachael swallowed the suspicious lump in her throat and aimed for nonchalant. "Mom, you don't have to apologize."

Her mother waved a hand again, batting the comment away.

"Tell me, what is happening with you and Gabe? You two have been spending time together. Seems like I'm always hearing about one of his cars pulling up to the house."

"Not much to tell. We're friends. He mentioned he'd like us to make a go of things, but I'm not ready." Rachael knew he had arrived back in town last night, but she had been hesitant to reach out after their last conversation.

Her mother's bright blue eyes blinked in surprise and she studied her daughter. "He was fine with that?"

"Yes."

"What do you want?"

Rachael thought back to the afternoon with Rick.

"I want more," she replied with a shrug, staring down at her desk. Gabe didn't make her feel the way Rick did. No one had ever made her feel that way. Rachael frowned, wondering what that meant. Was this what Kim went through with Owen every time they split up? No wonder they kept getting back together.

"That's my girl." Her mother smiled as she walked to

the door, patting her sleek blonde updo, then paused. "You've surprised me, Rachael."

"How's that?"

"You let yourself be happy with someone new; you took a risk outside of your comfort zone. I like seeing you happy."

Rachael watched her leave the office and sank back against her leather chair, thinking. Was she unhappy before? She didn't think she was at the time, but now she wondered. She thought about her own parents' full life of work and family. And Carlie and Brent. They all seemed to be able to manage things. Maybe she had always considered relationships unimportant as an excuse to avoid getting hurt.

What did she want?

Rick. I want Rick.

Massaging her temples, Rachael closed her eyes and relived that stolen afternoon with Rick for the millionth time. Was it even real? Why couldn't she let it go? She had to be romanticizing her time with him. She desperately needed to move on.

Carlie entered the office, leaning against the door frame. "You okay?"

"Yeah." She answered Carlie's inquiry without opening her eyes, holding onto the fading image of Rick.

"I passed Mom in the hallway. What was she up to this early in the morning?"

Resigned, Rachael met her sister's eyes and shrugged. "Honestly? I have no idea. Same old cryptic mom stuff." They were used to their mother's different ways. It was their normal.

"My Keurig is on the fritz. Come get coffee with me."

"As if I'd stand between you and your caffeine," Rachael teased, grabbing her bag. Carlie had very few vices. Caffeine was the one she allowed free reign in her life.

Trudging along in the midsummer morning, Rachael swiped at the heavy, soupy air surrounding them. "Ugh, this humidity is insane," she whined. "And you still want hot coffee?"

"Of course. It's the morning nectar of the gods."

They swam down the humid sidewalk, her sister's tall, lean shadow and Rachael's petite form stretching ahead of them. The Starbucks was crowded and hot, so she shooed Carlie in alone.

"Sure you don't want anything?" Carlie asked.

"No, I'm good. I'm going to wait out here."

Rachael sat on a low brick retaining wall in the shade, watching the people come and go on this hellishly hot Friday morning.

"Rachael?"

It was the voice she longed to hear. She closed her eyes and shook her head, unsure and unprepared.

"Rachael?" he asked again, closer.

Rachael looked up. His brown eyes were full of hesitation. He had new lines under them that she didn't recall when they were last together. "Rick?"

He smiled uncertainly. "How are you?"

"I . . . I'm okay, I guess. You?"

His gaze swept the area, looking anywhere but at her as he answered. "I've been better, but . . . you know how it goes."

She looked down and fidgeted, wishing she could find something to say. But nothing came to mind.

"What are you doing here?" Rick asked.

"Waiting for Carlie," she gestured toward the hopping coffee shop.

"Oh."

Time stood still in their little bubble; the world moved around them. She longed to touch him, smell him, just be with him. Was this the chance she had been waiting for? Not one to squander an opportunity, she took a deep breath and got to her feet, ready to close some of the distance between them. "I am so glad to see you. I want to tell you—"

"No, Rachael. Stop." He looked away.

She felt like she'd been slapped. *Just spit it out, Car!* "Gabe and I are just friends. I miss you."

He swallowed and turned. "It was good to see you."

"You too . . ." she trailed off as he walked away, the bottom falling out of her world.

So that's it then.

It's over. Really over.

She tried to keep her shit together, to not show how fragmented she felt inside. Eyes burning and stomach churning, she struggled to breathe, the humid air oppressive and imprisoning her in the moment. How could this be happening? It wasn't supposed to go that way. Clutching her stomach, she staggered back to the brick wall, sitting down to stop the world from smothering her.

She sat until she could no longer take it, texting Carlie, *Too hot. Heading back to the office.*

"He didn't even give me a chance to explain," she said aloud, angry with herself for being so upset, angry with him for giving up, and angry at the world that continued to stream around her.

Dashing a bitter tear from her cheek, she sent out

another text. She hoped he wasn't bogged down in meet-ings. *Need to talk. Can you meet me?*

At the office or your place? Gabe replied immediately.

Home.

Meet you there in 20 minutes.

16

Rachael sat on her parents' sofa, a full glass of wine untouched on the table in front of her. She heard the front door open and close, but her gaze remained fixed on the flat surface of the wine.

"What's going on?" Gabe asked, jogging into the house, concern written all over his face.

"It's time," she muttered, staring at the glass. "I'm convincing myself to move on."

He sat down next to her, reaching for the wine glass. Gabe sniffed then took a drink, cringing. "Christ, Rach. What is this? What are you drinking?"

"I don't know. It's the only bottle I could find in the pantry. Cooking wine?"

"I don't think this would be called wine in any country. Come on, let's get you a real drink."

Pulled to her feet, she followed along numbly, grabbing her bag and phone on the way to his car.

"Where to?" Rachael asked.

"My place, if that's okay with you?"

She nodded and stared out the window, seeing Rick's face over and over. Could she have said something different? Made him listen?

"What happened?" Gabe asked.

"I saw him. And it was awkward. Awful. Like stepping into a cold, dark shadow."

Gabe swore under his breath as he zipped along the side streets, ending up in front of his downtown condo. She'd heard rumors that he owned the building, but it didn't really matter to her. He tossed the keys to a valet and escorted her inside. They took the elevator up to his penthouse, and he pointed her to the living room as he beelined to the kitchen. Rachael heard him working in there, opening and closing cabinets, the refrigerator.

"Music?" he called.

"Sure."

Soothing, mellow tunes filled the air, a relaxing musical number that was heavy with strings and piano. She'd been to Gabe's place before, briefly, but this was the first time she'd really studied it. The black leather sofa set and geometric area rug were masculine but tasteful. The walls were decorated with framed artwork in shades of blue and gray, contemporary pieces that made her think of waves crashing over a seascape. A wall full of entertainment options opened before her: a huge curved television screen, an impressive audio system, and not a single wire visible. Also missing were photographs, trivial knick-knacks, or anything else that could reveal the real Gabe.

"Of course," she murmured, then kicked off her shoes and leaned back into the leather sofa, closing her eyes. She felt him settle on the sofa beside her. He remained silent.

After a while, Rachael turned to see him watching her attentively.

He handed her a glass of wine, and she sipped, humming at the accompanying fruit and spice explosion in her mouth. "This is good," she noted.

He nodded.

"Thank you," she whispered, feeling a tear run down her cheek.

He leaned forward, wiping it gently from her face. "Please don't cry, love. He isn't worth your tears."

She smiled at his words, his concern. "Gabe, I'm sorry. This is so unfair to you."

"There is nowhere else I'd rather be right now."

"Why does everything have to be so complicated? So confusing?"

"It doesn't have to be that way." He trailed a finger down her cheek, drying the path of a runaway tear.

He was so close. So warm. So supportive.

Rachael knew what he wanted. Part of her wanted that too.

She took a shuddering breath. Could she do this?

Gabe leaned closer, watching her eyes. His own pale crystal-blue eyes were pulling her in, and she wanted to swim in the coolness, lose herself. He moved closer still, his fingers cupping her chin, tilting her face up toward his.

"Rachael, I . . . you know I want you."

She knew it was wrong. She didn't want what he wanted. Rachael wasn't sure she ever would. Yet, there they sat together, and the temptation was inescapable.

"I want to be close to someone, to feel something real." She studied his face, the hope and tension warring. They'd been there before. As good as it had been during that illicit interlude, she knew it would be better now. But as a friend, she had to be honest. "You know I can't commit to anything beyond right now, this moment. I can't do a relationship, Gabe."

He closed his eyes, and she forced herself to remain quiet, not console him. It would be his choice.

When his gaze returned to her, they were ablaze with icy fire. "If we do this, I don't know that I can go back. I want you, all of you."

Another tear escaped and he leaned forward, kissing it away.

Shuddering, she turned away from him. "I can't, Gabe. I can't do this to you. You deserve more. I can't offer you something that isn't there." Her tears continued to trickle and he wrapped his arms around her, pulling her against his chest. "I need my friend. I need this, just for you to hold me. Help me forget things for a little while."

He chuckled, his chest rumbling against her. "It figures," he murmured aloud. "The one woman I want, and she just wants me for my body."

"The irony," she laughed sadly against him.

"What do we do now?" he asked.

She leaned back and wiped her eyes. "We drink excessively and you tell me about San Antonio and Boston."

17

---

*T*hree bottles later, she was beyond the point of giving a damn. She struggled to recall why this couldn't happen. Would it be that bad?

"Why isn't it you that I'm this upshet about?" Rachael pouted, poking him in the chest. "I remember. You were soooo good. *We* were good. Mmmm . . ."

"Christ, Rach." Gabe reached to take her glass away. "I think that's enough for you."

"I'm sherioush," she paused and giggled. "Serious."

He shrugged, a half-smile on his lips. "I wish I knew, love."

"Life is so messed up."

She sprawled across the sofa, stretching her legs across his lap. "Comfortable?" he teased, rubbing a hand up and down her shin.

"Yes, as a matter of fact. Though you wouldn't happen to have some sweat pants I could borrow? This suit is killing me."

Gabe lifted her legs and dropped them behind him,

sauntering to his bedroom.

"You know these are going to be about two feet too long on you, right?" he said, tossing them to her.

"Turn around," she ordered, darting around to the backside of the sofa to change into his pants.

He chuckled and turned away. "You could have just gone to the washroom or my room."

Rachael tossed her slacks and jacket on the side chair and shuffled back around, wearing his dark-blue sweats and her fitted black camisole. "I clash."

"You do. But you're cute enough to get away with it."

She crawled across the couch and leaned against him, her feet tucked under the square pillow at the end of the sofa. "Gabe?"

"Yes?"

"I still want to kiss you. Can I do that and us still just be friends?"

He was quiet for so long that she looked back up at him. "Gabe?"

His long hair formed a dark curtain between them. Rachael reached up to pull it back, a goofy grin lighting her lips. "Hellloooo?" His face was unreadable, his eyes flat on the surface. What was going on in there?

She sat up and put some room between them. "Gabe?"

"I should take you home, damn it," he muttered, brushing his hair back away from his face.

"You don't want me to kiss you. I understand. I do. It's awful of me. I'm sorry I asked." She started to stand and he reached out, closing his long fingers around her wrist.

Gabe flexed his arm and she flew backward, falling into his lap. Rachael stared up at him and stopped breathing. Warring anger and desire filled his beautiful face. "Of course I want you to kiss me, Rachael. I've never wanted something so fucking bad in my life. I want that and a hell of a lot more."

She scrubbed a hand across her face. "I'm so sorry, I know. I remember what you said earlier. How are you so much better at all of this than me? I'm such a mess, and this is so unfair to you. Even now, when I'm essentially throwing myself at you, you are . . ." She shrugged helplessly and tugged her wrist free of his hold. ". . . and I shouldn't have—"

He cut her off with his mouth, crushing her, suffocating her. The force stunned her and she reflexively pushed him away. Gabe cursed and backed up, torment ravaging his beautiful features. She held her fingers to her mouth, shocked. What would this do to them? She hesitantly reached up to touch his lips. His eyes dropped closed and his breath stuttered as her fingers traced his lips.

He turned his head, a dark angel leaning into her touch, placing kisses on her fingers. "You are right where you belong. Maybe we just try this and see what happens," Gabe murmured, opening his eyes and locking them onto hers. He inched closer, waiting for her to stop him.

A contented sigh escaped her as he pressed his lips to hers, a much gentler attack of the senses. He slid a hand behind her to cradle her head, holding her body tightly against his chest. "Rachael, do you want me?"

Right now? Yes.

She nodded, and another tear slipped down her cheek.

He followed the trail of the tear and kissed it away before reclaiming her mouth. Closing her eyes, she curved her hand around his jaw as he ravaged her mouth. She felt like she was floating and realized he was quite literally carrying her away. She moaned, twining her arms around his neck.

He set her gently on his bed and followed, raised on his elbows, his body tensed. Gabe placed a hand behind her head and smiled, leaning closer. "I've dreamed of this," he said in a low voice. "Of you here with me in my bed, love. My beautiful golden girl."

"Gabe, this doesn't change anything. I still—"

"Shh . . ." he pressed a kiss to her forehead. "I promise we will talk later," he assured her, nodding into her eyes.

Rachael wrapped a hand around his neck and pulled him to within a breath of her lips. "So, what did we do in your dream?"

"We started with this," he said, licking the corners of her lips. Rachael giggled, then slipped her tongue out to meet his. "And some of this," he continued, before plunging into her mouth, tangling with her tongue. He leaned to one side to free his arm. His burning hand slid her hair back from her face before moving over her shoulder and trailing a searing path down her side. She wriggled as he tickled her. He tilted his head up and gave one last teasing kiss. Like a starving man, his gaze drifted down her body, his lips closing over her breast through the black shirt. "And this," he mumbled against her.

"Oh!" she gasped as his mouth dampened and heated the fabric over her, his hands roving.

His fingers worked to untie the laces at the front of her borrowed sweatpants and he jerked them roughly. He gave a frustrated grunt and sat back. "What the hell . . . ?"

Rachael giggled at his befuddlement. "They were too big, I had to tie a knot."

Instead of untying them, she wiggled her hips and let them slide down. She deftly reached down and kicked off the pants, leaving her lacy black underwear and now-moist fitted tank. With a smile befitting a fallen angel, his mouth greedily returned to her, his tongue working and licking her tight nipples through the thin material. A tingling behind her breasts connected with the heat growing in her middle, and she squirmed, wanting more. Rachael tangled her hands into his long hair and tugged at his head, trying to bring him back to her.

"Gabe," she whispered.

He worked his way up, biting and sucking, the deep suction marking her chest and doing funny things to her insides. He reclaimed her mouth and roved a hand lower, tracing the lines of the lacy black underwear. She reached for his hand, guiding it under the waistband, moving his expert fingers where she needed him. He touched her and groaned into her mouth when his fingers found her ready for him. She arched closer, wanting his touch, needing to feel him.

"Rach," he moaned, tearing his mouth away, watching her face as he toyed with her.

She squirmed beneath him. "I want you."

He smiled broadly, his dimple catching the light. "Say it again."

"I want you."

"Say you need me."

"I need you."

"Say my name."

Rachael stared at him, her fingers tracing the angles of his jaw. "I want you, Gabe. I need you."

"Good girl," he growled. He grabbed her panties and

ripped, tearing the fabric away. He grunted and lowered his weight between her legs, sliding his hand against her sensitive flesh, his thumb circling and finding her clit. She moaned and her head fell back. He dropped his head to follow, licking and biting her neck, chasing after her lips.

His thumb kept circling, and his index and middle fingers slipped between her outer folds and dipped into the warm, wet center.

"Gabe," she murmured, his thick fingers pushing in and out, his thumb working in circles as he pressed. "I love your hands," she panted, gripping his broad shoulders and holding on as his fingers continued to bring her closer to the edge, plunging deeper and faster, his thumb steadily moving, all building together. Soon she was thrashing her head back and forth, shuddering, trying to hold on.

"Come for me, love," he demanded.

And she did. She gasped and felt a violent trembling rush through her, shaking her core, catching them both off guard. "Holy crap," Rachael breathed, her body still clenching his fingers, refusing to let go.

Gabe smiled at her tenderly as the tremors subsided, and leaned down to kiss her. He slid his hand up her stomach, dragging the fabric with it. He continued up and tossed the black material over her head, throwing it to the floor.

"Touch me," he commanded.

She slid her hand under his shirt and pressed her palms flat across his bulky, ridged muscles. She traced the lines, following the trail down a deep V, reaching the waist of his pants.

She reached lower and unfastened his pants, sliding the zipper down.

"Too slow," he growled, ripping his pants and briefs down and tossing them to the floor too. She arched an eyebrow at him.

"What?" he asked.

She laughed and shook her head. "Nothing, Mr. Impatient."

"Hell yes, I'm impatient. Look at you. Perfection laid out for my enjoyment. Now touch me again."

Smirking, she continued exploring, roaming lower. He hissed when she touched him, wrapping his hand around hers encouragingly. Locked around him, she marveled at the velvet heat and how responsive he was to her touch. "Condom?"

Gabe pressed his eyes closed for a heartbeat, then jerked out of her hand and rolled over, digging into his dresser drawer. In less than a minute, he returned, fully sheathed, and crawled over her. She reached for him, skimming her hand along his wrapped length. He groaned and buried his head in her shoulder.

"Rachael, I need to be in you," he rumbled. "Now."

She wrapped her arms around his shoulders and tossed her hair back. "Then do it."

He groaned and spread her legs farther apart. He leaned on his elbows, watching her face as he pressed into her, his thick girth stretching her beyond her limits. She moaned, closing her eyes against the invasion.

"Open your eyes, damn it. Look at me as I take you," he demanded. Her eyes flew open and he nodded, holding her gaze with his own.

Gabe continued pushing into her and she winced at the pressure. He noticed and slowed. "Do you need me to stop?"

She shook her head. "No, just give me a second."

"What's one more second," he teased, staring at her mouth. He reached between them and massaged her, circling gently, stirring her as she relaxed to accommodate him. Rachael nodded and he dipped to kiss her as he moved in her, his dark curtain of hair closing the world off. He withdrew and returned, pushing deeper each time. She hissed as he surged in again, filling her.

"All in." He chuckled, kissing her damp forehead.

She wrapped her arms around his neck as he started the dance, slowly at first, moving gently, rocking her whole body back and forth. He braced his elbows on either side of her, wrapping his fingers into her long tresses. He continued easing in and out, kissing her with infinite skill, his tongue twirling to his movements, black hair tickling her cheeks. She dug her nails into his shoulders and unwrapped her legs from his waist. Bracing her feet against the bed, she pushed up to meet him. He grinned and moved more forcefully, slamming and surging deeper, over and over, their bodies sweating and sliding together. Panting, she bit his shoulder, following the sting with a lick. He grunted and groaned, his body swelling further and tightening up.

"I have you," he panted, crashing into her, over and over. She felt it coming, felt her own climax cresting.

She gasped, her body breaking into a million pieces under him.

"You're mine, Rachael," he shouted in triumph, straining forward as his body heaved and shuddered, losing himself in her.

He dropped to her side, cradling her, and whispered, "I love you."

18

Did he just say he loves me?

She couldn't say anything. Rachael closed her eyes and relaxed against him.

"You're bleeding," Gabe noted as he tossed the condom away. "Did I hurt you?"

"No, I'm fine."

He rolled over to look at her, worry creasing his forehead. "You don't have to say it. I understand." The love was clear in his face.

A thread of uneasy concern ran through her. "Gabe, I care so much for you. I don't know what I'm feeling right now. But I do care about you. You're one of my best friends."

He ran a hand down his face. "I know."

"And who knows. Maybe this is how things start?"

He smiled sadly. "Love, I don't know that I'm the one for you."

She frowned in confusion. "What do you mean?"

Gabe sighed and looked up at the ceiling. "I love you, Rachael. I can't fucking believe it, but I do. That's not easy for me to admit." He turned back to meet her eyes. "I want you to be with me, stay with me, be mine. But I think I'm the right person at the wrong time. Or maybe the wrong person at the right time."

"Gabe?"

"Shh. Just come here and rest."

Rachael slid off the bed, and he held his hand out to her. "Where are you going?"

She pointed to the restroom and he nodded.

Shutting the door softly behind her, she leaned heavily against it.

Fuck, fuck, fuck. Rachael, what have you done?

She washed up, glaring at herself in the mirror.

What is wrong with you?! Gabe is perfection. How can you not love him?

"You should have a sign on your forehead: 'Rachael Eller, world's biggest screwup,'" she hissed to herself.

Tossing down the hand towel, she flipped the light off and returned to the bed.

He held his arms open and she rolled into him, breathing in his spicy scent and the smell of their sex. She settled in and relaxed, finally finding her voice.

"Gabe?"

"Mhm?"

"Are you upset with me?"

"Yeah. But I'm more pissed at me."

"You didn't do this, Gabe. I'm sorry. I shouldn't have—"

"Stop, Rachael. It's done."

What did that mean? The friendship? The sex?

Rachael breathed and stared at his firm chest, debating what to say, how to make this right. The sex was incredible, but she knew he was a substitute for who she wanted to be with but couldn't have. And she was pretty sure he knew that too.

"Gabe, I—"

"Damn it, stop, Rachael."

"Are you sure?"

He kissed her forehead and groaned. "I'd like to be more angry. But being used by you is the most fun I've had in quite some time."

Rachael flinched at his description and heard the truth in his words. She was so going to hell.

"Can we still be friends?" She couldn't imagine not being friends with him.

Gabe was quiet for some time. "I don't know."

She nodded against his chest. "I'm sorry."

"For fuck's sake, Rachael. Please stop apologizing. I did this of my own free will. I wanted you as much as you needed me. I don't regret it. I would appreciate knowing that you didn't either."

"I don't. In fact, I'd say it was the highlight of my day," she teased.

"Of your day? Damn. I'm losing my touch." He tickled her sides and they both rolled onto their backs.

"I do love you, Gabe. Just not that way."

"I know, love. Now zip it and let me catch my breath before I take you home."

Relief washed over her and she kissed him on the shoulder. She was a selfish mess, but he seemed to understand what she was going through better than she did.

Acknowledging the truth, she owned that she was an

absolutely terrible person. Rachael just hoped it didn't cost her his friendship. She might not be in love, and she definitely didn't deserve it, but she was loved. And right now, she needed to know she was loveable.

19

The next week flew by with work and meetings. She tried not to think about how quiet her phone had been. Nothing from Gabe, not that she expected it. Nothing from Rick, no surprise there. And it seemed like half the country was on vacation. Her Instagram feed was full of beaches and palm trees.

Deciding it was time to find her groove, Rachael doubled down and threw herself into her work, tearing through the stacks of contracts and proposals she had let accumulate during her meltdown. Maybe she could forget everything that happened and find her blissful workaholic escape. She loved her job, truly. But right now, it didn't fill her with the satisfaction she had known before.

Time. Time would help.

Her mom stopped by her office a few times, but never stayed for more than a minute. They remained mum about things at home. Maybe her parents knew, maybe they didn't. Either way, she was grateful her mother never brought it up.

In the mornings, Rachael and her dad fell into a routine, each of them enjoying their coffee in companionable silence. She would let the dogs out. He would grumble and complain, but would always agree to let them in so she could leave early. Olive and Martini were undoubtedly working their magic on him. They were kind of impossible not to love.

Olive was due for her next checkup, and Independence Day was approaching. Rachael wondered how the dogs would handle it. Some dogs got severe anxiety and hid in the bathroom or under furniture to get away from the booming displays. She glanced down at Olive in the passenger seat and frowned. How would she and Martini respond to the fireworks?

Laughing quietly to herself, Rachael reflected how different her life was now than a few months ago. While she had loved animals and working in the shelters, she never considered herself to be the maternal type. Maybe after hitting the snooze button so many times throughout her twenties, her clock had finally started ticking. But instead of babies cooing, she melted over dog kisses.

They arrived at the animal hospital, and she parked in the shadow of a large oak tree, willing to suffer whatever droppings the birds had planned. It was still hot as Hades outside, and sitting in a sun-scorched patch of leather upon her return to the car was so not going to happen today. Attaching Olive's leash to her collar, Rachael told her furry companion how lucky she was to be getting her cast off today. The dog looked at her curiously, head tilting and tongue lolling.

Rachael opened the car door, letting Olive hop down to the shaded pavement ahead of her. Rachael slid her bag over her arm and followed the trotting girl toward the entrance. She chuckled at Olive strutting her stuff, the little cast on her hind leg hardly a bother at this point.

"Olive?" came a cheerful voice.

Rachael turned and smiled at the young college student. Olive panted happily. "Cora! It's so good to see you again."

"How is she doing?"

"She's good. The stitches have healed over perfectly. You did a great job."

Blushing, Cora adjusted her glasses. "I'm sorry I didn't recognize you when you were here before, Miss Eller. I tend to zero in on my patients."

Rachael brushed off the apology. "And that's why you're going to be an amazing doctor. Have you applied to veterinary programs yet?"

Cora knelt to greet her patient, who soaked up every blessed moment of attention.

Cora and Rachael chatted for a few minutes about graduate schools, and the future vet promised to visit the animal shelter where Rachael volunteered. Cora would love it there, and they could use someone with her dedication.

Waving goodbye, Rachael met Olive's impatient, adorable face. "Ready, girl?"

She pranced ahead and Rachael shook out the leash, switching it to her other hand. It was somehow tangled up in her purse strap. Crap. Glancing down at Olive, Rachael pulled her to a halt in the shade of the entrance's small awning. Surveying the jumbled mess, she tried to unknot the two strands and sighed in frustration as it only got worse. For God's sake, how did that happen? She must have been toying with it while talking with the intern.

Bending over her handbag, she examined the intricate cluster and twisted the leash, this way and that. If she could figure out how to weave her purse through a tiny loop she'd managed to loosen up—

The world went black.

SHE WAS LYING DOWN, but the world was dark. Where was she? The surface underneath her back and hips felt uncomfortable, but her head throbbed to the point that everything else faded to insignificance.

"What happened?" Rachael groaned.

"She's waking up, Rick," she heard a female voice murmur.

Rick? What?

"Where am I?" Rachael groaned, the words echoing in her head.

"Now, now, honey. You're safe. It appears you took a nasty couple of bumps to the head."

"Nancy?" she mumbled, straining unsuccessfully to open her eyes.

"Yes, that's right."

Nancy. Animal hospital.

Olive!

"Where's Olive?" She felt a cool, damp cloth pressed across her face. She peeled it back, flinching at the way it pulled at her tender skin, and cringed at the bright lights.

"She's fine. Gil took her back to remove the cast."

Rachael heard Nancy bustling around the room and

felt the wet cloth in her hand being swapped out with a soft, dry towel.

"Gil? Rick?" Nancy called.

Rachael slowly adjusted to the light and could still only open one eye. She gingerly touched the closed eye and cringed, fingering a puffy mess.

"You're going to want to keep ice on that for a while," an achingly familiar voice said, approaching the row of padded chairs she was laid out on. His warm hand touched the side of her face before he drifted away again.

"Rick?" she wondered aloud, shifting her head to try to see him. What was happening?

"It's okay, dear," Nancy patted her hand.

Head throbbing, the room began spinning faster, and to her horror, she vomited profusely before thankfully passing out again.

"RACHAEL? Rachael, you need to wake up. I need you to wake up."

She groaned and tried not to move her head. If she could arrange it, she never wanted to move again.

Animal hospital.

Right.

She stretched her hand out and felt a sheet. Nancy must have covered her up. That was thoughtful.

"Rachael, wake the fuck up."

What?

"Nancy?"

The woman sighed, muttering under her breath. "No, I'm not Nancy, you moron."

"Kim?!"

Rachael's head spun again and she struggled to catch the whirling globe, halt the world if possible.

"Where?"

"You're at the hospital."

"What?"

"Hos-spit-al," Kim exaggerated.

"Animal hospital," Rachael amended groggily.

"Seriously? The hospital-hospital, the people-hospital. You got knocked out cold at the vet's office, then I guess things went downhill so they sent you here. Carlie asked me to come check on you. You look like hell, by the way."

"Olive?"

"Is this your new thing? One-word questions? To be honest, I wouldn't mind the change. You talk too damn much for my liking."

"Olive!" Rachael barked, the sound richocheting around her too-full, throbbing head.

"Jeeze, no need to bite my head off. The vet people have her. She's fine."

"Thank you." Rachael closed her eyes, wanting to go back to sleep.

"Hey!" Kim shouted at her, nudging her arm. "Did you not hear me? You need to wake up, girlfriend."

"Why?" she mumbled.

"Because the damn doctor said so."

"Why?"

"'Why, why, why?' You're like a two-year-old. I don't know why. Artist here, remember? If it were up to me, you could sleep all day and night."

She heard heels clacking down the hallway and the metal-on-metal screeching of a curtain being dragged opened very nearby. Could anyone else hear how obnoxious that was?

"Rachael?"

Jesus. Was she dying? What took Mom out of the office at this time of day? Or . . . "What time is it?"

"Holy shit. More than two words. I think she's going to make it."

"Kim," Mary Eller warned. She turned to Rachael. "It's nearly seven o'clock."

Rachael tried to calculate. Olive's appointment was at four. Three hours had gone by.

"My bag? My car? What happened?"

Her mother sat on the side of the bed. "Dr. Thomas said you took a hit to the head with a door, of all things, then again to the back of your head when you hit the pavement. Why were you crouching in front of a door?"

Rick. She talked to Rick?

Rachael shook her head, then immediately groaned. "Shit."

Gritting her teeth, she willed the room to stop spinning. Once the rotation ebbed, Rachael thought through the question and rolled her eyes. "Her leash. The leash was knotted around my bag's strap. I was trying to undo it."

"Well, thank God you weren't standing in the middle of the street. Honestly, you girls need to pay more attention to what's happening around you . . ." She rattled on about how terrible this generation of young people was. Nothing Rachael hadn't heard before. Easing her eye open, Rachael took in her surroundings. Kim was hunched over in a gray plastic chair against a bland beige wall, and her mother was sitting at her side, both still dressed for work.

Her mom's voice drifted back into her ears. "I hope you learned a valuable lesson from this."

Rachael smiled numbly and mumbled what her mom expected to hear.

Kim winked and mock-strangled Rachael's mother. Rachael choked down a laugh.

"How long do I have to stay here?"

"Doc said a CT scan then you should be good to go. But you have to stay awake," Kim repeated.

"Why?"

"Don't start this again. Do I look like a doctor to you?"

Mom glared at Kim and gave an exasperated sigh. "Just until you get the CT scan, honey. You'll be able to sleep soon."

As if on cue, a pair of nurses and a doctor entered the room. Mom and Kim waved goodbye as the nurses wheeled Rachael from the room, the doctor in tow.

The medical staff brought her to a different room where they performed the CT scan. It felt like ages until it was over, but when Rachael thought she was finally free, she was transported back to her hospital room.

Carlie entered the room, sitting in the seat next to Rachael's bed and waving a weak hello. Carlie thanked the doctor and nurses as they left the room.

Rachael groaned. "I've had the CT scan. Why am I still here?"

"Soon. I told everyone that I would bring you home." Carlie fidgeted in the seat and looked generally uncomfortable. More so than usual.

"Car?"

"Hmm?"

"You okay?"

"Me?" She laughed nervously. "You're the one in the hospital bed."

"I'm also your big sister. Spill."

Tears welled up in her eyes. Damn.

"Just an argument with Brent. It's fine."

Fine, huh?

She examined her little sister's face, looking for clues. Nothing. "What happened?"

"It's no big deal," Carlie said, staring at her hands.

"Spill," Rachael demanded.

Carlie glanced at her and sighed, resigned. "We were grabbing an early dinner with Gina and Brian—you remember them?—when I got the call about you. I wanted to leave right away, but Brent was being a complete asshole. God, I'm so sorry I wasn't here for you. At least Kim was able to come."

"Car, I'm fine. A few bumps on the head. And I wasn't exactly awake most of the time anyway."

She nodded miserably. "Still," she paused, "if it had been someone in *his* family, we'd have been out of there right away. I'm just irritated. And the way Brent and Gina were talking, you'd think *I* was the one in the wrong. *I* was the selfish ass. Ugh."

"What happened?"

"I threatened to call an Uber, then suddenly I was pressuring him too much. If I asked him to leave, I was being unfair. If I called an Uber, I was being unfair. It was absurd. And Gina had the nerve to tell me *I* was being unreasonable and should consider Brent's feelings. Arrrgh!"

Bastards.

Rachael watched her sister and was completely at a loss

for words. Carlie was too patient, too sweet, too kind. To see her this miserable was infuriating. The best she could do was change the subject.

"It's okay, CarCar. You're here now, and I assume you're my getaway driver. Can we escape?"

She laughed. "Not until we get the green light."

20

$\mathcal{I}$t was nearly nine o'clock before Rachael was discharged from the hospital. Carlie drove her home and escorted her into the house, going straight up to her room. "You sure you're okay?"

"Yeah. Thanks. I owe you one."

After coddling Rachael to within an inch of her sanity, Carlie finally left her in peace. Rachael sat quietly on the bed, looking around the room. She'd been living there for a couple of months now, and while it was not her place, the guest room was starting to feel like home.

So not good.

"I need to get out," she mumbled.

Exhausted, she lay down on the bed, fully clothed in the sweatpants and t-shirt Carlie had helped her change into at the hospital. Tomorrow, shower. Tonight, sleep.

Before sleep could claim her, and in a very surreal throwback to childhood, her parents checked on her and repeated all the smothering before they also retired for the night.

She tried to sleep but kept tossing and turning. Each toss or turn caused the world to spin out of control. Once the spinning stopped, her mind would refuse to let her sleep, wanting to replay every single moment of every conversation—and experience—with Rick, then Gabe, then Rick again. So, she'd toss and turn and the whole damn thing would start again.

Martini slipped into the room and whined on the floor next to the bed.

"I hear you, buddy." Groaning, she slid off the bed and tip-toed down the stairs. The house was blessedly quiet. Surprisingly, the clock on the stove said it was only half past ten; she could have sworn she had been tossing and turning for hours. Rachael cracked opened the back door, flipped on the deck lights, and stepped out into the night. Martini rushed down to the grass to do his business as she eased into a patio chair, watching the sky.

After a few minutes, the little rascal returned and leaned up on his hind legs. She picked him up and he snuggled on her lap. Poor baby boy. "Probably wondering where Olive went this time, huh?" She scratched behind his ear and he exhaled, laying his head down and drowsing.

Rachael stared between the stars, hunting for the faint movements of satellites. When she was little, she and Dad would sit on the deck at their old house and search for them for what felt like eons until they'd see a small white light far off in the distance, steadily tracking across the dark night sky. The trick was to not focus too much on any one star, but to let the subtle movements capture your attention. Rachael used to squeal at every airplane, convinced she had found one. Dad would chuckle and redirect her to the farther lights. You had to be still and quiet, focus on not focusing. With only one good eye right now, it was pretty much impossible, but it was still soothing.

"Too late for a visitor?" a voice called from the fence's gate.

"Gabe?"

"Your sister left a message with my office." He joined her on the deck and winced. "Looks painful."

"Feels like a breeze." Rachael was surprised Carlie thought to do that, but then again, her sister knew how close she and Gabe had gotten. Well, the platonic part at least.

He laughed dryly. "At least it didn't steal your delightful sense of humor."

"Have a seat," she offered.

Dragging a chair over next to hers, he sat and took her hand. "You all right? What happened?"

"Had a run-in with a door," she mumbled.

"Must have been a hell of a door. Any permanent damage? To you or the door?"

She groaned and smiled weakly. "It hurts, but I'll be fine. Concussion." She pointed to her head.

"You didn't have to go all kamikaze. I could have told you there was something wrong with your head," he said, smirking and squeezing her hand.

"Ha, ha. Very funny." It occurred to her that it was the first time they'd talked since the night they spent together. Rachael was relieved he appeared to be willing to let it go.

They sat silently, enjoying the quiet night.

"I'm going to leave town for a while," he said at last.

"Oh?" This wasn't terribly surprising. She figured something like this would need to happen. She felt a little guilty that it was because of her, but understood they needed some distance. Though part of her wondered if he was actually leaving, or just saying he was. Either way, the result was the same.

He nodded, staring out into the dark. "Need to do some traveling. For work."

She glanced at him, but he stared steadfastly into the dark. She turned back to the sky.

"Where to this time?"

"Both coasts, then check on progress in Germany and Sweden. See how my brothers are adjusting."

"Oh." Maybe he really was leaving. She knew he had a pair of half brothers, twins.

The silence stretched again. He ran his thumb across the back of her hand and took a deep breath. "Come with me."

Surprised, her gaze flew to his face. He was watching her intently. She swallowed and looked away. What was he thinking? Hadn't she made her position clear already?

Rachael closed her good eye and mindlessly stroked Martini's coat. "Gabe . . ."

"Think about it. We could explore New York and LA together. Berlin, Norway. Come with me," he pleaded. "After those, we can tour Paris and Rome, take in the sights. Do all the touristy stuff."

Her head was spinning again, and not from the injury.

"I can't," she whispered.

"Rachael, I want to take care of you. I want to show you the world. I want to be with you."

Her emotions waged war. Anger that he was putting her on the spot. Hurt that he would pursue this after their last discussion. Fear that he would leave for good. Anxiety that she couldn't be what he wanted. A thread of excitement at the opportunity he outlined. Confusion. It was all so frustrating and overwhelming. Her heart hurt. A tear slid down her face; she pressed her eyes closed to keep more from falling.

"Gabe, I can't."

He sank down in front of her, and Martini looked up curiously. Gabe grinned at him, then took both of her hands. "I know you've been waiting on him. But he's not here. I am. And I love you. You said you don't feel the same way about me right now. But I think you do—or at least could. If we spent more time together. If we got away from here, from him, you would see how much you love me. We'll be great together."

The tears overran her eyes, trailing down to her chin. "Please," she whispered, heart in her throat, knowing this was her fault. She did this. To him. To them. The pain lanced through her. "Please don't do this. Not now. Can't you just be my friend?"

"We can leave tomorrow, and—"

"I believe the lady said no."

Olive came racing toward her, cast gone. Rachael gasped as she saw a familiar shape walk toward her from the darkness.

Gabe jumped to his feet. "Who the fuck are you?"

Frozen, she could only stare as Rick walked into the dim circle of light from the deck. His light-brown hair caught the soft glow of the porch light, his eyes unreadable in shadow. He nodded toward Rachael. "I thought you'd want Olive back home."

"Now?" She stared, stunned to see Gabe and Rick.

Together. Here on her parents' deck. Her heart was pounding louder than her head.

"I was planning to drop her off in the morning on my way to the office. But since I was passing the neighborhood, I thought I'd swing by and see if anyone was up. Saw the deck lights from the front."

They both looked at her, then Gabe stalked down the steps toward Rick, two huge menacing forms in the darkness. "So. You're the vet."

"I am," Rick said, tossing a questioning glance at Rachael before turning his attention back to Gabe.

"You don't deserve her," Gabe spat at Rick.

"And she doesn't want you," Rick said calmly, holding his ground.

"*She* is sitting right here," Rachael yelled, grasping her throbbing head between her hands.

Both men ignored her.

Martini jumped down from her lap, and he and Olive stood guard together in front of their human. A soft growl came from Martini, directed at the fools in the yard.

Oh lord. All the males in the yard had gone insane. Way too much testosterone flowing way too freely. What should she do? Her eyes flicked back and forth between the men, and she glanced at the closed patio door behind her, seeing the house was dark and quiet. She could leave now and let those two figure out their issues.

But she couldn't walk away. Not with Rick finally back in the picture. God, what if he'd decided to give her another chance? Please, she prayed, wishing Gabe would leave and she could talk to Rick.

"You lost your chance with her, Doc," Gabe continued, crossing his arms over his chest, muscles flexing. "You turned your back on her for having fucking dinner with me. During which, I might add, she did nothing but talk about you, and why she and I could only be friends."

Rick spun his head to look at her again, and she nodded once.

What was happening?

"It doesn't matter," Rick dismissed. "What matters right now, is that she is concussed and you are pressing her to make a major life decision. She said no once. Don't you know how to take no for an answer?"

"You have no idea," Gabe growled. "You have no idea how many times I've stood by her side, helping her try to make sense of your abandonment. Christ, you practically threw her into my arms and she still only wanted you."

Rick stood utterly still, hands resting at his sides, as Gabe moved into his space.

Gabe poked his finger at Rick's chest and continued, "*You* left her a mess. Didn't even give her a chance to tell you what happened. You don't think *I* know how to take an answer? At least *I* give her a chance to talk. To tell me what she's thinking. Even if it wasn't what I wanted to hear. You are a coward."

"That's enough," she said, wearily pushing herself up. Olive skittered closer to her feet, as though herding her away from the men.

Rick glared at Gabe, his anger visibly rising. "And what about you? Are you a scavenger, McAllister? You think *I* don't deserve her? I know your kind," he sneered at Gabe. "You'll keep after her until you get what you want, then move on to screw over the next girl. I may not deserve her, but you sure as hell don't either."

167

Gabe swung before Rachael even saw it coming. He threw a punch and caught Rick in the chin.

"Rick!" Rachael cried.

Rick recovered and dove at Gabe, and soon they were both rolling on the ground outside the circle of light, Martini and Olive barking from the top step of the deck.

She couldn't see what was happening but heard enough thuds and grunts to know it wasn't good.

"Stop!" Rachael shouted, frustrated and exhausted, the world spinning off its axis. "Stop it!"

A floodlight turned on in the yard, and her dad's booming voice halted the fight. "You had better have a damn good reason for tearing up my yard in the middle of the night."

She turned and fled into her dad's arms. He wrapped her up in a bear hug, kissed the top of her head, then shooed her into the house. "Go inside, pumpkin. Go back to bed. I'll take care of this."

Nodding, she crossed into the kitchen, Olive and Martini chasing after her, tails high in the air.

"Rachael," called Gabe. "Please."

Pausing in the kitchen, she hesitated before casting her parting words into the yard. "I can't do this right now."

Dad shut the back door, cutting her off and going out to deal with the madness. Rachael wasn't sure what he would tell them, but she was done. Finished. These Neanderthals could pummel themselves into oblivion for all she cared. She was going to crawl into her bed and stay there for the remainder of her days.

21

———

$\mathcal{U}$nfortunately, the remainder of her days didn't take into account coffee and other necessities. Time to brave the morning light.

"Care to tell me what that display was about last night?"

She grimaced and looked at her dad through her good eye over the rim of her coffee mug. "Not particularly."

His newspaper sat folded next to him. He had yet to pick it up since she came in. Rachael sat morosely, nursing her coffee.

Charles switched tactics. "Quite a shiner you've got there, honey."

"You should see the other guy," she joked. "I just hope the swelling will go down enough to see out of it again."

"Mom said it was a door that got you?"

"Yup."

"I hope you did some damage to it."

He's trying.

"Dad." She took a deep breath. "It's a personal issue.

Okay? I don't know what to do yet. But I'll work it out. No need to worry."

He patted the top of her hand. "Someday when you have children, I'll remind you of this conversation and we'll both have a big ol' laugh."

She smiled at his sentiment. Charles Eller was a genius mastermind and a tough nut to crack, but at home, he was a softy and her rock. She and Carlie had always found comfort in his warm hugs, sage advice, and humble gourmet cooking. It was amazing how different her parents were from each other, but they were perfect together, each providing their own unique, unfailing love and support for each other, their daughters, and the family business.

"I know you worry. But no need to worry about the guys from last night. It'll all work out."

"Am I correct in assuming the dark-haired one was McAllister?"

She blushed. "Yes."

"Mhm. Promise me you'll be careful."

"I will."

He picked up his paper and Rachael heaved a sigh of relief, grateful to have survived the inquisition.

"Who was the other one?" inquired her mother, brusquely walking to the table.

And there went her sense of relief, screaming out the back door and running for the hills.

"Rick."

"Rick . . . ?"

"Rick Thomas," she gave up. "Dr. Richard Thomas. Olive's vet."

She caught the look her parents shared over her head, but chose to remain silent.

"Dr. Thomas? I spoke with him on the phone yesterday. He seemed very concerned about you."

Rachael remained silent.

"I didn't know he planned to bring Olive home."

She shrugged. She had no answer. Or at least one Mom wouldn't pick apart.

Mom huffed aloud and Rachael smothered her grin behind her mug.

"I have to get to the office. Rachael, I've had Larry reschedule all your appointments for the next two weeks. Those that can't be pushed off are being covered."

"Two weeks? Mom, I'll be fine in a couple of days." She shuddered thinking of her mom's assistant, Larry, who had the personality of a dead frog, contacting her clients.

"Yes, dear, but I want that black eye to heal a bit, too. No sense in making people think we're beating you into submission."

Rachael stared into her mug.

Two weeks. No way. What was she supposed to do without her work to keep her busy?

"Maybe I'll check out some apartments."

"No driving yet," her mother tacked on. "Not until you get permission from the doctor."

Great. Two weeks. Stuck at home. No work. Clients left dangling in the wind with Larry Grant. And the two most important men in her life were out there hating her. Fantastic.

"Yaaaaay," Rachael mockingly cheered. "And maybe I'll learn how to cook."

Dad glanced over his paper in mock horror. "Maybe that concussion is worse than we thought."

"Once she stops sulking, she'll appreciate having this time to relax," Mom added.

Sulking? I have a freaking concussion, an eye the size of a grapefruit, a love life in tatters, and am stuck at home for the foreseeable future. Who wouldn't be sulking?!

Mom kissed Dad on the cheek and left for the office while Rachael shot daggers through her eyes. Or eye.

"She's just trying to get a rise out of you, honey. No need to be angry with your mom."

Dad could be pretty perceptive sometimes. Not always, but it was there.

"I know."

"If you need anything, you call or text any of us. We'll get you taken care of, pumpkin."

"Thanks, Dad."

After showering, she poked around and half-heartedly tried to locate her bag. She hadn't seen her phone at all. While it was liberating, she did need to find it.

When checking the obvious places proved fruitless, she picked apart the house, but there was still no sign of it. *Well then.* This would certainly make calling for help a bit more challenging. She grabbed her laptop off the bedroom desk and brought it out to the living room. Noting the gathering rain outside—*et tu*, Mother Nature?—she settled into the recliner.

She shot out emails to her mom and Carlie, asking if they knew where her bag and phone were. Staring at her computer screen, she couldn't help but think of the terrible moment that started all of the drama—that damn photograph. Ever since EHL Global became a household name, her family had been in the media spotlight. Staying in Ohio had kept the circus largely at bay, but when they traveled there always seemed to be stories that followed them, especially as she and Carlie came of age. Speculation and headlines were sometimes vicious, but they learned to ignore most of it. Unlike Gabe, who thrived on it and used it to his advantage. Rachael rolled her eyes. Gabe was a purebred media darling.

Blinking away the memories, she pictured the bizarre scene in the yard last night. Those two morons were ridiculous. Fighting in the dark as if she wasn't even there. At least Rick was forced to hear a taste of the truth, though whether or not he believed it was largely irrelevant. *Or was it? What brought him here in the first place?* She drummed her fingers on the chair, considering the multiple possibilities. *What would happen if . . . ?*

"Stop it, Rachael," she muttered. Best not to get her hopes up. She needed a distraction. She tapped a few keys and sighed in satisfaction. "Hello, Netflix." Might as well Netflix and heal.

Four episodes of *The Office* later, she broke the cycle and pulled up her email. No responses. Great.

She wandered around the house, played with the dogs, and ran out of things to do an hour later. Only a few hours in, and she was already at a loss. These two weeks were just going to *fly* by.

Stupid concussion.

The doorbell rang. Rachael was half hoping for a door-to-door salesperson, someone to chat with for a little while. She would totally blame it on the concussion. Instead, she stood stunned, wondering why Nancy was here.

Nancy smiled at her nervously, arms full. "Hello, there."

"Hi?"

She handed over Rachael's missing handbag. "You left this at the office. I thought you might need it. I didn't realize it was still there until it beeped earlier. Nearly scared the pants right off me." Nancy chuckled and blushed.

"Thank you. I had no idea where it was."

"And this is from all of us. We're all hoping for a speedy recovery," she added.

Rachael accepted the cheery vase of flowers and set it on the entryway table.

Nancy shifted back and forth on her feet, and Rachael stared at her for a moment too long before remembering her manners. "I'm sorry, would you like to come in?"

"As long as I'm not interrupting . . . ?"

Rachael cackled. "Not at all."

Nancy watched her for a moment with concern, then crossed the threshold.

"Coffee? Water? Liquor?" Rachael offered.

Her eyes widened, but she refrained from commenting. "No. No, thank you."

Rachael led her guest into the sitting room, and Nancy looked around, settling on the edge of the sofa cushion uncomfortably. Olive came running from the other room and sat next to Nancy's feet, gazing at her adoringly. Nancy scooped Olive up into her lap, cooing and petting her. She took a deep breath and met Rachael's eyes. "Rachael, I owe you an apology."

Not one to be left behind, Martini came chasing after Olive, checking out what the fuss was about. He sat on the floor a few paces away, not trusting this stranger who held his sister.

Rachael sighed and sat back in the recliner, her good eye watching Nancy. "No, you don't."

"I do. I misjudged you. It was wrong of me, and I apologize for my words and behavior."

Where did this come from? Did Rick tell her about last night?

Rachael cleared her throat and changed the subject. "Nancy, did I . . . did I actually throw up on you?"

Her cheeks pinkened as she laughed. "Heavens, yes! But don't you worry, I raised four children. A little vomit never hurt anyone."

It was Rachael's turn to be embarrassed. "Now I'm the one who owes you an apology. Or at least a cleaning service."

"Nonsense, honey. We all have our moments. It's already cleaned up."

Tapping her fingers on the arm of the chair, Rachael couldn't stop herself from blurting out: "Did Rick tell you what happened?"

She sniffed and looked away. "No. But I did have an interesting conversation with your mother."

Of course.

"She called you?"

Nancy nodded.

"I'm sorry. My mother has boundary issues."

Among other things.

"All good mothers do, honey. She's just worried about you."

"She needs a hobby."

Nancy laughed and shook her head, rising. "Well, I've said my piece and I don't want to get you overtired. You look like you could use some rest. And you, sweet thing." She tickled Olive's jaw. "You come back and see me soon!"

She set Olive on the ground next to Martini and stretched her hand out to him, palm down. He inched forward and sniffed. Evidently deciding the patient stranger was safe, he edged closer so she could pet him too.

"You come and see me too, Martini."

The dogs and Rachael led her to the door, where Nancy turned to wrap Rachael in a surprisingly comforting and maternal hug. "I hope to see you again soon, Rachael. And I believe Rick would like to see you too, though he won't admit it. Yet." Her eyes sparkled as she turned and shuffled back to her car.

Well then. That was interesting. So, did he or did he not want to see her? Of course there's never a damn daisy around to pluck petals from when you need it. She watched Nancy's car pull out of the driveway and debated what her next move should be. Did she want to talk to Rick? Should she call him? And if she did, would he answer?

Life was so much simpler when her only passion was her work.

22

_____

*H*er phone was dead. While waiting for it to charge a bit, Rachael checked her email on her laptop and saw a note from Mom saying her bag was at the animal hospital. Rachael replied and let her know it was delivered. She didn't bother adding anything about her conversation with Nancy. It would only encourage her mother's bad behavior. Once enough juice was returned to her mobile, she hit the button to power it on and headed into the kitchen.

She grabbed a bottle of water and some painkillers, returning moments later to see her phone vibrating and lighting up like a freaking UFO. Watching it warily, she sat and waited for the notifications to cease. Rachael closed her eyes and leaned back. The glow from the computer was really bothering her. This concussion could take a hike.

After a while, her phone was silent and she remained still, not ready to deal with it.

She would just rest a few more minutes.

~

OLIVE PAWED AT HER LEG, and she jerked awake, noting it was nearly noon. Rachael laughed to herself. *Well that's one way to kill more time.*

Letting the dogs out, she stood in the overhang of the patio door and watched the rain. This weather was so ridiculously fitting. The dogs came rushing back, leaving wet footprints all across the dry part of the deck. Glancing at the clean kitchen floor, Rachael groaned and closed the door, trapping them outside while she grabbed a towel. Either wipe their paws now, or clean the floor later.

Once they were inside and dry, she snagged a bag of grapes from the fridge and stared at her waiting phone. It looked malevolent.

What if he called?

What if he didn't?

And which did she expect?

Popping a plump green grape in her mouth, she continued to eyeball the phone.

Rachael, you're being a chicken. Woman up, girl!

Tapping the touchscreen, a slew of notifications popped up. Multiple missed calls and texts. Primarily from one of last night's prizefighters.

Apologies. Accusations. Demands. Pleas. All from Gabe. Poor guy.

And one lone text from Rick: *Sorry about last night. I was out of line. Hope you're feeling better.*

What could she do? She royally fucked up. She'd like to blame it on the wine, but that wasn't the truth. God help her, but after the run-in with Rick, Rachael wanted to sleep with Gabe. She wanted to be wanted, to be held. She wanted to forget.

She wanted to be with Rick.

You, Rachael Eller, are a terrible, awful, immoral human being. You don't deserve either of them.

Popping another juicy grape in her mouth, she read Rick's text over and over again. Nancy's words kept circling in her mind, and she wondered if things were as finished as she'd thought they were. Plus, he was at the animal hospital when she cracked her head like an egg. Presumably, he knew she was coming in. Maybe there was another act to this drama? And if there was, she now likely owed a thank you to Gabe. He surprised Rick last night with his admission of what happened—and didn't happen—between them at dinner that night.

Olive and Martini were snoring on the sofa, and Rachael smiled at their contentedness. What would it be like to be so at peace? To know you were exactly where you belonged?

It wasn't going to get any easier.

The phone's bright screen went to sleep in her hand as she wondered what to say to Gabe. Two more grapes, and she finally woke the device and typed out a message. *Thank you for stopping by last night. I really appreciate it. I am glad I can count on you to be there for me. You are my friend, and I love you for that.*

That sent, she sat and debated what to say to Rick. This was harder. Infinitely harder. She munched on her grapes and watched the screen, searching for inspiration in the blank text bubble. Every time it started to go dark, she tapped it, refusing to let it go away. Wadding up the empty snack baggie in her hand, she took a deep breath and started typing.

Thank you for bringing Olive home, and I'm sorry about everything else.

Might as well give him carte blanche in determining all of her mistakes. And, she reminded herself, he was not pure and innocent in all this either. He seriously freaked out at the first hint of trouble, a photograph with a business client-turned-friend. *Sorry, buddy, but that's not the first time, and probably wouldn't be the last time with a family like mine.*

Though usually it wouldn't be with a man like The Playboy.

Can I come see you? She got back from Gabe.

File this under conversations she definitely didn't want to have but desperately needed.

Yes, I'm home. For the rest of my life it seems.

Thank you, be there soon.

Here goes.

GABE PARKED his black Audi in front of the door, and ran through the rain, entering without knocking. His long black hair was pulled back and he had a few scrapes and cuts that made him look dangerous and sexy as hell.

Get ahold of yourself, Rachael!

He leaned down, looking at her swollen eye and pressing a kiss to the other cheek. "Damn, Rachael, you look like shit."

"You sure know how to sweet talk a woman," she

teased, trying not to be self-conscious. She knew she looked bad. But still. Ugh.

"Sorry." He sat on the couch and leaned forward, resting his forearms on his knees.

She jumped in before he could talk. "I've been thinking. What I did, seducing you, was terrible and unfair."

Gabe barked out a laugh, highly amused. "Love, you can't play a player."

"Excuse me?"

"I knew exactly what you wanted. And I was more than happy to oblige, once I figured it was what you actually wanted."

"But . . . ?"

"But what? You got what you wanted and I got to be with you. It's a win-win."

She sat quietly, absorbing this. "And your words? Your invitation?"

"I meant every word. And I do want you to come with me," he forced out, standing and pacing. "At thirty-one years old, I fall in love for the first time in my life, and it's with the one fucking woman who is completely closed off to me."

She flinched. "I am so sorry, Gabe. It's killing me that you're suffering because I am so screwed up. I don't know what's wrong with me. You are perfect. Funny and charming. Kind and patient. And obviously amazing in bed."

He grinned, but the smile didn't quite reach his eyes. "You don't have anything to be sorry about, love. You know you are still my favorite girl in the world."

Rachael hesitated, knowing he wasn't being completely honest, but if he was trying to move past it, so could she. "You're not mad at me?"

"When will you stop asking me that?"

"I guess when I stop doing awful things that would make most people incredibly angry."

He crouched in front of her recliner, holding her hands. He looked beautiful and calm, but the storm hadn't yet dissipated in his eyes. She glanced around, half expecting to see Rick come barging in again.

"Rachael, I know you are entangled in something else, someone else right now. I knew it that night. I see that better than you do. I had hoped with our intense physical connection, it might be enough to turn your head. But now? After last night? I know that isn't going to happen any time soon."

He bent his head and kissed the top of each of her hands, rubbing his thumbs over the moisture left behind. She leaned forward and kissed his cheek, blinking away the unshed tears in her eyes.

"Gabe, I don't deserve you," she whispered.

"This trip is coming at a good time for us. I need to get away from you, my little siren." He wiped the tear from her cheek, and cupped her chin, kissing her softly. "One for the road."

"I do love you, Gabe."

"I know, love. But I need to go. I can't stay and watch what happens next. I'll be back, and . . . and we'll see what happens."

He rose to leave and it took everything in her to remain in her seat, to not follow him out and ask him to stay. He needed to go, and she needed to let him.

It didn't make it any easier.

It felt like goodbye.

Unable to talk, she tracked his progress to the door.

Bitterly, she realized too late that he was perhaps the first true best friend she'd ever made outside of her family and Kim. When had he nudged his way into the core of her world? And how could she bear the loss of his comforting companionship?

The phone calls, the quick incognito meals, the friend who seemed to know what she needed before she did.

She'd ruined it. All of it.

The tears chased each other down her face, and she choked on a sob when the door closed behind him. He paused on the doorstep, turning back slightly. Her breath caught and she wondered what she would do if . . .

But he didn't come back. He dashed out into the rain and jumped into his car, perhaps driving out of her life forever.

"Goodbye, Gabe," she whispered.

She laid her head down on her arms and cried, letting this fresh heartbreak wash over her.

23

---

*N*umbness claimed her, allowing her to pass the days in a haze. Her family thought the concussion was really bad. But she knew it wasn't her head. Well, not only her head.

Rachael didn't hear back from Rick and her hurt was doubled.

What if she had sent Gabe away for nothing? Could she have loved him? It hurt to have him gone, so maybe she did love him. Was this love? She missed him.

No Gabe. No Rick. Nothing else to occupy her thoughts, her time.

She moved through the motions, showering, eating, reading when her eyes didn't hurt too much. Mostly she just thought, reliving the stolen moments with each. Feeling fresh pain when she thought of Gabe's words. His pleading. Fresh pain when she recalled Rick's anger over Gabe, thinking she had left him to be with another man.

The sizzling passion, the unbelievable sex. If she had to pinpoint what went wrong, that's where she epically screwed up. She lost herself in the physical, failing to see how important the connections outside the bedroom were to her as a woman. As a person.

Rachael was terrified that she had ruined the two paths that could have led to real happiness. Considering her track record, that might have been her entire life's allotment.

"Honey, I'm worried about you," Dad said, sitting down next to her at the breakfast table. No newspaper in sight.

"I'm fine, Dad."

"No, you're not. You spend all day brooding in the house, crying when you think no one hears you. What's going on? Can't you tell your old dad?"

Her eyes filled with tears, then she began abruptly sobbing, gasping for breath. He reached around her and tucked her against his side, and she cried. She cried for what felt like hours. He rocked her back and forth and didn't say a word.

"It's Gabe. He said he loves me. And I . . . I can't be what he needs me to be. I can't be his girlfriend. I don't want to be," Rachael admitted, hiccupping in the telling.

"Mhm," he replied.

That's it?

She looked up and was surprised to see that he was grinning broadly. Like, sunshine and rainbows grinning.

"What?" she scowled.

"I'm sorry, honey, but I'm so relieved. I thought you were going to say you're pregnant."

Pregnant?!

She stared at him in shock.

Then she felt it. A rumbling that started deep in her

stomach. Great, booming laughter erupted. Rachael laughed until her stomach hurt and fresh tears streamed down her face. She laughed and whatever haze had enveloped her at long last began to dissipate.

"Oh, my God!" she wheezed. "No, I'm not pregnant!"

More laughter ensued and a wave of pained relief crashed over her.

"Thank goodness. But honey, you are one hundred percent crazy. You know this, right?"

Rachael grinned at his response and leaned up to kiss him on the cheek. "I came by it honestly, Daddy dearest."

He blinked with an owllike expression, and then they were both laughing.

They finally calmed down, and he considered her. "Are you okay? This Gabe, was he pressuring you?"

Rachael shook her head. "No. He wanted me to choose him, be with him, go on this world trip with him. And seeing him so upset . . . It's killing me because I love him, but not like that. Does that make sense?"

"He's not the right one for you. When it's right, you'll know. I did with Mary. From the beginning, I just knew. Your mother and I were inseparable. I don't believe in love at first sight, but it was definitely a connection."

She tried to picture her mom and dad, young and in love. It touched her heart to hear him talk about it. If only things hadn't gotten so screwed up in her own life.

"And what if I felt the connection with someone who doesn't return it?"

"If you call the wrong number?"

She laughed. "Yes, like that."

"Then you hang up and try again. Or you don't. You

don't need a man or anyone else to make you happy, Rachael. You just need to be happy with yourself."

My dad. He's the best.

She hugged him tightly and stood up, a new determination growing.

It was time to shed this funk and work on her.

SHE CHEWED on her thumbnail and waited for Carlie's answer. She *had* to say yes. Who else was going to help with this?

"You want to do *what?*" Carlie squealed, astonished.

"Come on, Car. It's not like I want a tattoo or something. I just want to get fit. Can I work out with you? Or run? Do goat yoga? Whatever it is you fitness freaks do now?"

Carlie snorted like Rachael had lost her mind, which was probably not far off. "Goat yoga? You have never, ever worked out before. Which is so unfair, I might add. I look at a piece of bread and have to switch to an elastic waistband. You eat the whole loaf and stay a size six."

"Four," Rachael mumbled.

"Whatever," she chuckled. "When do you want to start?"

"Now."

"Rach, it's almost midnight."

"Fine, in the morning."

"If you say so. I'll be by around six thirty. See you in the morning."

They hung up and Rachael glanced at the clock. She

was actually excited. A change was needed, and this fit the bill.

Dropping into bed, she closed her eyes and visualized what she was going to do. Rachael was going to make a change. She would be better, do better. She was an Eller, damn it, and she didn't need anyone else to make her happy.

Far too soon, her alarm went off, and it took some serious mental acrobatics to get up. Who on earth woke up this early just to exercise?

"I guess I do now," she muttered.

She grinned and rolled out of bed, happy to note both eyes were fully open.

See, Rach? It's all about your attitude. Be positive and heal faster!

Less than an hour later, the positivity had been bitch-slapped right out of her.

"How . . . much . . . further?" Rachael huffed as she tried to keep up with her long-legged gazelle of a sister.

Carlie looked back with a comical expression and slowed. "Sorry, short stuff. We'll go around the bend and pass the shelter house, then back out of the park. Almost there!"

She watched her younger sister with envy; she was barely sweating.

Bitch.

As they approached the shelter house, Rachael snagged Carlie's arm. "Stop, please. Just a short break," she pleaded.

They walked over to the picnic tables—well, Carlie jogged and Rachael dragged her sorry self over—and Rachael sprawled across the top of a cool wooden table.

"You should stay standing, walk around a little," Carlie suggested.

Rachael rolled her head to the side and glared, not speaking.

"Or not," Carlie said, shrugging and sinking down onto the tabletop across from Rachael.

Slowly, Rachael caught her breath and the world stopped spinning. "Thanks, Car."

"You probably shouldn't be out running yet," Carlie commented about thirty minutes too late, watching Rachael with concern.

Rachael smirked, amused by the strange imbalance of intellectual versus street smarts her sister had been dealt. "Probably not. But it feels good to get out of the house."

"Want to talk about it?"

She sighed and crossed her arm over her sweaty forehead. "Carlie, I'm an emotional wreck."

"And that's new how?"

Rachael glanced over and saw the affectionate smile, halting her indignant reply. "It's new because I don't know what to do."

"Gabe?"

"That's part of it. He told me he loves me. He wants me to go travel the world with him."

"Wow," Carlie breathed. "What did you say? Do you love him?"

"I don't know. I don't love him the way he loves me. He's one of my best friends. I had to say no."

"Why?"

"Because I can't stop thinking about Rick."

Carlie blinked. "The vet? Is he back in the picture?"

"Yes. No. I don't know."

Rachael told her about the night after the hospital, their fight. "Granted, I was on some serious hospital meds and more than a little out of it, but it was crazy, Car. They literally got into a knock-down, drag-out fight. Only I don't really think it was about me. It was some weird stone-age shit."

Carlie squinted her eyes and watched Rachael for a minute, looking remarkably like their dad. "Rach?"

"Yeah?"

"I never dreamed I would have to say this to you, of all people. I love you, but you're being a complete and total wuss."

Rachael sat up and swung her feet to rest on the bench. "What?"

"You heard me. You are too scared to go talk to the guy."

"I am not!"

"And he's a pussy, too freaked or butthurt to come talk to you."

Staring at her shy, quiet younger sister, Rachael grinned, wondering what their mother would think if she knew Carlie had even half this moxie. "Who knew," she teased, "that you could lash out like that?"

Carlie winked. "Where do you think I learned it?"

"I would say me, but Mom would murder me if I had ever talked like that around you. Which leaves . . . Kim. Such a good influence on my baby sister."

Carlie laughed and started stretching. "Come on, Rach. Let's finish this and get some coffee. Are you okay to run, or should we walk?"

Rachael's head felt a little less end-of-the-world woozy, so she decided to punish herself.

24

Clacking heels approached the kitchen, stalking after Rachael's younger sister.

"Carlie Lynn Eller! Did you really take your sister running all over town?!"

Rachael hid her grin behind her coffee cup, watching Carlie nonchalantly put a single-serving pod in the coffee machine.

"Mhm. And guess what? She didn't die."

Their mother looked close to throwing something, but instead shook her head and stalked out of the room.

"Coffee?" Carlie asked the room.

Dad shook his head over the top of his paper. "You girls are going to send your mother to an early grave."

"Nah, she'll outlive us all," Rachael said, grabbing a banana from the counter.

"I've got to run, Rach," said Carlie. "But think about what I said, okay?"

"I will. Thanks, Car."

"Bye, Dad. I'll return the mug later. Love ya!"

Carlie walked out to the front, and Rachael heard her talking gibberish to Martini and Olive. Carlie was a sucker for those dogs. Not that Rachael was one to talk.

"What did you and your sister talk about?"

"Boy stuff," Rachael answered, tossing the banana peel into the garbage.

He turned his paper over and made a show of scanning the top of it.

"What?" she asked.

"Just checking to see what year it is. Have we gone back in time? Please don't tell me we have to relive your teenage years again. I don't think I could take it."

She laughed and walked over, dropping a kiss on his temple. "Love you, Dad."

"You too, pumpkin. And glad to see you got out of the house a bit. One foot in front of the other." He nodded and turned back to his paper.

The dogs begged the last bits of banana from her, and she obliged as she ran upstairs, stripping off her sweaty running clothes and taking a long shower. Carlie's words kept echoing in her head. She *was* being a coward. Rachael. The same person who fearlessly walked into boardrooms and convinced stodgy relics to move into the new era of technology.

What had happened to her?

And why was she waiting for him to make contact? Sure, she'd sent him a couple of texts, but otherwise . . . nada.

She finished rinsing out her hair and gently scrubbed her face. This eye needed to heal up, pronto. While it no longer looked like a squished meatball, it was now approaching cosmic-color scale.

"Highly accentuated single eyes are all the rage this season," she mocked into her microphone, a.k.a. loofah, imagining a wonky fashion magazine trying to sell this crap. "Don't just have starry eyes, be celestial!" She groaned and finished washing up.

After drying off, she pulled on some capris and a baggy t-shirt, then looked closely at her face. The skin around her eye was certainly colorful, but the swelling had all but disappeared. Camera avoidance had gone from code red to caution. She gently dabbed on some concealer. Still discolored, but it didn't look hideous.

Feeling marginally better about her appearance, Rachael returned downstairs to an empty, quiet house.

What to do?

She flipped through her email and messages, then brought her computer to the back patio, turning on some tunes and letting the dogs run around. Frowning at her screen, she skipped past the Sia and Train and went straight for classic rock. A dose of Aerosmith was just what she needed.

First, was she absolutely sure this was what she wanted to do? Her life was so full with work and the dogs she hadn't even been able to find a new place to call home. Rachael had never wanted a relationship before. Could she pull this off?

Her mind pulled up Rick's smile and their walk around the dog park, his generous spirit and passionate nature.

Yes. She wanted to do this. She was ready to do something different in her life. She wanted change, and she wanted Rick.

How to get him back in the picture?

Come on, think Rachael. You are good at this. Who are the players? The people? What do they want? Piece it together.

Gabe was leaving today for his globetrotting, so she could rule him out. Considering she didn't know if she'd ever hear from him again, she doubted he was going to affect what happened with Rick. She could probably eliminate him as a player at this point. The loss still stung, but it was for the best.

Rick. He was the lead. The person who would make the decision, sign the dotted line. He was the person she needed to focus on, directly and indirectly.

Who influenced him? Nancy. Gil. His family.

Family was out of state, so they were out. Which left Nancy and Gil. And Olive and Martini?

As Aerosmith gave way to Journey's "Don't Stop Believin'"—that had to be a good omen, right?—she opened a fresh doc and started making notes. Then trashed them. Then made plans. Then scratched those out again.

Why is this so hard?

Who was going to influence him in this decision?

After eliminating all the players, Rachael realized the person who held the power in this equation wasn't Nancy. It wasn't Gil.

It was going to have to be her.

Under other circumstances, once she'd identified the primary influencer and target, Rachael would request from the prospects' office a full write-up on the individuals, learning what made them tick, what they wanted. She was aware she had many blind spots where she was concerned. Rather than focusing on the unknown, she targeted growth areas where she could be more confident and stronger.

Spending the next few days working on herself, Rachael got a little less headachy and a little more headstrong. She finally got permission to drive, opening up the world to her reach again. But she made herself keep walking; she liked feeling stronger, increasing her endurance.

RACHAEL HAD plans to meet Carlie and Brent for dinner later, but had enough time to squeeze in some more "therapy." She grabbed her armband, phone, and a bottle of water and hit the pavement for a walk. Securing her phone on her arm and cranking up the volume to her earbuds, she settled into a steady pace, swinging her hips and arms to the rhythm of the upbeat Latin music.

What do you want?

She smiled, recalling when Rick asked her that. His voice, his lips forming the words. Her mind keyed in on this. Rachael's smile faded as she considered her own actions since then. While she didn't do anything that night, she and Gabe did eventually move things way beyond the platonic level. Would it matter? Did he even need to know?

When did I want to act?

Soon. She didn't want to lose her chance with him. But Rachael was also irritated at his mixed messages. He couldn't be completely disinterested if he had been willing to interrupt things with Gabe, right? Or was that just his pride? What if he wasn't trying to interrupt, but simply felt bad for her? Rachael took a swallow of water and tried to visualize all the ways this could go. What if he refused again? But what if he didn't? Was he worth it? Yes.

But would it work?

So many questions, but that was the million-dollar question.

A light sheen of sweat formed on her brow and she wiped at it as she kept moving. A bug grazed her upper arm and she swatted at it, keeping her pace steady. The fat, lazy bumblebees were all over the place this time of year. A tap followed and she shooed it away again. *Persistent bugs.*

A moment later, a hand wrapped around her upper arm and she screeched in alarm, jumping back, trying to free herself. "What the . . . ?"

She stumbled in her escape attempt and windmilled as she started to fall, before strong hands firmly grasped her upper arms, holding her steady. One of her earbuds fell out, and the world slipped back into her ears.

"The last thing you need right now is to knock yourself unconscious or worsen your concussion."

Rachael blinked, bewildered to see him and simultaneously noting the concern in his eyes. His hair was darker, wet. A light flush colored his cheekbones. She absently made sure her phone was still in place while her brain tried to make sense of this.

"Rick? What . . . what are you doing?"

He shook his head and dropped his arms to his side. "Sorry, I didn't mean to scare you. You okay?"

A laugh bubbled up and she unscrewed her water, mind racing. "I'm fine. But what are you doing here?"

"I was on my way back from the gym and saw you. I waved, and you weren't responding." He frowned and ran a hand through his damp hair. "So I pulled over and tried to catch you. I didn't know I'd literally have to catch you." He raised a brow.

"Sorry. Music," she mumbled, holding up the errant earbud. "You were at the gym?"

Rick nodded. "I swim laps between shifts, or as time allows."

Ah. That explained the long, lean muscles. She mentally fine-tuned her quarterback/baseball player to a stud swimmer. Yum. "Was there something you wanted?" She smothered her wince. That did not come out the way she'd intended.

He hesitated, looking uncertain. "I waved hello as I passed you. I wasn't going to stop, but when you didn't acknowledge me or respond, I thought . . ." he trailed off. He must have been nervous; he was repeating himself. She noticed the faint bruise on his chin.

"From Gabe?" she asked, touching the mark gently.

He winced. "Yeah. Sorry again about that whole thing. I don't know what happened."

"I'm sorry, too. I didn't know he would hit you." She reflected on her time with Gabe. Should she have seen that coming?

They stared at each other awkwardly, and miles of unasked questions ran through her mind. One was bothering her more than the others. "Have you been avoiding me?"

He considered, weighing his words. She had no idea what he was going to say, and the uncertainty made her anxious. Patience was not her strong suit, but she waited nonetheless.

"I wasn't avoiding you. Well, maybe I was at first, but . . . since your accident, since that night, I've been giving you time to recover and consider what you want. Frankly, I had to figure out some stuff too."

"You haven't responded to my texts."

"I didn't know you were expecting responses. I wasn't sure if you wanted to hear from me. You and McAllister . . ." he grimaced, "seemed like there were some unresolved issues there."

So Gabe was gone because she wanted to try things with Rick, and Rick was avoiding her because he wanted her to figure out what the deal was with Gabe? And men thought women were the sensitive ones. Sheesh.

"And today?"

Rick's cheeks warmed and he held his hands out, gesturing to her. "And today I saw you, and I—I was tired of waiting, wondering what you were doing. Damn it, I miss you."

"Oh." She smiled shyly up at him, hope soaring in her chest and butterflies preparing for liftoff.

"And just now," he said, clearly puzzled, "*you* were ignoring *me*. I thought maybe you had made up your mind; you didn't want to talk to me. That I had waited too long. Next thing I knew, I was pulling over and chasing after you."

"I wasn't ignoring you."

"I know that now," he said, rolling his eyes.

"I miss you too," she added.

Stepping closer, he brushed the hair back from her damp forehead and ran his hand through her hair, sending a frisson of awareness racing through her spine. His contented sigh warmed her soul.

"Now what do we do?" she asked, putting the ball firmly in his court. She was done trying to figure this out.

"Now?" He looked up at the sky and back down to her. "Now you tell me if you'd like to have dinner with me."

Joy and relief filled her. "I thought you'd never ask."

"Tonight?"

Rachael shook her head, wrinkling her nose. "Can't tonight. Tomorrow?"

"Pick you up at seven?"

"Sounds like a date," she said, wishing she knew what he was thinking.

"I'm glad I saw you." He smiled, eyes crinkling at the corners.

"Me too."

Rick shuffled his feet and flicked a look over his shoulder at his waiting car. "I need to get back to work. I'll see you tomorrow." He hesitated for a moment, then kissed her on the cheek, reminding her of the first time he'd done that, outside of the bar.

As she watched him return to his car and drive away, Rachael found herself praying that this was the opportunity they needed.

hh, the glorious freedom of being behind the wheel of your own car, the elation of knowing the world was within reach again. The wind poured in through the open windows, heavy with the scents of barbecues, cut grass, and mulched flower beds. Rachael took her time, cruising down the side roads, listening to the radio, and enjoying the summer breeze. Her wet hair was pulled back in a ponytail, the warm air pulling at the loose tendrils. She plucked the hair away from her eyes and pulled into the parking lot under the faded red sign for Pam's Diner. Sliding her sunglasses into her bag, she scanned the lot and was happy to see Carlie's car parked already.

Rachael strolled into the diner, one of Carlie and Kim's favorite spots. Somehow, she had never been here for dinner before, but they had awesome round-the-clock breakfast. Pancakes for dinner? Totally doable.

"Over here!" Carlie waved from one of the large booths in the two rows that lined the long and narrow diner. That particular booth ought to have a plaque saying "Property of Carlie and Kim." Rachael passed the breakfast bar and absently spun one of the old-fashioned metal barstools nailed to the ground. The sound of spinning metal clashed with the classic bubblegum pop music, and her shoes squeaked on the black-and-white-checkered tiled floor.

Rachael gave her sister a quick hug before sliding into the booth across from her. For as much of a dive this place could have been with the wrong owners, it was very clean and there were no rips in the red upholstery. "Where's Brent?"

"He had a late meeting," Carlie mumbled, pushing a menu toward Rachael.

Was she upset? Rachael couldn't get a read. "How are things going with you two?"

Car fidgeted with her silverware roll and eased off the self-adhesive paper wrap, spinning the white ring around her finger, staring at it like it was the most fascinating thing in the room. "Fine. We're both so busy with our jobs and stuff. You know how it goes."

"Sure, sure." Rachael placated. "Whatever works for the two of you, I guess."

Carlie frowned but moved on. "How are *you* doing?"

"Good. Head is better. I can't wait until I no longer look like a bar brawl champion—or loser—but otherwise, I'm feeling more like myself."

"Hear anything else from Gabe?"

She shook her head. "No. I wonder if I ever will. He was pretty great about everything as a whole. But, I don't know. I messed up big time by sleeping with him. What was I thinking?"

"Rach, you can't beat yourself up about this. You're both adults. If you want to make mistakes, then at least you made them together. Just tell me it was worth it." Carlie smiled wickedly.

Rachael laughed and felt her cheeks heat up. "All I can say is it was a very nice time."

"Ha! I knew it!" Carlie continued to fiddle with the silverware wrap, so Rachael jumped into the other bit of news. "I ran into Rick today."

Carlie's mouth made a perfect O. "What happened? Did you talk?"

"He chased me down while I was walking. It was kind of funny, actually. He said he was giving me time to decide what *I* wanted."

"And?"

"And we're going to dinner tomorrow."

Her lips curved in a satisfied smile. "I knew it."

Rachael hesitated before asking, "Should I tell him?"

"About?"

Rachael cleared her throat meaningfully. "Gabe."

"Does it matter?"

"I don't know. I've gone back and forth several times now." Rachael watched the condensation pool on the white Formica table at the bottom of the water glass. She trailed her finger in it, dragging a thin liquid ribbon across the table. Carlie watched, puzzled.

"Rachael, what are you thinking?"

"Just going through different scenarios."

"Can I offer a tiny bit of advice?"

Focusing on her sister, Rachael wiped her wet finger in the palm of her hand. "Shoot."

"I have always admired your go-get-em attitude. I know the other day I told you to go talk to him. But you do have to realize this isn't a sales pitch. You're not going to get him to sign on the dotted line. There is no dotted line. There's no algorithm, no formula. This is life. It's full of unknown variables, things we can't even begin to imagine. And relationships, well, they're less predictable than anything else."

Damn, Carlie knew her too well. "Your point being?"

Her sister blew out her breath impatiently. "You can't plan for every move and countermove. Some things you just have to feel out. You can't fill a void with the closest tool around. Find the one that is a good fit for you."

"To clarify, we're not talking about sex, right?" Rachael teased.

It was Carlie's turn to blush now, and she threw her paper ring at her. "No, you crazy person. We're talking about heart-stopping romance. Love."

"Love, huh? And what's that look like?"

She shrugged. "You'll know it when you feel it."

"Jesus. That's so freaking poetic, Car."

"I know. I should totally start my own advice column."

"Or a talk show."

"Yes, I'm definitely the next Oprah."

"Or Dr. Phil."

"Shut up. I'm starving, and I've got carbs on the brain."

"Pancakes?"

"Pancakes."

TODAY WAS THE DAY. Date day. Rachael smiled and stretched across her bed before bouncing down the stairs like a kid on Christmas morning.

"Ready to head back to the office next week?" her dad asked, voice drifting over the newspaper boundary.

Rachael nodded as she poured a giant mug of coffee. "Mhm," she said, curious that her date tonight was roughly an excitement level of Jupiter, making work feel like Pluto, which depending on who you asked, was not even a planet.

"Your mom and I are going out of town for the holiday weekend. Will you be okay here by yourself?"

"Really? I'm twenty-seven years old. I'll be fine. I'm more worried about what trouble you two will get into."

He smiled over his paper. "You could always come with us."

"Nah, you and Mom go do your thing. I've got Martini and Olive to keep me company."

"Feel free to invite Grey Goose and Twist of Lime, too."

"Funny. Aren't you the comedian today?"

"Someone has to be," said Mom, strolling into the kitchen.

"Morning, Mary." Dad smiled.

"Morning, Charles." She smiled back, sweet as sugar. Sometimes you'd almost forget she was a high-powered attorney. "Everything set for New York?"

"Yes, I was just asking Rachael if she'd like to join us."

"Oh, good! Are you coming, honey?"

"No, sorry. Dogs and need to prep for next week's meetings."

"Work can wait, Rachael. Life won't," her mom commented.

She blinked. "Who are you and what did you do with my mother?"

Her mother laughed and kissed her dad's cheek.

"Think about it?" she added, locking eyes with her daughter as she picked up her bag.

Dad nodded at Mom and Rachael got the feeling they had planned this conversation. She groaned and grabbed her mug. "Martini! Olive! Let's go outside."

She walked out the back door and heard her parents laughing. Whatever.

Sinking into the oversized deck chair, she watched the dogs roll around in the damp morning grass and sipped her cup of joe. She pulled out her phone and skimmed through her social media feeds before opening her texting app. She saw Gabe's name dropping lower. It had been a few days since she had last heard from him. The more time that went by, the more she began to think it might be possible to pick up as friends, once enough time passed. Rachael missed her best friend. But it wasn't fair to keep interrupting his life. Someday he would meet someone else, someone who would love him in return. Things would be so much simpler if she could have been that someone. But she wasn't. She loved him only as a friend. Even if he did know how to work it between the sheets.

God, Rach, you are awful.

Taking a long drink of creamy coffee, she let her thoughts move on. She couldn't change the past.

Rick. Did she love him? Was that what this was? She hardly knew him, but when he wasn't there, she was miserable. Everything about him appealed to her. His work, his passion, his humor, his smile. Him.

How was this going to work? She was afraid of him freaking out again about Gabe. And Gabe was important to her. When he came back—she refused to say if—and was ready to resume a platonic friendship, she still wanted him to be part of her life. Would Rick be okay with that? Even if he never found out that they slept together. It's not like she and Gabe were dating.

Did Rick need to know?

Would she want to know if the situation was reversed?

"Gah! This is ridiculous. I'm being ridiculous, thinking in circles," she mumbled, scratching Olive behind the ear and brushing some loose grass off her furry head. The dog tilted her head and panted. Rachael knew what the furry duo wanted. She pushed herself up and slipped in ahead of them to get a towel to dry off their paws. Martini sat patiently, waiting for his turn. She loved how good they were. They knew each other and trusted her. They had their routines, and they all played their parts to perfection. Usually. Why couldn't everything be that simple?

"Who wants a treat?" she asked, and they both pranced happily outside the door.

They entered the quiet kitchen and she saw Dad had picked up and left, too.

"Just us again, Martini and Olive. What shall we do?"

They gobbled up their treats and settled into a sun-warmed patch on the floor, informing her that she was on her own. She grinned at them and went back to her room, picking up her laptop to catch up on a little work before letting Netflix take her away for a while.

26

———

"**W**hat are you going to wear?"

Rachael watched Marie in the salon mirror, her lips pursed as she concentrated. Rachael's mind was clicking through the options as Marie maneuvered her comb and scissors, parting and flipping up the wet lengths of blonde, tugging this way and that.

"I haven't decided yet," Rachael finally replied.

"You like this man? You want to see more of him?"

Rachael pictured Rick as he gently tended to Olive, remembered the possessive feel of his hand on her lower back at lunch, considered how much they had in common and how everything just seemed to click. "Yes."

Marie paused her work and smiled gamely at Rachael. "Then you go and find yourself a nice little black dress. But you make him work for it, you know what I'm saying? No need to make things too easy for him. You know what they say about cows and milk? It's true!"

Rachael laughed nervously, knowing it was too late for that, but it was none of Marie's concern. "I know."

"Though with your coloring, you really can wear just about anything, bluebird. He'd be a fool to let you go."

"To let me go *again*," she clarified softly.

Marie frowned and resumed trimming. "I don't know if you ought to be wasting your time with an insecure man. That's no fit for you or your life."

Rachael thought about Rick and what happened. "Could you honestly see me choosing an insecure man? I don't believe he's insecure in the slightest. I think he's unaccustomed to the little taste of what passes for Cinci paparazzi. He's quiet but confident. He takes things at face value."

"If he takes things at face value, then he should already know you are priceless, honey." She tapped under Rachael's chin with her comb. "I don't know. This man, he may not be deserving of you."

"I think he is, Marie. I haven't been able to stop thinking about him. He's the first thing I think of when I wake up, and the reason I can't sleep at night." She frowned, wishing she could figure this out.

Marie stopped working and dropped into the chair next to Rachael's, swiveling her astonished face toward her. "My little birdie, I cannot believe what I am hearing."

"What?"

She smiled. "Junior is out of luck. Unless my ears deceive me, you, my dear, are in love." She nodded once, emphatically.

Love? "If this is love, it's kind of shitty."

Marie cackled and leaned back, crossing her arms across her chest. "Love in real life is not like the books you read, honey. True, it's full of unbelievable highs, but the lows can be equally devastating."

"Why does it have to be so confusing? I don't get it. Sometimes I think he can't stand me. But other times . . ." Rachael blushed, recalling their afternoon at his place. "I know he wants to be with me. How do I know if it's more than physical? If it can last?"

Marie rapped her comb on her knee and leaned forward. "There is no guarantee that anything can last. If you want him and he wants you, you like each other, you respect each other, then you work it out. You make the choice every day to be together. If you stop working, stop choosing to be together, then you move on. But I don't remember you ever acting this way before. I think this one may be something special. You want to work on it."

Warming at the memory of his messy hair and lazy smile as he drowsed in bed, Rachael knew Marie was right. She wanted it to work. For better or worse, she was deep into new territory. And it was more than a little terrifying. Nothing like jumping from a desert into an ocean.

"Is it worth it?"

Marie stood and patted her shoulder. "I'll not lie, honey. Not always. But yes. With the right person, it is worth it."

Rachael thought about Gabe. He was a good fit, but she didn't feel the need to be with him like she did with Rick. Rick made her feel more. She wanted to be more, do more, experience more. She wanted to share things with him. She wanted him at her side as she conquered her next mountain, and to cheer him on as he met his goals. Rachael wanted them to celebrate together. She wanted to fall asleep with him, and wake with him in the morning.

Oh. My. God.

She glanced at her wide eyes in the mirror, looking for

a change, a noticeable difference. Something that said: This was a woman in love.

Marie unclipped the last section of wet hair and finished the cut. She glanced up. "How do you want it for tonight, honey? Up?"

Rachael nodded and watched Marie's fingers weave in and out, drying and styling, and contemplated how on earth she was going to convince Rick that she was worth it for him.

27

*I*t was Friday night and a three-day holiday weekend. Could this be the night that brought them back together?

Rachael slid on the black dress and tugged at the fitted material, making sure it was just right. Her hair looked perfect, a side-swept updo, a sprinkling of long, shiny blonde hair softly framing her face. Carefully curling her lashes and finishing her makeup—she was getting better with the concealer—she stood back and admired the overall look. Very nice. Flattering and revealing without being over the top. As Kim would say, *classy with just the right amount of trashy*.

Nervously confident, Rachael ran downstairs to let the dogs out before Rick arrived. Her parents had finally left for the weekend after she assured them countless times that she was fine and perfectly capable of being alone. She'd promised to go stay with Carlie and Brent if she started feeling off. That seemed to mollify them.

She padded around the kitchen in her bare feet, her

heels ready to step into by the staircase. Smiling at the restocked wine fridge, she snagged a bottle of Carlie's wine of choice. A good sweet Riesling would hit the spot.

Cracking it open, she poured a generous dose and sat on the patio to enjoy the early evening sunlight and watch the furry duo wrestle and sniff for intruders. July already. It seemed the months slipped by faster every year.

The doorbell echoed through the house, and she danced through the rooms, greeting him at the door. Rick smiled and held out a bouquet of fresh flowers, taking in her bare feet and wine glass. "Am I early?"

Unable to prevent her giddy happiness from shining through, she bubbled with laughter. "These are gorgeous; thank you. And you're right on time. Wine?"

Taking the flowers, she led the way back to the kitchen and poured a matching glass for Rick. She arranged the flowers in a large white jar before joining him on the patio. Olive raced up the steps, excited to see Rick. He dropped down to a squat to pet her affectionately. He was dressed in dark tailored slacks and a black short-sleeve shirt. The material had a faint sheen and stretched across his back as he fawned over Olive. Martini slinked up the stairs and sat behind her, watching this new stranger pet his sister. He inched forward, sniffing in Rick's direction.

"You must be Martini," he said. "I've heard a bit about you. Can I pet you?" He held out his hand out for inspection and Martini obliged, sniffing and finding Rick up to par. He licked the back of Rick's hand and rolled over to give him permission to rub his belly.

"Friendly boy, aren't you?" Rick grinned, giving Martini a little extra loving.

Heart swelling, Rachael etched the scene into her memory.

Rick returned to claim the seat next to hers. "Olive looks great. She's healed well."

"Mhm. She had excellent care. I can refer you to the vet if you're looking for one. Gil's pretty good," she teased.

He chuckled, his brown eyes dancing. He tilted his glass toward her, and she met him halfway, the glasses clinking happily. They sipped and watched the dogs run around the yard.

"Where are we going tonight?" she asked.

"I have reservations at the fondue place, if that sounds good?"

"Are we getting the chocolate course, too?"

"Isn't that why everyone goes there?"

"Perfect! Of course it is." She laughed. "How are we on time?"

"Always enough time for a glass of wine with a beautiful woman."

Rachael blushed and felt butterfly kisses in her belly. This was a good start. Very good.

She cleared her throat. "How do you think they'll do? With the fireworks?"

He shrugged. "Like people, every dog is different. Might want to stick close by just in case, but most dogs handle them fairly well, especially when they're younger adults."

Watching him from the corner of her eye, she saw the sun highlight his soft brown hair, lending the edges a golden hue. He looked relaxed and content, leaning back into the seat and drinking the cool white wine.

"I am glad you're here, Rick. I wasn't sure you'd want to see me again."

He studied her, draining the last of his wine. "I couldn't stay away," he said, stunning her into silence before disappearing into the house.

"You coming?" Rick called from the kitchen.

Calling Martini and Olive to follow, she finished her wine and rinsed out the glasses, leaving them in the sink. The simple joys of temporarily having her own place.

THEIR HANDS MET as they ambled down the street together. His grip was warm and secure, his stride unhurried to accommodate her shorter, faster step. Rick held open the restaurant's door, and she brushed against him as she entered. Maybe not unintentionally. They were ushered to a private table for two, a hotplate set into the table between them.

"Good evening," greeted the server. She rattled on about the menu and specials while Rachael admired Rick's good looks and comfortable demeanor. He was so calm and patient with everything.

"Do you like fireworks?" he asked.

She nodded. "Yes, I've always loved them. They're kind of magical. You?"

"I enjoy them now, but I wasn't always a fan. I used to be afraid of them."

"Really?"

"Really," he said, a light flush on his neck. "My mother explained they were chemical explosions in the air. I was convinced they were going to catch the world on fire."

This touched her unexpectedly. She wanted to hug the child he must have been. "And now?"

"Now I know better, but I still don't like to be too close." He winked.

"We can see fireworks from my parents' backyard. Too far away to catch fire," she teased. "Want to watch them?"

"When?"

"Monday night. The township always does them on the Fourth."

"I'd like that."

The waiter returned with the drinks, and they ordered salads and cheese and meat courses.

"These always make me feel like a kid," she said, dipping an apple into the Wisconsin cheese dip. "Which is silly. It's not like we did this when we were little. It's just fun."

He smiled and wiped the cheese off her chin. She made a face and he laughed. "I believe it's the permission to be a little messy and play with your food. It brings out the child in all of us," Rick said.

"What were you like as a child?" she asked, picturing a quiet, shy boy cuddling with kittens and puppies.

He took a bite of gooey, crisp cauliflower before answering. "I was a bit of an explorer, I suppose. I'd run through the woods with my friends, and we'd hunt for animal prints and snakeskins."

"Really? I can't see that."

"Really. I was also into sports. Baseball, soccer, the usual. Until I found swimming. What about you?"

"I was every parent's worst nightmare. A saucy little girl who would not take no for an answer."

"A born negotiator?"

"Mhm. When I wasn't negotiating, I was in dance or some other activity that I obsessed over briefly. I dabbled in sports throughout school, but was never gifted with the height or speed for most of them."

They chatted and laughed through dinner, and the waitress cleared away the dinner mess. "Did you leave room for dessert?" she asked.

"Absolutely!" Rachael swooned dramatically.

Rick poured out the last of the second bottle of wine into their glasses and she sighed with pleasure.

"You are something, Rachael."

"I can't help it—I love food. And good wine." She tilted her glass toward him.

"I mean it. You are full of life and laughter. You make me happy to sit at the same table with you. I find myself at the edge of my seat, wondering what you'll say or do next."

"Marshmallow," she said emphatically.

Eyebrows raised, he stared at her in utter confusion.

"That's what I decided to say next. Dessert on the brain, you know."

Groaning, he leaned back, rolling his eyes playfully.

"Thank you, Rick. This is fun." She reached her hand out to him. He enveloped it in his own, sending heat racing up her arm. "And I think you're pretty wonderful, too."

He squeezed her hand and they both fell silent, enjoying the quiet and relaxing atmosphere.

"Your chocolate," presented the server, blending together the melting chocolate and toppings. Between them, she slid a plate of decadent treats to be dipped, and Rachael narrowly managed to suppress the impulse to squeal at the display of strawberries, marshmallows, pound cake, and brownies.

"This is heavenly," she murmured, sliding a chocolate-crusted marshmallow onto her fondue fork and drowning it in the divine pool of chocolate. "A chocolate-coated, chocolate-covered marshmallow. Poetry on a fork."

Rick was riveted as she twirled the treat to remove excess melted chocolate and brought it to her lips. She bit down on the confection, melted chocolate trailing down her chin. She giggled like a child and went after the remainder of the marshmallow. He watched intently and she paused in her enjoyment. "What?" she mumbled around the mouthful of sugar.

He shoved away from the table and towered over her. He slowly bent down to lick the chocolate from her lip and kissed her softly.

Oh.

Her silly grin split through the marshmallow and chocolate.

He pushed the dessert plate toward her. "I find it is quite enjoyable to watch you eat this."

Swallowing the rest of her treat, she nudged the plate back between them and laughed. "Nope! You don't get off that easily. You have to eat this with me or I may just drop into a sugar coma."

"The sacrifices I make for you, woman."

"And you love it," she teased.

"I do," he said quietly.

She stared at him, heat traveling all the way to her toes. "Then eat up, Doc. You have some catching up to do. But hands off the marshmallows—those are mine!"

28

They strolled to Rick's car after dinner, both full and happy. The sun had set and the cicadas were singing from the trees. Rick's arm rested across her shoulders, his hand gently clasped her upper arm, and she looped her arm around his waist, enjoying the summer evening. A rapid succession of popping sounded from the next street over, and a flash of bright light filled the sky briefly. Bottle rockets and rogue amateur fireworks displays would be common all weekend. She grinned up at Rick and he slowed to drop a kiss on top of her head.

"Don't worry about the fireworks," she whispered conspiratorially. "I'll protect you."

He laughed and hugged her tightly to his side.

"Thank you for dinner. That was delicious," she said.

"You're welcome."

"Where to next?" she asked as he opened the passenger door for her.

"Mini golf," he deadpanned.

She giggled as the door closed. "Really, where are we going?"

"I told you."

"You can't be serious. Dressed like this?"

He nodded. She went along, amused.

To her surprise, he turned into a miniature golf parking lot.

Huh.

They exited the car and Rick paid for a round from the painfully bored teenager at the front desk. Rachael surveyed the course. Giant artificial palm trees decked out a stone and plastic mountain with a shockingly bright blue waterfall trickling over it. She could smell the chlorine from the entrance. The water trailed through the rest of the course in narrow, open-topped plastic tubes, with large statues of jungle cats, giraffes, and other wildlife complementing the amoeba-shaped greens.

"What color do you want to be?" he asked, tossing an orange ball into the air.

"Blue."

"Light or dark?"

"Light."

He snagged the dimpled ball for her, then they collected clubs and waited for their turn. Around them, couples and small groups laughed and screeched, applauded and groaned as the low-stakes Putt-Putt playing continued. They were by far the best-dressed couple at the course. Or worst-dressed, depending on your point of view.

"Care to wager?" He smiled deviously, hand resting on the neck of a shiny gray plastic rhinoceros emerging from the shrubs at the lead up to the first hole.

She flicked the stained white horn on the animal. "On mini-golf?"

He nodded, spinning the brightly colored rubber-and-steel putter in his hand.

She forced her face to remain neutral. "I'm game. What do you have in mind?"

"Winner chooses the final destination on tonight's itinerary."

"You're on," she agreed, puzzled but intrigued.

He gestured for her to go first, so she set up her first shot. She would have to shoot it between the legs and under the body of a giant lizard. No problem. Slipping out of her high heels, she glanced back at him with a smirk, then stepped up, swung gently, and watched the blur of baby blue race up under the lizard and over the single bump in the green before charging directly to the hole. *Plunk!*

Take that, hot stuff.

"Okay, shorty. That was a lucky shot. My turn."

Settling the orange ball where hers had been, he tapped and groaned as the ball slid to a stop inches from the hole.

"You can still shoot for par." She smiled sweetly, straining to withhold her laughter.

His mouth firmed into a concentrated straight line and he knocked the ball home.

"One shot to your advantage. Shall we continue?"

Nodding, she ushered him ahead to the second green, where a pair of brown and black cartoonish monkey statues pointed to the tee area. Poor Rick had no idea who he was up against.

"You play golf?" he asked, watching her sink a long putt.

"All through high school and college. Though I don't get out nearly as often as I'd like anymore," she conceded. "Mostly I only get to play now when courting clients or at fundraising events. And those I frequently have to throw depending on the read I get from the group. A lot of men don't like to lose to a woman."

"Damn. I thought you said you didn't play sports."

"Not the usual stuff that required running or long limbs. But I've always loved golf. It's a mental game, all about strategy and execution."

Without her shoes, she felt the height difference between them acutely. "Plus," she teased, tapping him on the shoulder with her putter, "when you're this much closer to the ground, you have a clearer perspective of the lay of the land."

Laughing, he dropped onto a zebra-striped bench as they joined the line waiting for the next hole. "Now I'm closer to the ground. Is that better?"

"Much." She swung her heels from one hand, standing in front of him. "This is fun."

"It is. Even if you're kicking my butt."

"Aww. Does it bother you?"

"Nah. If I'm going to lose to anyone, I'm glad it's you. But I will definitely have to work on my game before the next round."

The butterflies took flight hearing him talk about a possible rematch, a future. Rachael pressed a hand to her stomach, willing them to settle. She still had to wrap up this game. They maintained a steady stream of chatter, carefully avoiding discussing anything to do with the photo or what followed. She knew they needed to discuss it at some point, but she shoved that thought away, focused on relaxing and learning more about him. Hole after hole, she wowed Rick with her putting game, and hole after hole he wowed her with attention and humor, making her fall for him even more.

"Ready to cement your victory, Miss Eller?"

She laughed and waved toward the last hole, which ended at the mouth of a giant anaconda that swallowed the completed game balls and presumably returned them to the course's front desk. "You first."

He groaned and went to his fate.

After depositing the clubs and finishing her soft drink, she sat on a crocodile bench and scanned the score card while slipping her shoes back on. "You're really not a golfer, are you?"

Rick's crooked smile was adorable. "It's hard to golf well when you're standing next to the hottest woman around."

"You're not so bad yourself. Looking, that is. At golf, you kind of suck." Laughing, she joined him on the walk back to the car.

"Yeah, yeah, yeah. Time to collect on your winnings." He smirked. "Where to, Miss PGA?"

She considered him beneath her lashes, struck again by how handsome he was. His body shielded her from the street. Even with her heels on, she was only as tall as his chin. She took in those wide shoulders, perfect lips, and warm brown eyes. Placing her hands on either side of his face, she pulled him lower. "Home?" she whispered. He watched her eyes and she smiled, lifting onto her toes to kiss him softly.

His eyes widened briefly before he engulfed her in his arms and returned the kiss, chaste but unbearably sweet.

When they returned to Rick's car, he unlocked the doors and ushered her in, closing the door and pausing on the sidewalk before coming around to the driver's side.

He took a deep breath. "Your place? Mine? Other?"

"My place if you don't mind. I need to let the dogs out."

Moments later, they pulled into Rachael's driveway and she unlocked the door. Martini and Olive were jumping around, wanting attention. She made baby talk to them, kicking her shoes off as she skipped through the house to let them out to the backyard.

They sat on the patio chairs, watching the dogs play and run. The night air was pleasantly warm, the evening crickets serenaded them and lightning bugs dotted the lawn.

"How long are your parents out of town?"

"They return Tuesday. Does it bother you that I'm living with them?"

"No, I was just wondering. What did you think of my place?"

"It was nice. I especially liked the bedroom," she added wickedly.

Rick chuckled and they let the conversation die off, both content and relaxed.

"Rachael," he broke the quiet, a reluctant tone adding to the gravitas. "What happened?"

She nodded slowly, sorting through her thoughts. "Gabe?"

Silence.

Sighing, she pulled her legs up onto the chair and

wrapped her arms around her knees. What to say, how to say it? He hadn't moved.

"So, that night after we . . . at your house? I was supposed to have dinner with him. We had made plans beforehand and I didn't want to break things off over the phone. That seemed rude, you know?"

He considered, then gestured for her to continue.

"We met and I was honest with him, right off the bat, that we could only be friends. I told him I met someone else, someone I wanted to explore things with. You. And he was pretty cool about it. We agreed to just be friends."

She stopped talking, wondering how to continue. How much to say.

"The next morning, my sister called to tell me about the photo and story. You have to understand, when you grow up with a family like mine—or Gabe's—people like to speculate. Make wild claims. Get the scoop. Earn a quick buck. But, Rick? Nothing happened."

He swallowed and looked away. "I'm sorry. I thought . . ."

"I know," she groaned. "It crushed me to know what you must have thought. What most people would have assumed. Did assume."

Taking a fortifying breath, she continued. "I'm going to be completely honest here. I don't want to lie to you. Gabe and I, we did have a little history. And he became a good friend to me. He was there for me when I . . . when you . . ." She shook her head. "Anyways, one night, just once after you and I met, we did become intimate. It was after I saw you downtown."

Face like granite, Rick stood and walked down into the grass, hands in his pockets. His back to her, he was quiet.

"After that disastrous run-in, the way you blew me off . . . It was obvious you weren't interested in seeing me anymore. That we were done."

Moving to stand behind him, she wrapped her arms around his waist and leaned her cheek against his back. "It was purely physical with Gabe. He's a good friend, but not someone I could love. Not like that."

"He loves you."

"I don't know. He says he does." She shrugged helplessly against him. "I can't control the way other people feel."

Rick pulled her arms from his waist and turned to look at her, putting physical distance between them. "I need to go, Rachael. I have to think this through."

She nodded, wondering if she had said too much. If she had ruined everything.

"I'm sorry. I am. If I had known, if I had thought there was *any* chance that we could try again, I would never have done that. But I was hurt. I was angry that you had discarded me so easily. I couldn't understand why you wouldn't even talk to me, give me a chance to explain."

He smiled sadly. "You weren't the only one hurt and angry. I jumped to conclusions and let my suspicions and insecurities carry me away. I'm sorry, too."

She didn't know what else to say, so she said nothing. She had done enough talking.

Martini whined at their feet, wanting attention. Rick absently reached down and scratched his ears before the dog rolled over for a belly rub. Olive ran over to join him, and soon Rick was crouched down with one hand on a furry belly and one hand scratching the other's silky ears.

Silently thanking the dogs, Rachael took a deep breath

and stepped forward, closing the distance between them. Rick's eyes were wary as he watched her approach while his hands were occupied. She framed his face with her hands and kissed each cheek before kissing him softly on the lips. "I would like to see where this goes. If you can forgive me. If we can leave the past behind us. I think this is worth trying. Us."

He stared at her wordlessly. Giving the dogs one last playful pat, he rose to his full height and returned to the patio without looking back. Stopping outside the kitchen door, he finally turned back. "See you tomorrow?"

She nodded and held still as he left, praying he could forgive her.

29

*S*leep eluded her. She tossed and turned, replaying the conversation in her head.

What was he thinking?

What was she thinking telling him all of that?

He didn't kiss her back. What did that mean?

But he was coming back tomorrow. She glanced at the clock. Today. *Ugh.*

Unable to tolerate her swirling thoughts, she grabbed her phone and messaged her sister.

Are you up?

It was almost one in the morning. Chewing her thumbnail, she watched the screen, praying for Carlie to be awake.

Restless, she got up and went to the restroom to wash up, then brought her phone downstairs to the living room. She flipped on the TV and scrolled through the channels, trying to find something to distract her. Her phone finally vibrated.

Kind of. What's up?

Can't sleep. Weird night with Rick.
What happened?
Date was awesome, but then he asked about Gabe
You told him?
I told him.

It took her a bit to respond. *I see. Need some company?*

The deafening stillness in the house was oppressive. Anyone else, and she would have said no. Rachael debated if it was fair to ask her to come over this late.

I'm on my way, Carlie messaged, deciding for her.

Ten minutes later, she knocked on the front door and let herself in. Olive and Martini didn't even budge. She dropped a backpack on the floor and hugged Rachael. "What happened?"

They sat at the kitchen table and Rachael grabbed some cold waters. What could she say? She went back to the beginning and spilled the whole story, telling Carlie everything. About the one-nighter with Gabe, then going out with Rick, then returning to Gabe again. And then last night's conversation. Carlie patiently listened to the whole story, only interrupting when she rehashed the fight between the men in the yard. "Did you ever find out what Dad said to them?"

Rachael shrugged. "I was pretty heavily medicated. I went inside and passed out in bed."

"Wow," Carlie sighed when she finish the story. "That's intense."

Rachael nodded.

"You're going to see him again? Tonight?"

"That's what he said before he left."

"Sounds like a good thing, right?"

"Maybe?"

"Think about it, Rach. Why else would he say he's coming back? He's probably processing what you told him. Really can't blame the guy. That's a lot to take in at one time."

"Maybe."

"Come on. That's enough sulking. Get your ass up and let's go watch some terrible movies and crash."

"What?" Rachael laughed.

"You heard me. It's after two. Let's binge on chips, ice cream, and cheesy movies and pretend like we're teenagers again."

"No ice cream."

"Then chips will have to do."

Family. She was pretty freaking blessed.

THEY SLEPT on the sofa and recliner and woke late. Carlie took off for a run and Rachael let the dogs out, waiting for Carlie to return for lunch. She checked her phone and saw no new texts.

Still want to hang out today?

She waited and watched, wondering if Rick would reply.

Please reply. Please reply. Please reply. The words orbited endlessly in her thoughts, driving her crazy. Her phone vibrated and she jumped, relief washing through her.

Dinner? I could cook something for you. At your place?
Sounds perfect.

She was damn near floating when Carlie returned, and her sister noted it immediately. "You heard from Prince Charming?"

"Yes! He's coming over later."

"Great. I'm going to go hog your bathroom and clean up. What do you want for lunch?"

"Your call," Rachael said, but she knew the destination before Carlie even answered.

"Pam's?" Carlie asked.

"Sounds good."

They took turns showering and then took off.

"Kim's going to meet us," Carlie hollered as she jumped into her car.

When they arrived, there was no sign of Kim. *Shocker*.

"Coffee, please," Carlie ordered.

"Same," Rachael said. "What's going on with her and Owen these days? On or off? Last time I talked to her they were done."

Carlie tapped her spoon against her mug. "Back on."

They both rolled their eyes and drank their coffee.

"I don't get it, Car. She's gorgeous, independent, and smart. What's she doing with that guy? He's a path to nowhere."

She shrugged. "Not my decision to make. If he makes her happy, then that's what matters, I guess."

"Happiness? I don't exactly see you beaming lately, Car."

She flushed and stared down at her mug. "What are you talking about?"

"I'm talking about you and Brent. What's going on?"

"Things are fine. We're just busy. Different priorities. It'll all settle back down eventually."

"Mhm."

"Leave her alone, Rach," said Kim, sliding into the

booth next to Carlie. "If she and Brent want to be miserable together, then that's their lot in life."

"What? You're one to talk," Carlie said, glaring at Kim then back at Rachael. "Shut up, both of you. I haven't had nearly enough caffeine yet to come up with a decent retort. So, consider yourself retorted."

Kim cracked up and planted a kiss on Carlie's cheek. "Fair enough."

"What are you girls up to for the Fourth?" Rachael asked.

"Nothing yet," said Carlie.

"Nada," echoed Kim.

"Want to do a cookout or something?" Rachael asked. "I kind of invited Rick over to watch the fireworks."

"Fireworks and we finally get to meet the vet?" Carlie asked. "I'm in!"

Rachael just hoped she didn't blow it with Rick tonight.

30

---

*D*etermined to find the perfect place for her and the dogs, Rachael spent the afternoon looking at rental properties. After visiting and doing drive-bys of more than a dozen, she was still no closer than before. From Cincinnati proper to Springboro, not one thing was perfect. So frustrating.

Massaging the back of her neck, she cranked up the radio as one of her favorite Billie Eilish songs came on. She was almost home, but she drove around the neighborhood, stretching out the trip and humming along. A few blocks away, she saw a "For Sale" sign in the yard of a beautiful colonial house with a large fenced-in backyard. Of course. All the good places were either not pet-friendly or not for rent. She stopped and grabbed an info flier from the plastic box on the sale sign. Maybe they would consider a long-term lease?

She returned home and dropped the flier on the counter, switching her brain into cleaning mode. If Rick was coming over to cook, she would make sure he had a clean kitchen to work with. She flipped on the kitchen stereo and cranked up the volume, dancing along as she washed the dishes and scrubbed the counters. The dogs pranced around her feet, and she sang to them and spun around the kitchen.

"Can I cut in?"

She froze mid-spin and turned to see Rick in the doorway, his arms heavy with grocery bags.

"Hope you don't mind," he said. "I tried knocking and ringing, but I could hear the music. Thought I would save a step and drop these off here."

"Sorry." She laughed. "Cleaning." Grinning, she danced her way over to him to help with the groceries.

He took in her faded leggings, tank top, and ponytail, then grinned. "Feel free to clean like that anytime." They set the bags on the counter and he turned to her, grabbing her hand and spinning her around under his arm. She giggled and spun back toward him, coming to a stop against his chest.

He caught her and wrapped both arms around her as the music transitioned to a monster ballad, and they began to slow dance. Rachael was covered in grime and there were groceries to put away, but she didn't care. They swayed together and he held her close, his hands sliding up and down her back. He dipped her over his arm, as the song gave way to a commercial. Rick leaned over her as she lay back over his arm. Time froze. She held her breath and saw the desire burning in his eyes. Suddenly, he stood and spun her around again, surprising a laugh from her.

Time resumed. She clicked the volume down and he turned his attention to the groceries, unloading thin, transparent bags full of fresh veggies and fruits, meats, and more.

"Planning to feed an army?"

Gauging the spread before responding, he lifted a shoulder and shot her a charming smile. "I wasn't sure what you'd like."

Amused, she helped put the bags away and leaned her elbow on the counter. "I need to grab a shower."

"Mind if I stay here and get dinner started?"

"Not at all," she said. She hesitated then leaned up and tugged on his shoulder. He bent down enough so she could kiss his cheek. "Be back down soon."

As she walked up the stairs, she heard him open the back door and let the dogs in. Was he always so thoughtful?

Relaxing in the shower, she scrubbed and scoured every last inch of skin, letting the exfoliation turn her a soft pink. She hummed as she shampooed and conditioned, then soaped up and stood in the hot spray, feeling her muscles loosen. When she finished up, she squeezed the excess water from her hair and wrapped herself in a thick towel. She then exited the steamy bathroom and crossed the cool hallway, freezing mid-stride once she saw Rick at the top of the stairs.

Immobilized, he stared, drinking in her appearance, before shaking his head and continuing down the hallway toward her. "I was wondering if you wanted a glass of wine?"

He held out a glass of red as she dripped water on the hallway runner. She tilted her head to the side, puzzled by his nonchalance.

"Thank you."

She took a sip and watched him over the rim, feeling his eyes rake over her towel-wrapped body.

"You're welcome," he replied, voice gruff.

Leaving her bedroom door open in invitation as she entered, she flicked on her light and waited, hoping he would follow. After an interminable pause, he appeared in the doorway.

"Rachael?"

Turning back, she raised her eyebrows, saying nothing as she took another long sip of wine, leaving the choice entirely up to him.

He walked into the room and crossed to her, taking her wine glass and setting it down on the dresser. Her skin heated at his nearness. She licked a stray drop of wine from her lower lip, and he watched, fascinated.

"I . . ." he trailed off, then cleared his throat and began again. "I'll give you some time to get dressed. I'll wait for you downstairs."

Nodding, she watched him retreat into the hall. Rachael was disappointed, but anticipation curved her mouth. This was good. She imagined him talking to the dogs as he cooked. Was he picturing her too?

She took her time getting ready, blowing out her hair and applying a light amount of makeup. Surveying her closet, she settled on a flowy red cotton skirt and a blue t-shirt. The combination felt appropriately festive for the holiday weekend.

When she at last returned downstairs, smoke was wafting from the patio grill and a variety of delicious scents assailed her from the pots simmering on the stove.

Wow.

Joining him on the patio, Rachael noted the juicy

steaks on the grill, beautiful cuts of rich red meat. "Looks good," she said, surprising *him* for a change.

Rick looked her up and down hungrily. "Not as good as you."

She couldn't stop the blush that rose, and shivered, excited to see where this was going.

Olive and Martini sat at his feet, watching him adoringly. They didn't even glance her way. "What's going on here?" she asked, nodding at them.

"Nothing," he said, sounding far too innocent.

Martini licked his chops and kept an eye on the grill.

"Uh-huh." She glanced at the side tray and saw tiny strips of steak cut up. "Buying their love?"

He laughed and tossed another small piece to each of them. "Theirs is easy. Humans on the other hand . . ." he trailed off and took a drink of water. "I forgot to grab a platter. Do you have one handy?"

She returned to the kitchen to hunt down Dad's platters and watched Rick through the window, chatting animatedly with the dogs, tugging at her heartstrings.

That's not cute at all. Definitely not.

Handing him the white tray, he flipped the cooked steaks onto it, the charred lines perfectly crisscrossing the cuts.

"Go sit down." He nudged her toward the kitchen door.

He filled two plates with steak, sweet potatoes, asparagus, fresh green beans, and grilled onions. He pointed to the dishes on the table already. "Cucumber salad, brown sugar, butter, a few sauces for the steak."

Dang.

She dug into the meal with gusto, entertaining him with her appetite.

"I would never have figured you for a big eater. Where does the food go?" he asked.

"I try not to question it." Rachael shrugged. "Someday my metabolism will slow, or so I'm told. But I keep watching my mom, and she hasn't shown a sign of it yet."

He took another bite of his steak, and she noticed two furry tails swishing beside his chair. "Martini! Olive! What are you doing?"

They slunk down and moved farther under the table.

"Busted. Sorry pals." He chuckled.

"What are you up to with my dogs?"

"Nothing that concerns you," he said teasingly.

"Sure, sure, Mr. Vet," she groaned, picking up her wine. "This is amazing, Rick. Where did you learn to cook like this?"

"My mom. She always had me in the kitchen with her, helping with recipes and testing out new dishes. All the barbecues and cookouts, dinner parties, brunches. If she was cooking, I was cooking."

"Is she a cook?"

He quirked his lips. "She's a chemist by profession, but an experimental chef at heart. Some of our meals were more, ah, adventurous than others."

"What about your dad?"

"A physician. Or as he'd say, *a real doctor*." He grimaced.

"That's quite the family."

"Well, they're not the Ellers, but then who is?"

"Touché," she laughed.

Swallowing another bite of sweet potato, he grinned. "My parents were a little older when they had me. I was a bit of a midlife surprise for them. They weren't exactly the parenting kind. But, for the most part, they always supported my decisions and we actually get along better now that I live out here."

She wrinkled her nose. "I can't imagine living far away from my family."

"I can't imagine living close to mine."

Rachael sliced into her tender steak, absorbing this and again thanking her good fortune for having the family she did. "You don't miss it? Having family around, your hometown?"

"Of course. I miss my friends and the convenience of popping in to see Mom and Dad on occasion. Strangely, I really miss the food. Sometimes I get a hankering for some real barbecue. You'd love Pappy's," he said, closing his eyes to savor the remembered flavors of home, "and Imo's ravioli."

"That I can totally appreciate," she said, hoping she'd get the chance to go with him sometime.

Her phone vibrated on the counter and she ignored it, keeping her attention focused on Rick.

"You don't need to get that?" he asked.

Looking between him and the phone, she finally rose and checked the screen: *Call me, please.*

"It's my sister." Rachael stared at the screen, puzzled. Carlie knew she was seeing Rick tonight. Sighing, she glanced back at him on her way to the deck. "Be right back."

Her sister answered almost before it rang.

"Rachael?" A staggered gasp and crying filled her ear.

"Car? Are you okay?"

She sniffed, and Rachael heard her fast, panicked breath.

"Where are you? What's happening?"

Rick joined her on the patio, his concern evident.

"Can you—" Her sister choked on a sob. Rachael struggled to contain herself, forced herself to not push Carlie. "Can you come get me? The park—the shelter house."

"On my way. Stay there!"

She hung up and turned to Rick. He nodded and returned to the kitchen, turning off the oven. "Shall I drive?"

She hugged him and they ran out to the car. "The park off of Main."

He nodded and drove off. She fidgeted in her seat, wondering what happened, kicking herself. God, what if she hadn't checked the phone? If Rick hadn't encouraged her to get it?

"Please be okay, CarCar," she whispered to the passing lawns, a knot tightening in her stomach.

31

---

hey spun into the park and Rick pulled up to the curb. She was out the door before he stopped, skirt flying in the wind as she searched for her little sister.

"Carlie?"

Her slender form was sitting alone at the table, shaking and overcome by a terror-filled panic attack. Okay. Rachael could deal with this. She wrapped her arms around her sister, who was cold and shaking, pushing away from Rachael.

"Listen to me, Carlie. Listen to my voice. Close your eyes. Put your feet flat on the ground. Feel the ground beneath your feet."

Carlie struggled against her, but Rachael wrestled her down to the lower bench of the table. Rick paced by the car, clearly unsure of what to do. She waved for him to stay there. He nodded and leaned back against his car.

"Deep breath. Hold it. Exhale. In and out. Focus on your breathing."

She slowly started to calm down, and Rachael stayed by her side, stroking her hair, talking soothingly.

"Focus on what you can control. Deep breath. In . . . and out."

She walked her sister through the attack as they used to do, so many years ago. Rachael wondered what happened to set her off. This hadn't happened in a long time.

Carlie took a long, shuddering breath and leaned heavily against Rachael. The shaking eventually subsided and fatigue set in.

"You're okay, stink bug. I've got you." She reverted to her childhood nickname for Carlie, hating the helpless feeling her attacks stirred in all of them. She caught Rick's attention, motioning for him to come help.

Exhausted, she hardly noticed when Rick joined them. "We're going to help you to the car. We're going to take you home," Rachael murmured.

"I can't go home," Carlie said despondently. "Not home. Anywhere but home."

"All right, honey. We'll go to Mom and Dad's, okay?"

Rachael struggled to support the weight of her taller, younger sister as they stumbled along the path to the lot. She tripped, nearly knocking them all to the ground. Rick took over and picked Carlie up, carrying her the rest of the way.

Carlie mumbled something as they settled her into the back seat, and Rachael couldn't make it out. Something about Brent.

"Do you want me to call Brent? Is that what you want?"

Carlie sat up in a panic, grasping Rachael's shoulder painfully. "No! No!" she shrieked. "You can't do that!"

"Shh! Carlie, it's okay. I won't call him." Rachael pried Carlie's fingers off her shoulder and squeezed her hand tightly, wondering what was going on. "I won't call him," she repeated.

Carlie sat back, still mumbling. Placing Carlie's hand in her lap, Rachael closed the door and took a deep breath. Rick stood beside her, uncertainty and worry lining his face.

She walked him around to his side of the car. "She'll be fine. I just need to get her home."

He nodded without question and drove them to her parents' house.

Once there, he didn't ask any questions as he opened Carlie's door and carried her inside. Olive and Martini were dancing around the living room, and Rick gently set her on the sofa.

"I'm going to go take care of the kitchen," he murmured. Rachael squeezed his hand, grateful for his understanding.

Grabbing a blanket from the closet, Rachael tucked it around Carlie and watched her pale face. She was sitting numbly, not paying attention to anything around her.

"Carlie?"

Her dead eyes stared through Rachael, who shivered at her cold blankness. Whatever had happened was major. This was worse than she could recall in the past. Rachael wondered if she should call the doctor. Glancing at the time, she realized the doctor's office was closed. Besides, Carlie would hate her for it.

Not knowing what else to do, she sat down and hugged Carlie to her. Rachael resumed stroking her hair rhythmically, waiting for the warmth to return, her breathing to steady. Eventually a little color returned to Carlie's cheeks. Her weariness was evident, but she was relieved her sister was returning.

"Want to talk about it?" Rachael asked softly.

Eyes tightly closed, Carlie hung her head and shook it slowly.

"Can you at least tell me what happened? What triggered this attack?"

A tear ran down her cheek. "I walked in on them," she whispered faintly.

No. No, no, no.

"Who?" She knew what was coming, but prayed she was wrong.

"Brent and Gina."

THE FRONT DOOR slamming signaled Kim's arrival. "Where is she?"

Rachael pointed to the living room. Kim ran to her best friend. Her sister. They clung to each other tightly and cried together, mumbling and speaking the language the two of them had always shared.

Taking advantage of the moment, Rachael slipped through the living room and continued into the kitchen. Rick sat at the table, his phone in his hands.

"What happened?"

Shaking her head, the angry tears started falling. "That son of a bitch!"

He stood and wrapped her in his embrace, patiently waiting.

She shook her head again. "Carlie's boyfriend. She walked in on him in bed with one of her friends."

"Christ. I am so sorry, baby," he said, holding her as she cried tears of anger and frustration. "What can I do?" he murmured in her ear, sweeping her hair back from her face.

"I don't know. I have to figure out what she needs. What she wants to do."

"I'll leave. You need to be with them."

"I don't want you to go, but you're probably right."

"If you want me, if you need anything at all, just call or text and I'll be here."

Another tear ran down her face. "You're amazing, Richard Thomas."

He returned the smile and wiped her tears away. "So are you, Rachael Eller."

He collected his wallet and keys and she walked him out to his car. "Sorry to have to cut the evening short. Dinner was delicious."

"You should have seen the dessert," he said with a devilish smile.

"Rain check?"

"Yours, anytime."

He opened his car door, then shut it and turned back. "Rachael?"

She raised her eyebrows.

He ran his hand through his hair nervously. "I know this is terrible timing, with your sister and all, but . . ."

Pulling Rachael against himself, he kissed her hungrily, his hand sliding up her jaw and into her hair. Rick moved his lips against hers and she opened to him. He tilted her head back and angled deeper into the kiss, fire forging a blazing path through her.

Groaning, he stepped back and she stumbled forward against him. He chuckled and caught her, dropping a kiss to the top of her head.

"I wish I had stayed upstairs with you earlier," he whispered regretfully into her hair, breathing in her scent and rubbing her arms.

"Me too." Rachael wished they had more time, but he was right. She needed to be with Carlie.

He exhaled, then tilted her face up to his. "I am not done with you. I don't know that I will ever be ready to let you go."

Rachael smiled warmly up at him. "That's good."

He leaned down and kissed her gently before turning back to his car. "I'll be back. Go take care of your sister."

Watching his receding taillights, the words surfaced to her lips, unable to be kept inside any longer. "I love you," she whispered to the darkness.

32

*H*ours of crying, screaming, laughing, and silence followed. Rachael and Kim took turns sitting with Carlie, trying to provide comfort in any way they could.

Carlie held herself together better than many would in her situation. It was as though she concentrated the misery in the panic attack.

"Is it wrong that I want to go hunt down his sorry ass and string him up by the balls?" Kim muttered, twisting her hands over each other in the air as she followed Rachael into the kitchen.

"Not at all. I'm also thinking that bitch deserves to be dealt with, too."

Kim grumbled approvingly as she hugged Rachael.

"God, I can't believe this."

Carlie and Brent were together for four years. How could this happen to them?

But then again, there were signs. It had been apparent to Rachael—and Kim, too—that the pair had been having issues for a few months. All the times Brent was a no-show at family functions. The canceled plans. The late nights at work. It all took on a darker slant now. She knew Carlie had been miserable the last few weeks, that something was wrong. Rachael wondered if her sister had suspected it.

She poured a big glass of orange juice for Carlie, and brought it back to the living room. "You said it always makes you feel better?"

Kim followed with a bottle of vodka, waving it back and forth. "And if the OJ doesn't cut it, we can always screw it."

Carlie wiped her red nose and rubbed Olive's back, curled up next to her on the couch. "I don't know what I would do without you guys."

"Fortunately, your crying ass won't have to find out. Now hand me your glass so I can make a proper screwdriver," said Kim, reaching for the juice.

Carlie shook her head, clutching the glass. "No, thank you. I don't really feel like drinking."

"That makes one of us," Kim said, retracing her steps to the kitchen to mix her own drink.

Rachael smirked, watching Kim disappear on her mission. "What do you want to do, Car?"

She took a long drink of OJ and stared into space. "I need to find a new place. I can't stay there."

"We can take care of that. I've actually been looking at rentals all over."

"And I need to get my stuff. I can't believe this," she said, clattering the glass onto the tabletop, splashing a small puddle of juice across the furniture. "How can this be happening?" She buried her face in her hands, her breath heaving.

Rachael wiped up the juice and felt helpless. Carlie's misery was so acute it was tangible, a haunting figure in the room. Rachael's heart broke for her.

"He's sent text after text," Carlie whispered miserably. "He wants to talk."

"Do you want to talk to him?"

Shaking her head, she met Rachael's eyes. "No. I can't."

"Then don't."

She rocked forward over her knees, and Rachael sat next to her, running her hands through her little sister's wavy caramel-blonde hair, over and over.

Her red-rimmed, slate-blue eyes peeked up at Rachael through her cascading hair. "That was Rick?"

"Yes."

Carlie thought for a minute. "He's cute."

"He is, isn't he?"

She smiled. "He seems nice, too."

"He is." She hesitated. "Sorry, Car."

"What are you sorry about?"

"This conversation, talking about Rick when you just walked in on Brent like that."

"In case you missed it, I'm the one who brought up Rick. And besides, I like seeing the effect he has on you. You're gushing, practically radioactive with this mushy glowing."

"Am I?"

"Yup."

"Well, he's pretty amazing."

"Sorry I interrupted your date."

"No need to apologize. I'm glad I could be here for you. Rick understands, too. He's actually the one who insisted he should leave."

Carlie nodded slowly. "He probably thinks I'm a complete nut job."

"No, not at all."

The sisters sat in silence, both lost in their thoughts.

"It smells good in here," Carlie finally sniffed. "He cooked?"

"He did. Steaks, veggies, all kinds of stuff."

"Any leftovers? I'm starving."

Rachael laughed and pulled Carlie to her feet. "Yes, let's get you some food."

Kim had already dug into the fridge, pulling out the leftovers. They took turns heating up dishes and settled down for some calorie indulgence and Brent bashing.

THE ANNOYING BUZZ of her phone's alarm woke Rachael. She mumbled and grumbled, slapping her hand all over the nightstand trying to silence the damn thing.

Finally locating it, she realized it was not an alarm, but a phone call. She focused on the screen and saw Rick's name.

She fumbled to hit the answer button, just as the phone switched to voicemail. *Crap.*

Yawning, Rachael looked blankly around the bedroom and noticed she had fallen asleep on top of the bedspread. She rubbed her eyes and forced them to focus on the phone's screen, discovering it was almost ten. She counted backward. Not quite six hours of sleep. That would have to do.

Her phone vibrated. A picture of her front door with a

tray of coffees and a bag graced the screen. She hummed happily and called Rick. "Morning."

"Good morning. I never heard from you, but figured you could do with some good coffee. Want me to leave?"

"No, just give me a sec to brush my teeth. Go around back. The door should be open."

"See you in a minute."

She washed quickly and brushed her teeth, grabbing a hair tie and pulling her blonde nest back into a knot. Better. She ran down the stairs and saw Rick in the kitchen, picking up the mess from last night. "The food was great the second time, too," she said, walking up to him. He smiled and wrapped his arms around her. Inhaling his warm, uniquely Rick scent, she snuggled against him. He smelled of fresh laundry, soap, and soft spices, with a hint of lingering chlorine.

"I wanted to see you. Hope that's all right."

"Very. I missed you already," she replied, peeking up at him. "How cheesy is that?"

"Pretty cheesy, but perfectly acceptable. How's your sister?"

She pointed over her shoulder to the living room. "Passed out on the couch. I don't know what to do. I'm so angry at Brent, but I also think this is ultimately going to be good for her. They've been drifting apart for a while now."

"Sounds like you don't need to do anything but be there for her."

"She did say she needs to find a new place to stay. And so do I. Guess we can house hunt together."

She could see his wheels turning, when he suddenly widened his eyes and shook his head. "Coffee, pastries."

He jogged through the house and opened the door, picking up the carrier and bag. Rick held up the tray for her inspection. "Take your pick."

Scanning the labels, she grabbed a vanilla latte. "Mmm . . . Thank you."

"You're welcome."

"What have you got going on today?" she asked, adding another splash of vanilla creamer, savoring the sweet scent.

"You're looking at it. Only thing I had on my schedule was to hit the pool to swim some laps. Already done."

"Is Gil working this weekend?"

He nodded then stepped behind her to rub her shoulders. She loved that he wanted to keep touching her.

"If you could just keep doing that for the next two hours, that would be great," she closed her eyes to enjoy the moment, and a thought occurred to her. "Who works the holidays?"

"Gil and I take turns, along with our partners you have yet to meet, Alan and Theresa. I have tomorrow off for the Fourth, but may still drop in and check on a couple of the patients."

"We were thinking about doing a cookout tomorrow before the fireworks, but not sure if that's going to happen now."

"Why wouldn't we still do it?" Carlie asked, yawning as she shuffled into the kitchen.

"You still want to?"

She nodded and inspected the coffees. "Can I have this?" she asked, holding up a regular coffee with cream and sugar.

"It's yours," Rick granted.

"Thanks. I'm Carlie," she said vaguely in his direction while pulling the lid off the coffee and checking the color.

"Rick."

"Hmm? Oh, yes, I know," she said into her cup.

"Creamer is in the fridge, Car," Rachael said, grinning at her sister's pre-caffeine aloofness.

"Please, God, tell me you have something with caramel or white chocolate," Kim said, stumbling in after Carlie.

"Rick, this is Kim. She's basically my other sister."

"There's nothing basic about me, Rach," she winked in classic Kim sass. She let out a tiny squeal and picked up a caramel macchiato. "There is a god, and his name is Rick."

He laughed and bowed in her direction.

"I like this one, Rach. He's a keeper," Kim said, inhaling deeply over the drink's opening.

"The pastries were pretty picked over, so it's just cinnamon rolls."

Rachael pulled out a stack of napkins, and they tore into the rolls. "Thank you, again," she mumbled around a mouthful of food.

"You're welcome," he said, taking the remaining cup.

"What's that one?" she asked.

"Black coffee."

Her nose wrinkled. "Want some cream or sugar?"

He shook his head. "No, this is fine."

"Suit yourself."

Clutching her cardboard cup of heaven, Rachael let the dogs out and stepped into the sunshine. The humidity was trying to build, but it was still decent enough outside for now. Rick followed her onto the deck.

"How'd you sleep?" he asked.

Rachael dropped into a chair and sipped her latte. "Not especially well, but I got enough for today."

"I was worried about your sister. Does she do that, have panic attacks, often?"

"Not anymore. She used to get them when we were younger—and super intense dreams, too—but it's been a long time." She stared off into the yard, recalling how scared she had been when Carlie woke up in the middle of the night, sobbing. The doctors said it wasn't sleep terrors, but she had emotionally devastating, vivid dreams. Shivering, Rachael pushed the memory away.

"Does she take anything for it?"

"No. She always refused meds. Mom took her to a specialist for a little while, but she's found success relying instead on running and meditation."

He took a drink of his coffee, considering. "She seems better today."

Rachael nodded, and glanced back toward the kitchen. She couldn't see them; they must have gone back to the front room. "It's going to be a long road for her. They were together for four years, ever since they met in college. She had even begun talking about getting married, so I imagine this came out of left field." Or had it? She frowned as she thought again about how odd things had been lately.

"Did you suspect anything?"

"No. Yes. I don't know. They used to be so perfect together, like sickeningly so. Over the last few months, maybe more, he started flaking out, not showing up for family functions, working late. Lots of little things. She never said anything, but I think they had been having some problems. It's still so shocking though. And to cheat on her like that. It makes me so angry!"

He frowned and took the chair next to her. "What's she going to do?"

Massaging her temples, she shrugged. "Move on, I guess. What else can you do in a situation like that?"

"Therapy. That's what I did."

She looked up at him, surprised.

He smiled somberly at her expression. "I was engaged once. Went through something similar."

Mind. Blown.

"You were engaged?"

So many questions.

"Five years ago." He nodded slowly, brown eyes gazing across the yard. "We were together for two years. I was in love with her. She was in love with money." He looked back at Rachael, a bitter smile in place. "It didn't end well."

Processing this, she watched the dogs chase each other in the yard.

He glanced at her curiously. "Does it bother you that I was engaged?"

Rachael thought about it. "I guess not. I mean, we have both had relationships in the past, right?"

"We have."

"None of mine have ever really been serious though," she added.

"None?"

"No," she said, watching as Olive tackled Martini, rolling in the grass. "I've never even been in love."

He was stunned. "Never?"

"No. I dated occasionally, but I never got that doe-eyed, lovey-dovey feeling. Not that there were many men in my past, but it was never . . . right."

To her amusement, he was wide-eyed and his mouth opened and closed a few times, but nothing came out.

"Does that bother you? It looks like it bothers you," she observed, trying not to laugh at his fish-out-of-water expression.

He smirked and leaned over the armrests between them, breathing into her ear. "Hell no. I'm glad no one has stolen your heart yet."

Oh, but someone has.

She swallowed and looked away.

"Tell me more about your fiancé. Is she still around?"

"*Ex*-fiancé," he corrected. "No, she's back in St. Louis. Worried?"

"No," she said aloud.

Umm . . . Yes! Wouldn't any person want to make sure their significant other's ex was far, far away? And even then, farther yet would be better. Perhaps she was a bit possessive.

"How did you two meet?" Rachael asked.

"College. I was in the veterinary medicine program, and she was finishing her bachelor's degree. We didn't have all that much in common. But we had fun. I thought she was the one." He brushed invisible lint from his leg. "But when I told her I was accepting the job at the animal hospital out here, she was furious. She wanted me to open a private practice there and be exclusive to high-dollar clientele. I scoffed at that. She had no idea what I wanted to do, what was important to me."

"But you were engaged?"

"I was so naïve," he said. "In my mind, it was the

logical thing to do. I wanted to get my career started, get married, and have a family right away. Maybe that's an only-child thing? I had hoped that being engaged would help her feel more connected, somehow help her share my vision. I thought it was starting to work, too, until I walked in on her with a classmate of mine. Guess he was willing to start this money factory."

"That's awful. I'm so sorry."

Rick opened his eyes and looked at her. "I'm not. It *was* awful at the time. But now? Now I'm damn glad I didn't marry her."

She was quiet as she thought about his words, his desire to start a family right away, then tugged at the thread connecting the past to the present. "Is she why you freaked out and quit talking to me? After the photo and the story?"

He looked out across the yard and took a deep breath. "I couldn't let myself go through that again."

"Rick?"

He turned to her, and she caught her breath at the exposed hurt in his eyes.

"I'm sorry. I promise I won't do that to you. If I could take back that dinner, that photo, everything else, I would."

Rick leaned toward her. "I know." He kissed her softly.

Kim strolled out to the deck, glanced at them, then walked back in the house without comment.

Laughing, they headed into the kitchen.

33

———

"What's the plan?" Rachael asked.

"I'm going to the store to buy boxes and tape," Kim said. "Then you and I are going to go pack up her clothes and toiletries."

"Does Brent know we're coming?"

"No," Kim looked away sheepishly. "You're going to call him while I'm at the store."

Fuuuuuuck.

"What's the address?" Rick asked.

"Why?" Rachael asked.

"So Gil and I can stop by and rough him up a bit."

They all stared at him and time paused briefly. When it resumed, they laughed like mad women.

"Seriously," he said. "What is the address?"

"Twenty-five Maple."

He nodded and grabbed his phone. "Wait here."

Mystified, she watched him walk away, phone to his ear.

"What's that about?" Kim asked.

"I have no idea."

Carlie was sitting on the sofa, a fuzzy blanket stretched across her lap. "Sorry to put you guys through all this," she said.

"No problem, sunshine. You'd do the same for us," said Kim.

Rachael bit her tongue to stop from mentioning they had done this several times now for Kim. Sometimes it was better to let it lie.

"Still, thank you."

Rick strode back in. "All taken care of."

"What's taken care of?"

"One of Nancy's kids runs a moving company. He's going to contact the ex to schedule a time today when he will not be there. They'll arrive with boxes and packing tape. You just need to go tell them what to pack."

Rachael's jaw dropped. "Seriously?"

Kim and Carlie mirrored her expression.

"Who's Nancy?" Kim finally asked.

"His receptionist at the hospital,"

"She's somewhat more than that, but yes, that's the general consensus." He smiled. "I do need his name and phone number to send them."

She texted him the info, and sat down, blown away by his generosity.

"Now we just need to find you a new place, Car," said Kim. She glanced at Rick uncertainly. "Unless you've covered that too?"

He laughed. "Sorry, no apartments up my sleeve."

"You could always move in here with us," Rachael offered. "Mom and Dad won't mind."

She shook her head. "No. Mom and I would kill each other."

"Okay, then. Let's go drive around, see what's open," Kim suggested. "Unless you want to stay with me and Owen?"

Carlie cringed. "No, thank you."

"I hate to be a killjoy, but it *is* Sunday and tomorrow is a federal holiday," Rachael reminded them.

"I still say we go drive around. Carlie and I will take the south end of town, and you two take the north end," Kim said.

"Works for me." Carlie perked up.

Seeing her become animated for the first time in twenty-four hours, Rachael couldn't deny Carlie the opportunity to take the first step in her path to freedom. "Okay. I'll grab the folder Mom put together. Several good places in there that I had to rule out for not being pet-friendly. Unless you're planning to get a pet?"

Carlie made a face. "No. I prefer being an auntie."

She pulled out the leads and split them geographically. Kim and Carlie took off with the lion's share. Rick took the remaining info sheets, skimming through and planning a route. "You don't have to do this, Rick," Rachael offered, giving him a chance to escape.

"I don't mind," he said absently as he shuffled through the papers, reordering them.

"Are you sure?"

He put the stack of papers down and focused on her. "I'm positive. I personally appreciate a plan that allows me to spend more time alone with you."

"Well, okay then."

"Okay then." He grinned. "Ready to go?"

She grabbed her bag and slipped on some sandals. "Guess so."

They started with the rentals farthest away and marked notes on the pages. A few they could rule out immediately due to location or occupancy, but there were a couple that were strong possibilities. Rachael was still making notes when they pulled up to the next one.

"An open house. That makes it easier," he commented.

She blinked in confusion, then recognized the place. They were idling at the curb of the house she happened upon the other day. "No, this isn't a rental. It's just a house I liked. I don't know what I was thinking. I'm definitely not looking to buy right now, and I seriously doubt they'd entertain a lease offer. Not with the way the market is right now."

He looked at the house for a long moment, then back at her. "Want to check it out? It is an open house after all."

Glancing at the dwindling stack of rentals, she returned her gaze longingly to the house.

He unbuckled his seat belt. "Come on. Let's do a quick walk-through."

Holding hands as they walked up the driveway, they passed an orderly row of lush green plants on their way to the front door. White columns stood on either side of the entrance and an elegant metal knocker shone from the glossy door.

"Shall we?" he asked.

Rachael twisted the doorknob and they moved into a spacious foyer with pristine hardwood flooring and soft cream walls. Large windows cast bright, natural light on the wooden stairwell that led up to the second floor, while the first floor opened all around them. A pleasant real estate agent greeted them, handing her business card to Rick. "Hello and welcome! Kay McLin with Cinci Home Finders. Please look around. There are property specs and a sign-in sheet on the kitchen counter, if you wouldn't mind leaving your names."

"Thank you," Rachael murmured.

She walked from room to room, falling more in love with the house with each space she entered. The large windows in each room created sizeable patches of sun-warmed floor that Martini and Olive would love. The character in the home was perfection—beautiful arched wooden doorways, window wells that were rich with soft, weathered wood, and floors that were impeccable buttery wood. She could imagine setting up an office in the smallest bedroom. The hall bath was divine and perfect for guests who would come visit. The hallways and open spaces were ripe with opportunities to decorate and host holiday parties.

"Wow," she whispered as she entered the spacious and luxurious master suite. "This is beautiful."

Rick followed her around the house, watching her "ooh" and "ahh" over each new feature. He was smiling indulgently, and she squeezed his hand when she passed by to check out the enclosed yard.

"Oh, Olive and Martini would love this!"

The yard was flat and wide open, two large trees offering shade over the patio. Not quite as large as her parents' yard, but big enough to run, play, and get into plenty of trouble.

They finished up in the airy gourmet kitchen. Rachael skimmed through the pages of property measurements and tax info while Rick signed the register. "How long have you two been married?" Kay asked.

"Oh, we're not married," Rachael replied absently.

"No? Well, if you don't mind my saying so, you look quite charming together."

"Thank you," Rick replied. "I keep trying to tell her that."

The realtor laughed delightedly. "So charming."

They returned to the car, and Rachael sighed. "Someday . . ."

Rick started the car and shuffled to the next page. "Onward?"

Rachael nodded and indulged in a fantasy that they were indeed a married couple—or engaged—and house hunting for that perfect family home. A shiver reached her spine, as she considered what a future like that might entail. Could she imagine marriage, a big family home . . . a family of her own? For the first time, she didn't find the idea so foreign. Being with Rick had made her question her entire future; the plans she thought were cemented were now wavering like a mirage. A new path, a new plan, started to tease her from the edges of her mind.

She turned from the window and watched him as they made the short drive to her parents' home. What was he thinking now? Could he be thinking about the future, too?

34

They arrived back at her parents' house and saw no sign of her sister and Kim. Rachael bottled up her musings and returned to reality, picking through the papers in her folder and selecting the three most likely candidates from their stack. "I doubt she'll like these, but they're the best of the bunch we had."

"That was fun," he said, opening the fridge. "Water?"

She nodded. "Thanks again for coming with me."

He sat at the table next to her and shuffled through the stacks, finding the house they walked through. "You loved it, didn't you?"

"Yes," she sighed, looking at the pictures, wisps of dreams flitting through her mind's eye. "But completely unrealistic. It's too much for just me and the dogs."

He took a drink of his water and glanced at her curiously. "Someday it could be more than just you and the dogs."

"I suppose."

"Like . . . maybe kids?"

She smiled. "Kids?"

"Yeah. You know, little humans. They run around. Poop a lot. Cry. That kind of thing. Or so I'm told."

"I know what kids are," she laughed, slapping his shoulder.

"Do you think you'd want to have kids?"

Her laughter trailed off as she looked at him. "I don't know. I've never really thought about it. Maybe? With the right person. And at the right time."

He nodded, studiously avoiding her eyes, fidgeting with the papers on the table.

"And, of course, you'd probably want to be married, right?"

"More than likely. That would pair with the 'right person' part of the equation."

He glanced up briefly, then shuffled to the next page. "And what would the 'right time' part of the equation look like?"

"I have no idea."

"No?"

"No. What about you?"

He took a deep breath and closed his eyes. She saw his throat work, and he finally turned back to her. "When I was little, I dreamed about having a big family. My thoughts were always full of what life would be like if I had brothers or sisters. As I grew older, I knew I wanted to have kids, more than one. I wanted to have kids who had those brothers or sisters, the lifelong friend to always count on. I didn't want to just have them, but be young enough to play with them, run around with them, coach their baseball teams, soccer teams . . . get out and enjoy life with them."

She considered growing up with Carlie. They always had each other. And even Kim. Kim's homelife sucked, her dad was as absent as one could get, but she was always considered part of their family. For the first time, it occurred to her that she'd never heard Kim talk about kids, let alone a permanent relationship. So different from Rick. Picturing the lonely young boy, desperate for companionship and permanency, was painful. She imagined a little wilderness explorer, talking to imaginary friends and using animals as substitute siblings. Lost in her thoughts, she was surprised when his hand wiped her cheek, coming away wet.

"I'm thirty-four years old, Rachael. I've dated. I've been in love. I've been engaged. I've been hurt. I've learned a lot about what I do and don't want in a partner. And if I met the right woman, if we loved each other and it felt right . . ." His serious expression betrayed his casual shrug. "If that all happened, I would probably not wait long. I'd try to figure out if it was what she wanted too, sooner rather than later. And I'd probably act on it. Sooner rather than later."

He resumed shuffling through the pages, and she watched. Could she see herself not only getting married, but having kids? Soon? She didn't know. That was so mind-boggling compared to how she had pictured her life.

"Rick?"

"Hmm?"

Rachael sorted through their conversation. Did she miss something? "Are you trying to ask me something?"

"I'm just making conversation." A flush worked its way up his neck, and she was fascinated, watching his discomfort grow. He turned another page over and glanced at her. "Is something wrong?"

"No," she murmured, picking up her water. She took a long drink and stood, staring out the back door. Her heart was already his, but was she willing to change everything she had ever believed about herself. For him? Change her present, her future?

She jumped when she felt his hands close on her shoulders. "Did I upset you, talking about all of that?"

Leaning back against him, she twisted her head, kissing the top of his hand. "I'm not upset. Maybe overwhelmed. Like I said, I've never given it much thought. I've never met someone who made me *want* to consider those things before. Marriage, kids? It's all new territory for me."

"Think about it. Later. But for now, we have something else to discuss." He leaned down and kissed the side of her neck, his hands sliding down her arms and wrapping possessively around her stomach.

"We do?" she asked, crossing her arms over his.

"Mhm. Well, truthfully, less talking and more making up for lost time," he continued. She tilted her head to the side as he worked his way up to her ear, nibbling and tickling.

"Very much so," she agreed.

Rick hummed his mutual agreement and she turned her face toward him, searching for and finding his kiss. He brushed softly, his lips grazing hers, and she twisted in his arms, wrapping her hands over his shoulders. Sliding his hands down to cup her behind, he lifted her against himself and moved across the room, settling her on the hard granite kitchen counter. She snuggled against his chest as he deepened the kiss, his tongue probing the corners of her mouth. Entwining her tongue with his, she sighed into his mouth, teasing her fingers into the hair at the nape of his neck. Tugging her to the edge of the counter, he groaned, pressing intimately against her. She wiggled against him and felt deliciously naughty, sitting on her parents' counter. His arousal was straining against his jeans and she rubbed against him, enjoying the hiss of painful pleasure.

"You have no idea how much I want you," Rick rasped into her ear before reclaiming her lips. The kiss drew more heated, more demanding, and they were soon both panting.

He pulled back fractionally and swept her with his gaze. He slid his hands up her thighs, sliding between her shorts and skin. The teasing movements continued before he drew away and examined her shorts, unbuttoning and sliding down the zipper. Breathless, she watched his intentional movements. Grasping her waist with one hand, he lifted her slightly and tugged at the shorts with the other. Rachael giggled as he fussed with them, eventually succeeding. "You could have asked me to help," she teased.

Growling, he grasped her underwear and tugged them down swiftly. Discarding them on the floor, his hands moved back up, grazing her legs possessively as he neared where she wanted him. She hooked her ankles behind him, encouraging him closer so she could reach his waist, his jeans. Making quick work of his button and fly, she took pleasure in finding his scalding hot, firm erection and the feel of him pressing into her hand. He kissed her deeply, both relearning the other.

Rachael gasped for breath. Filling her lungs, she met his eyes. "I want you."

With a tortured groan, he pulled out of her caress and scooped her up, carrying her up the stairs and into her room. He kicked the door closed behind them before depositing her gently on the bed. She pulled her top over her head, and unclasped her bra, anxious to feel him against her skin. He matched her movements and they were soon fully exposed to each other. Rick took a deep breath and climbed onto the bed with her. "You don't know what you do to me."

"I know what you do to me." She pulled him closer, devouring him. She ran her fingers up his biceps, reveling in the conflicting strength and compassion he represented. Breaking their kiss, they stared at each other.

"I've never felt this way before," she admitted. "I have never needed to be with someone so much. Never felt so complete, so right when we're together. This is all new to me."

He stared and she could see him making connections. They didn't say the words, but Rachael could read them in his eyes; she hoped he could read them in hers. He stroked her face and lay next to her, watching her in awe, touching her. They met halfway in a sweet kiss. It was a first-kiss kind of kiss. A new kiss. A kiss that spoke of things to come. Of promises to be made. It was a kiss of new love.

Rick pulled her securely to himself, and she held him just as tightly, wanting to be as close as possible. She wanted this man. She wanted his body. She wanted his heart. She wanted his future.

Sliding his hand up her thigh, Rick grasped her hip and buried his face in her neck. Trusting him wholly, she closed her eyes, and gave him all the control. She needed nothing more than him.

He rolled her onto her back and kissed her deeply, his hand skimming and teasing the damp curls at her core. He swiped one finger deeper, parting and searching, finding an entry and easing in. She moaned into his mouth.

"What do you want, Rachael?"

"More," she whispered. "You. Just you."

His thumb worried her sensitive bud while he worked in and out of her, stretching and teasing. The tension grew, and she moved her body against him, straining for more.

She sensed him withdrawing and held him closer. "What? What's wrong?"

"Shit. I don't have anything with me," he said, pressing his forehead to hers. "I meant to stop on the way over. Damn it! Do you . . . ?"

Her mind blanked. Condoms were not really something she had anticipated needing in the guest room of her parents' house. She shook her head, frustrated.

His fingers were still teasing and tempting, and her senses were keyed up. But it wasn't just the physical connection she needed to share with him. Closing her eyes, she made a decision with her heart that she had never allowed herself to consider until this moment. She knew what it meant, what it could mean, what could happen. But she trusted him completely. This man.

Gazing into his eyes, she found the love she knew would be there. "Rick. I still want you. I want this."

"You know I want you." He stared at her longingly.

"I'm on the pill and I have always used protection. I have never tested positive for any STD. You?"

"No, I'm clean, baby. But are you sure? We don't have to . . ."

"I have never been so sure." She took a deep breath then bared her soul, giving him everything. "I love you."

He closed his eyes and stopped moving. "What did you say?"

"I love you, Rick. You're the only one I want to be with. I love you. And I'm not just saying it because we're here together in this room. I'm saying it because I have never wanted to share my future with anyone. Until you." The emotion filled her eyes, her lips trembling as she said it. But she didn't care. She was with him, and she was finally saying the words aloud.

With heartbreaking tenderness, he wiped a tear from her cheek. "I love you, too."

"This is crazy, right? I mean, how is it even possible?"

He smiled and kissed her, eyes suspiciously bright. "I don't know. But I'm not letting you get away."

Rachael wrapped her arms around him, embracing him tightly, their hearts beating against each other.

"Are you sure?" he asked again.

"Yes, if you're okay with it. I trust you and I love you."

Capturing her mouth with abandon, he drank her in. She met his passion, pouring all of herself into the moment. Settling between her thighs, he held himself still over her. He stared down into her eyes with so much love it made her cry again.

"I love you," she repeated in a whisper.

"Jesus, I love you," he said, pushing into her. He pulled back and moved in deeper. She grasped his shoulders and wrapped her legs around him as he surged in all the way.

"Yes," he groaned. She sighed with pleasure, and he watched her face as they moved together. Buried deeply in her, he rocked slowly, his coarse hair massaging her clit, over and over. The flames rose, the heat built, burning her, carrying her to the edge. They moved together in awe of each other. Nothing had ever felt so good, so perfect.

"Rick," she gasped as he kept moving, the pressure crescendoing. Unable to hold back, she cried out, her body bursting around him, brilliantly exploding into a million stars. And still he kept moving, pushing firmly against the clutching pulses of her orgasm. He drove deeper and deeper, and she felt him tighten, thicken further. He pulled back one last time and slammed home, the shuddering release racking his body. She wrapped around him tightly, her body, her heart, filled with him. He collapsed, and they stared at each other.

Rick pressed his lips to hers then stared down at her in wonder. "You're mine."

"I am. And you're mine."

35

They lay together completely entwined, still connected. Rick kissed her hand and trailed small kisses up her arm and across her chest.

"I never want to leave this moment, this spot," Rachael purred.

"Then don't. We'll stay here," he replied, licking and biting her neck, "forever."

"What happens now?" she asked.

He paused his kisses and turned thoughtful eyes toward her. "We stay together."

"I know that, silly." She laughed, running her fingers through his soft brown hair.

"I mean it, Rachael. I want you to stay with me."

"Stay with you?"

He stared into her eyes. "I know it sounds crazy, but I want you to think about it. I want you with me. Move in with me."

"Rick, I can't just move in with you."

He gathered his thoughts. "Look, if you were renting a place and I was in the middle of a lease, then I might not have suggested it so soon. But you're living with your parents. I only have two months left on my current lease. The timing couldn't be better. It seems like the perfect opportunity to feel it out. Try it."

"You are insane."

His crooked smile warmed her. "Probably."

"What if you hate living with me? I'm selfish and messy. I can't cook. I hate cleaning. I work all the time. I have my routines. And the dogs! I can't leave Olive and Martini."

"Of course you can't leave Olive and Martini. You know, I happen to be good with animals. Kind of comes with the territory. And the rest we'll figure it out."

Stunned, she stared at him, trying to make sense of this. "You're serious, aren't you?"

"Completely. I love you and I want you to be with me. Move in with me?"

He dipped his head down and kissed her witless, a decadent gift intended to persuade. He lifted his head and smiled at her breathlessness. "Say yes."

She shook her head. "I don't know, Rick."

Rick groaned and pulled out of her, rolling to lie on his side. He leaned up on his elbow and watched her. "What is worrying you?"

"What will my parents think?"

"That's what you're concerned about? Your parents?"

"I don't know. What about your parents? Won't they think it's odd?"

He laughed. "Rachael, I'm a grown man. That's not

really a consideration. Besides, I haven't talked to my parents since Easter. They don't care."

What on earth was happening? Rachael saw the sincerity in his eyes. He really wanted this. But did she? Could she actually live with him? She had never lived with anyone before. It was too soon. She needed time.

"Give me some time to think about it, okay? Let's take care of my sister and get her settled, then see if you still want this."

Rick chuckled and kissed her nose. "If I still want this? I can tell you that answer is not going to change. You've been on my mind since you walked into my office with Olive. You have taken over my heart, my life. Is it wrong to want you in my home, too? But take your time, baby. I'm not going anywhere."

Holy cow. How did you say no to that?

She shook her head and slid to the edge of her bed.

"Where are you going?"

"I left some clothes in the kitchen. Going to snag them before it advertises to Carlie and Kim what we've been up to."

He leaned back and closed his eyes. She ran down to the kitchen; her conscience required that she clean the granite counter. If her mom freaked out about dishes on the wrong rack, she could just imagine her reaction to her bare ass on the counter. She laughed before grabbing a couple of waters and her clothes. Olive and Martini were sleeping on the sofa and she smiled at their sweet smushy faces as she passed them. When she returned to the room, he was nearly asleep.

"Come here," Rick drowsily demanded, holding up the edge of the blanket.

She scooted against him. He wrapped his arm around her hip, tucking her against his chest. She laid her head on his bent arm and leaned into him, smelling his soap, his cool cologne, his sweat mixed with hers, and feeling his breath in her ear.

"I could get used to this," she murmured.

"That's the plan, baby. That's the plan."

Unbelievably happy and content, she dozed off and dreamed of the future.

A KNOCK on the door woke her a short while later. "Rach? You in there?"

She stretched and yawned, mumbling, "Be down in a few."

Rick was no longer there. Where did he go? Did he leave?

Frowning, she rolled off the bed and pulled on her discarded clothes. Checking her reflection, she noted she was flushed, but otherwise presentable enough.

Going down the stairs, she rolled her shoulders and stretched her neck. A tiny bit sore, but otherwise good. Her head didn't bother her anymore, which made everything easier.

Rick and Kim were sitting on the sofa, reviewing apartment leaflets. Carlie was in the kitchen on the phone. They all looked up as she entered the living room. "You okay?" Kim asked.

Rachael blushed and nodded, grumbling about not sleeping much last night. "Just wait till you're a few years older," she teased them.

"Funny. I just assumed the two of you were getting it on," Kim said, looking from her to Rick.

Ignoring her, Rachael passed through to the kitchen. Carlie covered the mouth piece. "Mom and Dad."

Oh. She gave her sister some privacy and stepped out onto the patio. Martini and Olive were out, and they raced to meet her on the deck steps. Sinking down to sit on the top step, Rachael scratched their ears and considered Rick's proposition. Could they? Should they?

The door opened behind her and she looked up as he sat down on the step next to her.

"You left me." She squinted up at him.

"Came downstairs and picked up a little. You girls were slobs last night."

She blushed and leaned against him.

He wrapped an arm around her and pressed his lips to her temple. "Say it again, please."

"I love you."

He smiled with deep masculine satisfaction. "I love you." He kissed her softly.

"How long have they been here?"

"About half an hour."

"Any luck?"

He nodded. "She found a couple she likes. One is only a few blocks from here."

Wow. "That would be perfect. Close enough to have us all nearby, but still private. She definitely needs her own space." Rachael imagined what would happen if Carlie and Mom were ever to live in the same house again. World War III. No doubt about it.

"I heard back from Nancy's son," he added. "We can get her stuff in about an hour. Guess they had to do some convincing to get Brent to leave long enough to allow her to move out. He, uh, doesn't want her to leave."

"This is all so hard to believe. Everything is changing in the blink of an eye."

"Are you talking about them or us?"

She smiled weakly. "A little of both, I guess."

They sat in companionable silence and watched the dogs.

"Thank you," she finally said.

"For what?"

"For organizing this. Getting her out of there."

He shrugged. "If you have the ability to help someone, you should."

"It means a lot to me."

"I'm glad. But that's not why I did it."

"I know, but it still means a lot to me. You're a good person."

He grinned. "I try."

Smiling back at him, she kissed him lingeringly, loving the feel of his arms around her, his body supporting hers.

Pushing herself up reluctantly, she held a hand out to him. "Hungry?"

"Starving," he practically growled.

"Food?"

"Not what I was thinking of, but food would be a close second," he conceded.

Laughing, she tugged him up and together they led the dogs in and collected Kim and Carlie. Her sister looked completely wrung out. She could imagine how the conversation went with their parents. Rachael hugged Carlie and, with Rick in tow, walked her to the door. "Let's go get some food, okay?"

She sniffed and nodded. "I could eat."

Rachael smiled. "The day you're not hungry is the day I really begin to worry about you. You're going to be just fine."

"You're one to talk."

36

$\mathcal{T}$he four of them crowded into a booth at their favorite sports bar. For all her bluster, Carlie barely touched her food. Rachael and Kim kept a steady stream of conversation flowing, and even Rick dropped a line or two, but Carlie sank further and further into an unreachable place.

Kim met her eyes and Rachael shook her head sadly. This was awful.

"We need a round of drinks, here," Kim hollered to the server. "Three—no four—four tall Miller Lite drafts with limes."

Rick raised his eyebrows and Rachael laughed.

"Tradition," she told him.

The beers arrived and they squeezed the tart limes into the drinks, dunking them and watching the bits of pulp float and mix with the carbonated bubbles. They raised their drinks and Kim quipped, "Here's to me, here's to you, here's to parents never finding out what—"

"And who," Rachael inserted.

"—we do!" Kim finished, and even Carlie giggled.

They clinked their glasses and cackled like mad. Rick turned to her, mildly entertained. "Tradition?"

"Yes," the girls said in unison.

Rachael pulled apart another flapper and tore into the meat. "I love these wings. I get to be ferocious and create carnage."

"Please. It's a little hard to pull off ferocious when you look like Alice in Wonderland," Kim teased.

"Eat me," Rachael scrunched her face up at Kim. "Besides, I can't help my genetics."

Carlie grimaced. "Genetic lottery loser right here."

Rachael patted her hand. "You got all the height, girl-friend. What I wouldn't give to have those long killer stems."

"Mhm," Kim agreed.

"I rather like your legs, especially when they're wrapped around me," Rick whispered under his breath, causing her to flush instantly.

"Enough, you two. What gives?" asked Carlie.

"What?" Rachael asked her sister innocently.

Narrowed slate blue eyes tangled with Rachael's bright blues. "What is going on here?" Carlie pressed.

"Here?" Rick asked.

Carlie pointed her carrot stick at Rachael then at Rick. "*You* and *you*. Don't think I haven't noticed. What's going on?"

Rachael glanced at Rick. He shrugged and tilted his beer at her. Guess it was on her to decide how to define this. "We're dating."

He nodded and gestured for her to go on.

"And we're happy?"

He swirled his fingers, encouraging more.

"And . . . ?" Rachael prompted, looking at him curiously.

"And . . . ?" Kim continued.

"And I'm in love with your sister," Rick said.

Carlie looked at them, stunned. "What?"

Rachael blushed at the public declaration and stared at Rick, who was waiting expectantly. "And I love him, too."

"The fuck you say," Kim whispered.

"This isn't funny, Rach," Carlie glared.

Rachael leaned against Rick and remained silent. He wrapped his arm around her shoulders and they waited. Let it sink in.

"Holy shitballs, I think they're serious," Kim said, shocked.

Rachael nodded at Kim and waited for Carlie absorb this, wishing the timing was different.

"No offense, Rick, you're lovely," she turned to Rachael, "but you don't *do* love."

Rachael glanced at Rick and replied with the only thing she could think to say. "I suppose I only needed to meet the right guy." Her words were incredibly cliché, but they were the truth.

"What about Gabe?"

Rachael winced and felt Rick tighten his grip. "Gabe and I are friends, Car. Nothing more. He understands that and accepts it."

Carlie's gaze shot to her plate. "Sorry. That was thoughtless of me."

"No need to apologize. You've had a traumatic couple of days, and now was probably not the best time to drop this on you," Rick said. "But I do love her, and I'm not planning to go anywhere anytime soon."

"Well then," Kim said uncertainly, lifting her glass, "Cheers to the new lovebirds?"

Rachael watched Carlie, worried. "Life can be unbelievably unfair. I wish I could take away the pain Brent caused you. I love you and will make sure that bastard never gets the opportunity to hurt you again."

A tear ran down Carlie's cheek and Rachael's heart clenched. Her poor baby sister. Kim leaned into Carlie's side, hugging her tightly.

Carlie picked up a napkin, took a shaky breath, and dabbed her cheeks, a devious smile breaking her sadness. "So, when's the wedding?"

Rachael choked on her beer, coughing and gasping, and started laughing. "God, Carlie. Seriously?" Grabbing a napkin, Rachael dabbed at the beer she'd sprayed all over her plate. *Married?*

Kim was snickering behind her glass. "Damn, Rach. I haven't seen a display like that since freshman year of college."

Rick helped her clean up, laughing at the mess. "Remind me not to let you drink red wine around them."

"On a serious note," Carlie said, a frown creasing her brow, "what's the plan for going to the house? How do we know Brent won't be there?"

"The moving company will text me when they have seen him vacate the premises," Rick assured her.

Carlie nodded slowly. "And if he comes back while we're still there?"

"He won't."

"But if he does?"

"He can try. But he won't get in."

"I just can't bear the thought of seeing him right now. I keep picturing him and Gina. God, how could he do that? With her? She's my friend!"

"Was, girl. She *was* your friend. And she clearly wasn't a good one," Kim spat out.

"Carlie, if it wasn't her, it would have been someone else," said Rachael. "He's a complete idiot for messing this up with you. You're the best thing that ever happened to him. Now someone else will get to see the love that you have to give. And he will be the luckiest man in the world." Rachael reached across the table, grasping her hand. "I promise, you will find someone who deserves you."

Kim added her hand to theirs. "And if he doesn't, we'll just introduce him to Gina."

Rachael groaned and Carlie winced.

"Too soon?" Kim snorted.

Rick snagged a carrot off Carlie's plate. "He's not worth your tears. People who cheat are among the lowest form of scum."

"I'll keep that in mind."

"I'm serious. I've been where you are, and it isn't easy. But it will get better. Just be grateful you found out before you took a bigger leap together. I nearly married the woman."

She watched him and shook her head. "I know I'll get there someday. But I can't talk about it anymore. So, tell me more about you two. I want to know how you went from flaking out after a stupid photo," Carlie looked at him suspiciously, "to suddenly having a date or two and are in love? What am I missing here?"

"I made a terrible mistake," he said. "I jumped to conclusions and nearly missed the chance of a lifetime. Thankfully, your sister has forgiven me."

"We *both* made mistakes, and we are working through them," Rachael agreed.

"We are," Rick said, kissing her temple.

"Wham, bam, you're in love?" Kim asked, still skeptical.

"Yes. From the moment she walked into the clinic with Olive, half-naked and screeching and cussing out Nancy, she's been on my mind."

Rachael slapped his side and bit her lip. "I wasn't screeching! And I was fully dressed—I had to use my jacket to wrap her up. But I did curse at Nancy. I was so awful."

"No, you weren't awful," he assured her. "You were distressed." He kissed her temple. "Somehow things led us back to each other. And I'm the idiot who almost lost her because I was insecure. That's what my ex left me with, Carlie. Don't let this joker leave you like that. You are not at fault in this."

"I see what you did there, turning it back around to me. Well done," Carlie golf-clapped.

"You two are disgusting," Kim said, looking between Rachael and Rick. "All this lovey-dovey crap is gag worthy. But I am happy for you. About time someone cracked that cold heart of yours open."

"Thank you?" Rachael offered, her nose curled up.

Rick's phone vibrated. "Eagle has left the nest, ladies. Shall we?"

They finished their beers and charged onward, ready to tackle some packing chaos.

37

_____

The chaos was exceedingly unchaotic. The moving team was already there waiting for them, stacks of flat boxes waiting to be assembled and filled. Stoically, Carlie went room by room, pointing out what was going, what was staying. Her part took less than an hour. The movers swept through like kids at an Easter egg hunt, picking up and packing the place clean of her belongings in record time.

"Dang, I need to hire them to just come clean up after me at the new place," Carlie commented, as the first room was emptied of her belongings.

"Did you choose one?" asked Rachael.

"Yes! I'm going to rent the one close to Mom and Dad's. Thankfully the owner is in town, but I can't get the keys until tomorrow morning. Guess I'll be crashing with you and the dogs for a spell."

"I'm glad. We can watch some terrible chick flicks and hate on men."

"Ahem," Rick interjected. "I hope you're not hating on *all* men."

"Just those whose names start with B and end with 'rent,'" Kim clarified.

After Carlie made one last pass through the apartment and was satisfied the crew knew what they were doing, Car looped her arm through Kim's and they walked out of Brent's life together.

"Rachael," Rick said, capturing her arm as she was about to follow them.

She smiled up at his heart-stoppingly handsome face. "Yes?"

He kissed her gently. "I'll never do that to you."

"I know. You're mine, remember?"

"I remember." He hesitated. "Have you thought more about what we talked about?"

"Not yet. We've been a little busy." She laughed, gesturing around them. "But I promise I will think it over soon."

"Come along then, Ms. Eller," he said, offering his arm to her. Rachael hooked her arm through his and they walked out the door. A shiver tickled her spine, a glimpse of things to come.

Carlie and Kim waited for them by Rick's car. "You two coming?" Kim yelled back at them.

"Coming," Rick hollered. He looked down at Rachael, then grinned wickedly.

"What? What are you—ahhh!" She squealed as he lifted and swung her in the air, catching her securely in his arms. "Rick!"

Her sister and Kim chortled, teasing her about being swept off her feet.

"Ha, ha. You made your point, caveman. Put me down."

He ignored her and kept walking toward the car. "Would one of you young ladies mind getting that door for me? Should be unlocked."

Carlie laughed and pulled open the passenger door with a flourish.

"Rick! What are you doing?"

He walked to the open door and set her in the seat, buckling the belt around her.

"Rick?"

"What?"

'What?'

"Would you mind telling me what you think you are doing?"

"Me?"

"No, the other Rick. Yes, you!"

He laughed and dropped down to kiss her again. "I'm just taking care of my baby."

"Your baby?"

"Yes. You." He punctuated with a pair of kisses on the top of her head.

"You're crazy," Rachael said with a laugh.

"Crazy for you," he crooned, shutting the door between them.

Carlie climbed in behind her. "Jesus, Rachael. What did you do to the guy?"

"I have no idea," she murmured, watching him practically dance around to the driver's door.

"You are in so much trouble," Kim laughed. "That is one lovesick puppy."

"Good thing he's a vet," Carlie giggled.

"Veterinarian, heal thyself," Kim commanded teasingly.

Oh, lord.

Rick opened his door. "Where to, ladies?"

"Home?" Rachael said.

Still grinning, he closed the door and started driving. When they reached her parents' place, he drove past it.

"Rick?" Rachael asked.

"Hmm?"

"Are you kidnapping us?"

"No."

"Then where are we going?"

"You said 'home.'"

"I meant my parents' house!"

Kim and Carlie were watching them from the backseat with matching giggles. Rachael threw them an evil look, which made them laugh harder.

"Oh? I must have misheard you," Rick said.

"You're being so weird. Are you okay?"

"I've never been better. You?"

She crossed her arms over her chest and watched him. He took another turn and she recognized where they were. "We're going to *your* place?"

"Mhm."

"Why?"

"I just wanted to show your sisters where I live. Just in case."

"In case of what?" Carlie asked, glancing at Kim.

"In case she says yes."

"Rick, stop."

"Yes to what?" Carlie asked, her eyes alight with fresh suspicion.

"Rick," Rachael warned.

"Yes to moving in with me."

"What?!" Carlie and Kim cried in unison.

"Rick!" Rachael shouted. "This is not funny."

"You're right. It isn't. Because it isn't a joke."

Carlie and Kim stared at them, mouths agape.

"Just a trial. You know, see how we do together," he explained to them. "She needs a place to stay and my lease is almost up."

"You have lost your damn mind," Rachael muttered.

He opened the garage door to his condo and pulled in. He hopped out, but everyone else remained frozen in their seats.

For the first time, he looked nervous. He pulled open the car door again. "Rachael? Please?"

She turned and looked at her sisters. They both watched her. Carlie nodded. "Let's go in. I'm curious."

"This is madness," Rachael grumbled as she opened her door.

They joined him at the garage door, and he motioned them ahead of him. They walked up the short flight of stairs to the kitchen and living area. Rachael glanced at the couch and remembered the last time she was here. How nervous he was.

"This is a great place," Kim said, walking around and checking out the few pieces of art around the room.

Carlie skimmed the texts on his shelves, then checked out the view from the windows.

Something new greeted them by the large back picture window. Two plush dog beds sat on the floor, the perfect size for a pair of crazy dogs she loved. Rachael blinked and turned to Rick. He was watching her, an expectant and cautious smile lighting his face.

"Those are *so* cute," Carlie gushed, bending down to press her palm in the plush padding. "Rachael, did you see these? Can we see upstairs?"

"Go ahead," Rick nodded.

At the top of the stairs, they all turned toward the master bedroom with the large four-poster bed. Rick walked up behind Rachael and kissed the side of her neck.

Kim let out a low whistle. "That is a gorgeous bathroom."

"Rach, you gotta come see this," Carlie called from the hallway.

"I've been here before," she said.

"No, really. Just come here."

Rachael left the master bedroom and met Carlie in the hall. Her sister pointed to the guest room. "In there."

The queen-sized bed was pushed back along the wall. Two modern computer desks and two more dog beds filled the rest of the room. One desk was clearly Rick's, covered with medical books. The other desk . . . Rachael walked over and saw a large monitor, a tablet, and a framed picture of her family.

"Rick?"

"It's just a placeholder for now. Something pulled off the internet. But I wanted you to imagine what it could be like. Here. Us."

"When did you do this?" She was stunned, unsure how she felt about this presumptuous move.

"Nancy did it earlier while we were packing up Carlie's house. Do you like it? She was stressed because she didn't have a lot of time, but I think it's a good start."

"Rick, this is . . ." She turned in a circle, her hands

clutched empty air as her brain clutched for the right way to phrase her thoughts. "Wow."

Kim walked in and looked at the photo on the desk. She raised an eyebrow. "You guys are crazy."

Kim and Carlie went back downstairs, leaving her to stare at Rick. "This is too much, Rick. It's too fast."

He sat in the broad leather computer chair before his desk and swiveled to assess the room. "I know. It's fast for me, too."

"Then why all this?" She circled around, eyeing the room.

"Hell, I don't know. I knew it was crazy—even while I asked Nancy to help me out. But I couldn't stop myself from asking."

"This is very sweet though. The little dog beds! I love them!"

"You don't have to answer me now. But I needed you to see that I was serious. I want to try this. Take the next step with you."

Rachael sat down on his lap and wrapped her arms around his neck. "I love you," she whispered before pressing a kiss to his lips. He gripped the sides of her head and intensified the kiss, sealing his mouth over hers and plunging into the softness of her mouth. A moan escaped her throat. He massaged the back of her head, the other hand sliding down her back. She nuzzled against him, his arousal pressing against her thigh. His hand eased its way up under her shirt, caressing her backside. Rick released her mouth and kissed his way down her throat.

"Really?" She laughed. "My sister is downstairs."

"So?" he mumbled against her chest.

"And Kim," she gasped, her objections wilting as he

lifted her shirt over her head and licked the top of her breast, tugging her bra down.

"And?" he mumbled, his chin between her breasts, mouth suckling her puckered nipple.

"Rick," she sighed, giving in and leaning back against his arm as he continued to lave her breast. She wriggled her behind against him and he exhaled harshly, his breath raising goosebumps across her wet nipples. Escaping his grasp, Rachael rose to her feet and quietly clicked the door closed before sliding her panties down under her skirt. She reached down to unbuckle his pants; he shifted to allow her better access. Sliding her hand down, she grasped him, freeing him from his clothing. He sprang to attention. Dropping to her knees, she bit her lip and raised a brow at his fascinated expression. His eyes were flicking back and forth between her hands and mouth while he clenched the sides of the chair. Rachael leaned forward, touching her tongue to him, tasting him. He inhaled sharply, his death grip on the arms of the chair turning his knuckles white. Intoxicated by his reaction, she turned her full attention to pleasuring him, running her tongue up and down the length of him before closing her lips around the throbbing crown.

"God, yes," Rick hissed.

She took him in deeper, letting her tongue caress the warm velvet skin of his erection. He moved his hands to her head, guiding her mouth over him. She hummed and licked her way up before taking him in more fully.

"Stop," he moaned minutes later. "Too much, I'm going to come." Licking her way back up along his ridged seam, she rose from her knees and lifted her skirt as she climbed on top of him, knees on either side of his hips. Rachael liked being on top, having control, being able to kiss him as she sat astride. He reached under her skirt and slid his hand to her apex, groaning as he felt how wet she was for him.

Kissing him passionately, she lowered herself to him as he positioned his bulging erection at her entrance.

"This," he panted. "This is what I want. You and me." He wrapped his arms around her waist, pulling her tightly against him as she slid down his length. She ground against him, her breath coming faster. Rick surged and stood. "Wrap your legs around me," he commanded. Leaning back against his arm, she gasped as his hips rocked into her, pelvis grinding. His pants dropped down to his calves and her skirt was bunched between them. But there was no stopping, no pausing to move them.

Rachael whimpered and he claimed her mouth and thrusted into her, making love to her mouth and her body.

"I'm close," he gasped. His body was thickening, the fever increasing, and the pressure hit her over and over at the perfect place. A spool of heat gathered, tightening, coiling painfully, relentlessly. It was close, so close. He kept moving, kept lifting and pushing, filling her. His hands pulled her buttocks apart, surging in even deeper.

"Oh, my God. Oh, God. Yes!" she shouted, and he quickly covered her mouth, grinning as she moaned and came hard, falling against him. He rocked into her again and again, finally joining her in their shared high.

He held her against himself, both shaking, panting against each other. "I love you. Please say yes."

She nodded breathlessly. "I love you, too."

"Was that a yes?"

"It's an almost yes."

"What's an almost yes?"

"Yes, I will probably live with you. But give me a little time to catch my breath and get used to the idea."

He smiled broadly and lifted her higher against his chest, kissing her. "I don't know what I did to deserve you, but I am so thankful."

"Me too," she whispered, kissing him back.

They dressed quickly and returned to the living room to find it empty. "Car? Kim?" she called. They checked the backyard but didn't see them. She passed through the garage and walked outside to the front, discovering them sitting on the curb, chatting.

"There you are!" she called.

They turned as one and Rachael could tell they knew what they were doing upstairs. She blushed but continued toward them. "What are you doing out here?"

Kim arched an eyebrow. "Giving you two a few minutes to, uh, discuss things."

"Getting fresh air," Carlie added, elbowing Kim.

Rachael glanced behind her to make sure he wasn't out there yet. "What do you think about Rick?"

They glanced at each other and started grinning.

"Well?"

"He's great," Carlie gushed. "Seriously, the way he's stepped in and helped with everything. Plus, he's a freaking doctor. This is like Love Story 101. I approve."

Kim nodded. "I don't know what happened to the two of you, but you've got it bad. And so does he."

"But it's too soon though, right? I can't believe I'm considering living with him." She plopped down on the curb with them, contemplating the absurd beauty of it all.

Carlie tilted her head, her mouth pursed for a moment.

"It is soon, and weirdly fast. I get the feeling that is not your doing. Why is he pushing for you to live together already?"

"Something to do with his childhood and his past relationships," she mumbled vaguely, not wanting to share his painful stories.

They absorbed this in silence.

"I can't believe this," Kim said. "I never imagined the day . . ." She shook her head.

"Dad always says that when it's right, it's right. Maybe this is *the one?*" Carlie said wistfully.

Rachael was so conflicted, torn in her desire to be with him versus her need for independence. Could the two coexist? Could she have both? All she knew was she desperately loved him and couldn't imagine not making a go of things.

"You ready to go?" Rick hollered, coming down the drive toward them. They jumped up and met him, Kim chatting about some of Owen's pieces that would work with his décor, and Carlie sneaking questioning looks at Rachael.

Packed into his SUV to return home, Rick held her hand as they wove through the streets. Rachael watched him, still unable to believe that he chose her. That they chose each other. That this was real. He squeezed her hand, sharing a private connection.

"How did the call go with Mom and Dad?" Rachael asked over her shoulder.

"About what you'd expect. Mom was angry, Dad was angry. Both had wildly different ways of telling me how to deal with it. The usual."

"How are you supposed to deal with it?"

Carlie stared out the window. "According to Dad, I should give myself permission to be hurt and sad, then find it in me to forgive him and move on."

"Forgive him? Hell no. And Mom?"

"'As the wronged party, you have every right to demand he move out and leave the property to you,'" she mimicked in Mom's voice. "Like I'd ever want to live there again, with the memory of them banging each other in my bedroom, wondering if they'd screwed in every room of the house. God."

"You do you, Car. Everyone else can hold onto their thoughts," Kim consoled.

They pulled into the driveway of Rachael's parents' house. Rachael stepped inside, immediately greeted by Olive and Martini. The two pups jumped around like mad, begging to go out. *Cripes, you'd think they'd been home alone all day.* Rachael walked back through to the kitchen to let them out and gasped at the scene that greeted her.

Roses covered the deck. Hundreds upon hundreds of them. Vases on the patio table, side table and scattered about. Loose roses carpeted the deck. Every color, every size.

"Oh. My. God." She stood frozen in the doorway, fingers pressed to her lips, trying to comprehend what she was seeing. Rachael turned back toward the kitchen, where the three were amicably chatting about tomorrow's cookout. "Rick, this is . . ." she threw her hands up, unable to say what it was. "When did you have time to do this?"

Puzzled, they joined her and stared at the sea of roses.

"I didn't," Rick said.

"What?" She looked sharply at him, his eyes not giving any indication of his thoughts.

She pushed open the door and cleared a path through the flowers so Martini and Olive could get through. A vase on top of the patio table had a card in it. Addressed to her.

"They're not from you?" she asked again over her shoulder, dread pooling in her stomach.

His face darkened as he looked around. "No."

Rachael plucked the card from the vase.

A flower for every moment I've missed you. I can't stay away. I love you. G

She looked at Carlie, who just shrugged.

Oh, no. No, no, no, no, no!

"Wow. These are gorgeous," whistled Kim. "A bit excessive, but gorgeous. Who are they from?"

Rick glanced at her. And walked away.

"Gabe," Rachael whispered, watching Rick leave.

38

_____

Rachael topped off her wine glass, frustrated at the damn roller coaster her life had become.

"What does that even mean, 'I can't stay away'?" she muttered.

Carlie shook her head, taking another drink of wine.

"I mean, we had a great conversation. We talked it out. He understood." Rachael groaned, wondering if the whole world had gone mad. Clearly, Gabe had.

Kim had to leave to help Owen set up his upcoming exhibit, so Rachael sent her off with a few bushels of roses. Maybe they could find a use for them.

Carlie remained, standing across from the sofa Rachael sat on, watching her older sister quietly.

"God, I'm sorry Car. This is so shitty of me to be complaining with all you're going through, but _holy shit_. Why is this happening?"

Carlie sighed and sat on the coffee table in front of her.

"Mom would kill you if she saw you sitting there," Rachael said absently.

Carlie squinted her eyes, giving a pretty darn good Mom glare. "Rachael, what are you doing?"

"What do you mean, what am I doing?"

"Are you leading them both on?"

"No! Gabe and I had a physical thing. That was it. I love him but as a friend. Not like Rick. Nothing like Rick." She frowned, staring into her wine glass. "What should I do?"

"First thing you're going to do is pull yourself together. This isn't the end of the world, Rach."

Eyeing Carlie over the rim, she nodded for her to continue.

"Second, you need to figure out what you want. Who you want. It seems pretty obvious to me, but you need to decide for yourself. Then, as much as it sucks, you need to cut ties with the other person. Cold turkey. Finished. Kaput."

Rachael sighed and set down her glass. "I know you're right. God. What a pair we are, right? You're dealing with the scumbag of the year and I've got to figure out what the hell I want to do with two guys. And a bazillion roses. Maybe I should just join a nunnery."

"Convent. They're called convents. And I doubt you would do well with celibacy, so we can rule that out as a viable option."

"Carlie, I love him. Real, terrifying, freaking-the-hell-out-of-me love."

"I know."

"His ex-fiancé left him for another vet from his class, one who was willing to go all-in on a money-making practice. She cheated on him while they were engaged. He knew the guy. This has to feel like another slap in the face to him. Me choosing the guy with the money and fame."

"But you didn't choose Gabe."

"I know." Rachael picked up her glass and swirled the wine around, watching it cling briefly to the sides of the glass before sliding back down. She took a deep drink and closed her eyes. "He wants me to move in with him. I told him I probably would, but I need some time."

"I assumed," Carlie grinned. "But I think it's wise to take your time. No sense rushing into something that has you this confused."

She smiled, tears in her eyes. "You know, he healed my girl. He took care of Olive and took care of me when I was a mess. We went out a couple of times and we had an amazing time before the whole Gabe thing. When we eventually got back together, it all clicked. It was immediate and unlike anything I've ever felt. I can't describe it."

"So why didn't you say yes?"

"I don't know. It's all so new. I don't know what I'm doing. Look at you and Brent. And Kim and Owen. Does this stuff ever last? What if it's just lust? Or a fling?"

"Is it just lust?"

"No."

"Is it a fling?"

"I don't think so. The way he makes me feel—"

A knock on the front door spooked them.

Gabe.

Rising to her feet, Rachael knew what she had to do. Time to close one chapter so a new story could unfold.

She took a fortifying breath and closed her eyes, not able to look him in the face—that beautiful face—as she put the final nail in the coffin. Rachael pulled the door open and started talking. "This is not going to work, Gabe. I can't do this." When she gained the courage to open her eyes, she was shocked to see blood-shot hazel eyes staring at her in confusion.

"Brent? What are you doing here? She doesn't want to see you."

"Is she here?"

"You need to leave."

"Is she fucking here, Rachael?"

She stared at Brent, shocked.

"Carlie!" he yelled into the house. "Carlie! Please, I need you. We need to talk."

Rachael put her arm across the doorway, bracing herself between the door and frame. "You are not welcome here. Go away."

"Caaaarrrliiiieeee!"

"Do not make me call the police, Brent. Go home. You messed up. You had the best girl in the world, and you fucked it up. You! She walked in on you screwing another woman. And not just any woman. No, you had to do her friend! And like the loser you are, you didn't even have the decency to do it somewhere else. Her home. How could you?!"

He dropped his head into his hands, moaning. "I know. I know. I don't know how it happened."

Carlie walked up behind her. "Go home, Brent."

"Carlie! Please. I'm begging you, give me another chance."

"No. Go home."

"It's *our* home. You belong there, Car. With me. Brent and Carlie forever, remember?"

Seeing the hurt and anger in her sister's face, Rachael

seethed. "Listen to me, Brent, and listen well. You lost her. You fucked up too many times. And you finally crossed the line and thought you could still keep her? Guess what? You. Do not. Deserve. Her." Rachael attempted to slam the door closed, but his foot was wedged in the frame.

"I'm not leaving without you, Carlie."

"It's done," Carlie said bitterly over Rachael's shoulder. "I can't do this anymore. I can't sit at home and pretend you love me, tell myself that you're just too busy with work to be with me. All those late meetings . . . I can't. I just can't."

"I'm not pretending, Carlie. I love you. You know that! Please, we can work this out. Talk to me. Come home with me. God, I love you. Please!" The haunted, pleading look in his red-rimmed eyes was unbearable. Rachael glanced over her shoulder, praying Carlie would stay strong.

You deserve better.

"I can't," she whispered before fleeing into the house.

"No! Carlie! You have to listen to me!"

"Brent, last time," Rachael cautioned. He squinted down at her, his eyes wild. "You are leaving now, or I *will* call the police."

"No need to call the police," said a deep voice. "He's leaving now, aren't you?"

Brent spun around, wobbly. "Who the fuck're you? She belongs with me. I am not leaving here without her."

"I think you are." Gabe stepped into the circle of light on the porch, his pale blue eyes promising destruction as his dark hair swirling in the wind.

Oh. My. God.

Her own freaking avenging angel.

"Carlie!" Brent tried again, straining against Rachael's outstretched arm.

The sound of Carlie sobbing in the house reached them, giving Brent the final push to insanity. He shoved at Rachael wildly, trying to get into the house.

"No!" Rachael screamed, pushing him back. He slammed her against the door frame and threw an elbow at her, landing it squarely in her eye.

Gabe roared. "You do not touch her!" He grabbed Brent by the scruff of the neck, throwing him to the ground outside.

"Go to your sister," Gabe said, breathing heavily and nodding to the house. "I'll take care of this."

Rachael nodded and pressed a hand to her face, stumbling into the house.

Carlie looked up from her tissue and stared, stunned.

"Rachael? Rachael! My God, what happened?"

Rachael sat in the chair and pressed her hands over her eye. "The same fucking eye," she groaned.

Carlie ran to the kitchen and came back moments later with a bag of ice. "Here, want me to hold it?"

Rachael shook her head. "No, I've got it."

They heard a door slam and a car take off down the road.

"He's gone," Carlie whispered.

The front door opened and Gabe stalked in, going straight to Rachael. "I could kill him. Rachael, are you okay?"

She pulled the bag away from her eye and looked at him through the swelling. "I'd really love it if the world would stop bashing the hell out of this eye in the future."

"Damn. You're going to have another doozy of a shiner," Gabe noted.

Thanks.

"Brent did that?" Carlie asked, appalled.

"He heard you crying and lost it."

"Oh, Rach. I am so, so sorry," she cried. "This is all my fault."

"Shh, it's okay," Rachael wrapped an arm around her sister's waist. "It is *not* your fault. It's over. He's gone now." She soothed her as best she could with a bag of ice between them.

Carlie nodded and hiccupped, tears running down her face.

"I need to . . . I have to go do my thing. I'll be back. Are you okay here?" She looked from Rachael to Gabe and back again.

"Yes. Go do what you need to do. Do you need me?"

"No, I can manage."

"Where's she going?" Gabe asked.

Rachael waited until Carlie was out of earshot. "She gets severe panic attacks. Something like this could set her off if she doesn't manage the stress. She's going to meditate."

He looked after her retreating sister. "She's all right?"

"She will be. She's stronger than she looks."

Gabe sat where Carlie had been and examined his knuckles. Bloody and bruised skin marred the tops of both of his fists. "That's going to hurt like a bitch tomorrow."

Rachael scoffed. "I'm hoping Brent's face will hurt worse."

He nodded, reaching to touch her chin, tipping it up so

he could see her eye better. "And a few other places. That son of a bitch deserved that and a lot more."

"He hurt my sister."

"He hurt you," he said furiously.

They sat silently.

"Gabe, the flowers . . ."

"Too much?"

"Too much. Much, much too much. It can't be like that with us."

He looked down at his hands again and flexed his fists. "I have never loved someone like this before. I don't know how to stop. How to go back to being friends."

Rachael took one of his large hands and gently pressed her bag of ice to the knuckles, wishing she could hold it to his heart and make that feel better.

"This is my fault, Gabe. I shouldn't have kissed you, encouraged you. I thought we could be physical again and let it go like the first time. I didn't think . . ." she trailed off, knowing there was no appropriate way to end that.

"The first time I didn't know you. The last time . . ." He cleared his throat. "That last time I did. I know you now, Rachael. You are beautiful and strong. Independent and hellfire, but soft. Smart and funny. Passionate. You are everything I want in a woman. In a partner. Jesus, in a wife. You are the one for me. I love you."

Gasping at his pain, she wrapped her arms around him. "I am so, so sorry. But I can't love you like that."

"Rachael—"

"No, please stop," she begged, a tear sliding down her face. "I can't listen to this anymore. It hurts too much. It hurts you too much. Please, Gabe. I can't bear it."

"I have to say it. I have to know I tried everything. I can't regret this for the rest of my life."

"Please don't," she pleaded, shaking her head.

He got down on a knee and looked up at her swollen face. His battered hands held hers. "I love you, Rachael. I will do everything I can to give you everything you want in life. I will be faithful to you. I'll support you, your family. Travel. Cars. Children. You name it. There's nothing I wouldn't do for you."

She couldn't move, couldn't breathe. The pain ripping her apart was an unbearable torment. "It is a beautiful dream, Gabe. A beautiful fantasy. But it can't be. If you love me . . ." Rachael paused, trying to say the words. "I need you to love me enough to walk away. I am in love with Rick. Completely. Irrevocably."

He watched her, the agony scarring her soul.

"In another life, in another time . . . In another world, this—you and me—this would be everything I could ever wish for, dream of. Your words, your beauty, your passion. You. You are wonderful and I don't deserve you. You deserve someone who loves you the way you love them. And that can't be me." She closed her eyes, unable to look at him anymore. "That can't be me, Gabe."

"Love, please." He lifted her chin, forcing her to look at him. "Don't do this."

"I can't give you what you want, what you're asking." Her chin trembled in his grasp. She loved him, but she would never be able to love him the way she loved Rick. There was no comparison. Yet knowing that didn't make this ending any easier to bear. It didn't lessen the pain or take away the brief history they had shared.

Two solitary tears slid down his cheeks and she wiped them away, fighting to keep her own tears at bay.

"Go now, please," she whispered. "I'm so sorry. I wish nothing but the best for you."

Gabe stood and wiped his face, leaving a line of red across his cheek. "I'll always be here. If you change your mind."

She shook her head, knowing what she had to do. Rachael met his eyes and remained firm, even as it broke her. "I won't. I can't leave that door open."

He swallowed and looked away, nodding to himself. "Then this is goodbye."

"I will always be grateful that you were here for me. Thank you, Gabe. Thank you for being my best friend when I needed one. Thank you for everything."

He reached for her and stopped, seeing the end in her eyes. One last time, he caressed her with his gaze. Then he turned and left, walking out of her life for what she knew would be the last time. It had to be.

She had lost a small, but important, piece of herself forever. It needed to be done. But she couldn't breathe. Couldn't move. Couldn't stop herself from praying for a wall, a barrier, something to isolate the hurt and barrenness. At last, letting the tears fall, she sobbed silently, mourning one lost future, one lost dream, until sleep finally claimed her.

With the morning sun came a calming sense of self-awareness. The loss would always remain with her, but it was a punishment she could acknowledge she deserved. It was of her own making.

Perspective was dawning on her. Here she sat in mourning while her little sister dealt with a much larger blow to her heart, her life. Rachael crept up the stairs to find Carlie sleeping soundly on the guestroom bed, the pale morning light slanting through the slats in the blinds. She didn't budge as Rachael crawled onto the mattress next to her, closing her puffy eyes to try to catch a little more sleep.

It was time to pull herself together. She still had her family. And she hoped she still had Rick.

39

---

*T*he Fourth of July usually brought explosions of color. This was just the first year they had shown up on her face.

"Fuuuuck," Rachael groaned, looking at her reflection in the mirror. "What is it about this eye that begs to be attacked?"

"It's not that bad," Carlie said absently from the couch, flipping through a copy of *Rewired*.

Rachael glared at her.

"At least it won't be that noticeable in the dark?"

"Silver lining," she mumbled and sat next to Carlie. "How are you doing?"

Carlie sighed heavily. "I don't know. I feel kind of blank," she cast a quick glance at her sister, "and guilty. I am so sorry, Rach."

"Carlie, you are not responsible for his actions. Not anymore."

"I know. But your eye." She cringed. "It's awful."

Rachael laughed. "So much for 'It's not that bad.'"

"Sorry," Carlie said with a not-so-sorry shrug. "So, um, are you going to tell me what's going on?"

"With what?"

"Oh, I don't know. The two million roses? The man on the porch last night? Rick? Take your pick."

Rachael checked her phone; still no messages. *Damn*.

"The roses were from Gabe."

Carlie nodded and spun her fingers for her to continue.

"And obviously that was Gabe last night. He took care of Brent."

"Meaning?"

"I suspect he looks far worse than I do this morning."

She accepted this with a grim nod. "Fair enough. What happened after I left?"

Closing her eyes, Rachael took a deep breath and counted to ten before slowly letting it out.

"That bad?" Carlie asked softly.

Rachael nodded. She thought she had cried enough, but fresh tears began to fall.

"Oh, Rach. What happened?"

Brushing the wetness away, she tried to think of how to say it. She finally threw her hands up and let them fall back to the chair at her sides. "I thought I could make it all work. That we could still be friends."

Carlie caught her hand. "And you can't?"

"No."

"Maybe with time."

"Carlie, no. He practically proposed to me."

Carlie's eyes grew wide and she sucked in her breath.

"I know, right?"

They both leaned back into the cushions, thinking and absorbing.

"What now?" Carlie asked, squeezing Rachael's hand.

"I don't know."

"Gabe?"

She shook her head. "Done. For good this time."

"What about the contract?" Carlie asked.

Rachael stared blankly for a minute, then shook her head. "I'll have Mom reassign someone else to McAllister. It would be best for all involved."

Carlie nodded slowly, calculating the risk and reward of such a move. "You're probably right. Sorry, Rach."

Rachael shrugged it off, the job component of their relationship being curiously the least of her worries. Diving into unfamiliar territory, she'd have to play it by ear as best she could.

"And Rick?"

Rachael glanced at her phone again. "I haven't heard from him since he walked out last night after seeing the flowers."

"Nothing?"

"Nada."

"Ouch."

"Yeah."

Carlie rolled her head to the side to look at Rachael. "Want to come with me? To get the keys to my new place?"

Rachael smiled with relief. "Very much so. I need to get out of here."

"Come on," she said, dragging Rachael to her feet. She turned them toward the kitchen. "Let's grab a bottle to christen my new bachelorette pad."

Collecting their things, then hopping into Rachael's black car, they drove the half mile or so to Carlie's new place. The interior had been painted recently and still bore the heavy scent of chemicals from a deep cleaning. The private entrance opened into a foyer with a roomy kitchen to the right and a short hall straight ahead to a generous-sized living room with large windows. A bedroom and large bath veered off to the left.

After a quick tour of the airy one-bedroom apartment, they sat on the hardwood floor of the living room and passed the wine bottle back and forth.

"Sorry, I didn't think to grab glasses," Rachael mumbled. "Or a bottle opener."

Carlie held the bottle eye level, and shrugged. "At least it was a twist-off. We could have had a real emergency."

"When do the movers get here?"

She checked her phone. "Less than an hour."

"I like this. It's nice, Car. Once you get your furniture and," she patted the floor beneath her tush, "maybe a few area rugs, it's going to be amazing. And I love that you're close to Mom and Dad."

Carlie handed the bottle back to Rachael, who took a long drink of the cool white wine. "Wonder what Rick's doing. Why isn't he calling me?"

"You could always call him," Carlie said, reaching for the bottle. "It's not like it's the 1950s. He might even be waiting to hear from you."

It was hard to know what the right thing to do was sometimes.

Compromise. Rachael grabbed her phone and typed out a text.

"What did you say?" Carlie asked, wiping the mouth of the bottle and handing it back to Rachael.

"Told him I was over here with you."

"That's it?"

"What else *should* I say?"

"Oh, I don't know . . . how about I love you?" She rolled her eyes and flopped back on the floor.

Rachael's phone vibrated and Carlie snagged it from between them. "Well, that's lame. But it's a start." She tossed the phone to Rachael.

Still on for the cookout?

Rachael frowned. Definitely not a declaration of love or intent, but at least he wasn't avoiding her. That was an improvement over last time.

"What do you think? Still game for a cookout at Mom and Dad's?" Rachael asked.

Carlie shrugged. "Sure, as long as you help me get my room ready before we leave here."

"Deal." Rachael started to type a message, then deleted it, thinking about her sister's comment.

If you're coming, then yes. Miss you.

What time, he messaged back immediately.

"What time do you think we'll be done here?"

"Dunno. Maybe three?"

Around 5?

I look forward to seeing you then.

He was being so formal. She didn't know how to take it. "Am I making as much of a mess of things as I feel like I am?"

Carlie lolled her head toward Rachael from her sprawled-out position on the wood floor and grasped the neck of the bottle. "Gimme a minute to think about that question." She grinned. "No. In fact, I'd say you're handling your shit pretty well, considering you've had a proposal to live together, a marriage proposal, and a black eye all within the last day or so. From three different men." She took a long drink, eyeing Rachael over it, before sliding the bottle back to her.

"Technically, Gabe didn't propose," Rachael said, rolling the half-empty wine bottle back and forth between her hands. "At least I don't think he did. There wasn't a ring."

"Then it doesn't count. A ring is a must."

"Since when? I know plenty of people who got engaged, then they went to pick out a ring together."

"No ring, no proposal. That's the law."

Rachael laughed at her sister's hard line in the matrimonial sand. "You're so old-fashioned, CarCar."

"Nope, just a romantic at heart," she said with a sigh. "That was part of the problem. I disappointed myself over and over by imagining all the incredible ways he *could* sweep me away. But he never did. I kept hoping Brent would turn out to be that romantic knight in shining armor. Surprise me one day with a candlelit dinner and propose. He could be romantic when he wanted to. But it had been a long freaking time since he showed it."

How often we set ourselves up for disappointment, wishing for the improbable outcomes. Rachael knew that was part of the reason she walled herself off from dating; it was too frustrating to discover their motives were never about her. "Is it really over, Car?"

"I can't trust him again after that. How could I? And I know things were different since we moved in together, but I chalked it up to work and being busy with everything. Life. Now every time I close my eyes I see them together. Gina wrapped around him as he . . . God. I can't believe how stupid I am. I wonder how long it's been going on?"

Rachael slid the cool bottle back to her. "You need this more than I do."

Accepting the bottle, Carlie closed her eyes and spoke aloud. "I keep thinking about Kim. How many times she's gone back to Owen. How can she do that? This is killing me."

"I don't know." And she truly didn't. She stretched across the space between them and chucked her sister on the chin. "But, Car, it *will* get better. For what it's worth, I think you're making the right decision."

"I'm so done with men. I can't go through this again."

"Turning to women?" Rachael joked.

"Why not?"

She looked at Carlie. "Seriously? Not that I'd mind, but that seems a little unlike you."

Carlie shook her head and giggled. "Alas, no. But could you imagine what Brent would do?"

"He'd probably be turned on. Maybe he and Gina can work something out with you."

She groaned. "Please. Gag. They can have each other." She sat up and looked around the space. "Let's figure out where everything is going to go. The movers should be here soon."

40

———————

The crew arrived on time, and after the whirlwind of the delivery, the sisters got to work. Carlie asked approximately three million questions about Rick, and Rachael tried not to gush too much. It was hard not to.

"Here, put this one on top," Carlie said, handing her a soft quilt as they finished up the bedroom.

"Wasn't this mine?" Rachael asked.

"Was it?" Car asked innocently, a light blush staining her cheeks.

"Thief," she muttered, spreading the blanket on top of Carlie's bed. "You know there are devil horns under that halo of yours."

Carlie giggled and slid the stuffed dresser drawers closed.

Rachael glanced around the bedroom. Still not decorated, but it was good enough for now. "What else do we need to do?"

"A few things in the kitchen. If you can help me locate

my Keurig. And a coffee mug. And maybe a water glass. And a bowl and some spoons." She shrugged helplessly. "Guess I should unpack all the kitchen boxes."

Rachael laughed and led the way to the kitchen. "Let's do it."

After they broke down the last empty box in the kitchen, they headed to the front door.

"Ready to go?" Rachael asked.

"You go ahead. I want to shower and feel a little more human before I come over."

"Okie dokie. See you in a few."

Rachael left and climbed into her car. As she pulled away from Carlie's place, she made a mental list of what they needed for the cookout. She rolled the windows down and let the wind blow through her hair.

What a crazy couple of days. She thought about Gabe and Rick. The unbelievable highs and lows, the emotional turmoil. Her heart clenched as she again thought of never seeing Gabe again, but it was countered and then some by the unexpected joy she'd found with Rick. She knew she could trust Rick. He would never destroy her like Brent had Carlie.

Carlie. She couldn't imagine how her sister must be feeling. To walk in on your life partner screwing your friend? Good God. It was enough to make her want to scream. Then all the apartments and houses. The proposals. The black eyes.

Black eyes! SHIT.

Once she parked at the grocery, she examined her puffy, colorful eye in the mirror. Maybe with some large sunglasses? Rachael pulled on her shades and loosened her hair, tugging some over the edges of her glasses. She could only groan and laugh at her reflection; she looked like she was trying out for a role in a bad made-for-TV movie.

Walking through the aisles, she pushed the shopping cart and listened to the squeaky wheels rolling over the linoleum and the bits of gossip that hovered in every supermarket.

Meat, buns, veggies, potatoes, drinks, desserts. She zipped back and forth, entering thoughtless oblivion as she scoured the shelves for anything she might have missed.

"Rachael?"

She turned and inhaled sharply at the pretty she-devil who stood there.

"Gina," Rachael growled.

Gina's black hair framed her olive skin and heart-shaped face. Rachael was surprised she had the nerve to approach her. They were close in height, but miles apart in how they treated her sister.

The traitorous jezebel smiled nervously. "How are you?"

Rachael removed her sunglasses and looked Gina in the eye. "Been better. How about you?"

Gina gawked at her black eye. "What happened?"

Sliding her glasses back on, Rachael turned away. "Ask your buddy, Brent."

"What? Why?"

Rachael walked away, pushing her cart down the aisle until she felt a tugging at her arm. She muttered under her breath then cut Gina with a glare. "What do you want, Gina?"

"What happened? Brent told me he got jumped."

Cackling, she shoved the glasses back on her face and walked away again, turning into the next aisle.

"Rachael?" Gina asked in a small voice.

She stopped and turned back. "What?"

"Can you tell Carlie that I'm sorry?"

"Go to hell. All the men you screw—yes, everyone knows—and you had to go and fuck Carlie's man. Go crawl back to Brent. You two deserve each other."

Furious, Rachael stalked off, leaving Gina standing by the ketchup and other condiments. She needed a bottle of mustard, but like hell she was going back anywhere near that bitch. They could do without. She stormed down the aisle toward the registers.

Calm down, Rach. Calm the F down.

"Rachael!"

Smiling, she turned toward a voice she needed to hear. "Marie!" Rachael glanced behind her and didn't see Gina. At least she'd finally gotten the message to leave her alone.

"There's my bluebird. What are you up to today? The boys are all in town. You girls want to come over? Carlie can bring Brent, too. We can watch the fireworks later."

Rachael cringed and shook her head slowly. "Um. Carlie left Brent."

Marie blinked. "What?"

"She found out he was having an affair. So she left."

Marie puffed up, her righteous anger rising. "That boy doesn't have one brain cell in his thick head. I always knew she was too good for him. Who was the hussy?"

"Hussy?" She giggled at the phrase.

"The tramp. She will not be welcome in my shop. Who was it?" Marie demanded.

My, my. This was a side of Marie she didn't get to see very often. Rachael loved it. "One of Carlie's friends. *Ex-*friends," she said.

Rachael heard a gasp and turned to see Gina had reappeared behind her. The woman was every-fucking-where.

"What?" Rachael snapped, ripping her glasses off to glare at Gina. "Did you think you were still friends? After that?"

"Rachael! My God—your face! What happened?" Marie cried.

Shit. "Ask this hussy over here. Brent happened."

Marie eyeballed Gina while Rachael walked to the open lane, ready to checkout in more ways than one.

"Brent did that?" Gina blinked in astonishment. Rachael shook her head at Gina's absurd blend of obtuse innocence and man-stealing prowess.

"Yes. Though to be fair, it was his elbow. He was trying to break into the house. To patch things up with Carlie. He begged her to forgive him, pleaded with her to come home with him. He said she was the only one for him. That you were nothing to him—you were nothing but a mistake." *Let her stew on that.*

Gina flinched, her cheeks stained with guilt.

"I hope to God she had the good sense to turn him down," Marie huffed.

"Oh, yes. A friend of mine helped to take the trash to the curb." Rachael turned back to Gina. "Now go away."

Her head pounding, Rachael swept the groceries onto the conveyor belt and leaned on the cart handle, willing the cashier to move faster.

Marie wrapped her arms around Rachael. "I'm here if

you or Carlie need anything at all. You girls come see me this week, yes?"

She nodded. "We will. Love you, Marie. Tell the boys I said hello."

"I'll do that, honey. Now you go home and rest. Dinner's at seven if you change your mind. The door's always open."

"Thank you."

"I have to go get some pie. But I'll stand here and make sure she doesn't bother you anymore until you're done."

Marie was truly the best.

"*Hussy?*" Her sister choked with laughter as she helped Rachael put groceries away.

"Hussy." Rachael confirmed.

Carlie snorted. "That may be my new favorite word. What happened after that?"

"Not much. But I think it's safe to assume that Gina will not be showing her face around that Kroger for a while."

"Which makes it my new favorite place to shop."

They dumped the chopped vegetables into the salad bowl and Carlie tossed it with the vinaigrette. "What's next?" she asked.

"I think we're all set. Now we just have to see if and when Kim and Owen show up. And Rick."

"Are you nervous?" Carlie asked.

Hell yes. "No, I'm good."

"Have you thought about what he asked? Living together?"

Nonstop. Rachael shook her head. "Been a little busy."

Carlie grinned. "Liar. But you have nothing to worry about. I know you'll make the right decision."

That makes one of us. Ugh. "I'm going to touch up my makeup. Can you let Olive and Martini out for me?"

Nervous energy coursed through her as Rachael jogged up the stairs. She sat on the edge of her bed, trying to force herself to calm down. Why did this have to be so overwhelming? Shouldn't it be easy? Dad always said when it was right, it was right. She knew without question that Rick was the right man. But why didn't everything fit together? It was all wonky. Like puzzle pieces that hadn't been cut properly.

She picked up her phone and hit send.

"Charles Eller at your service," he answered on the second ring.

"Hi, Dad. How is your vacation?"

"It's great, pumpkin. How are things at home? Feeling well? I assume you're taking care of your sister?"

"Mhm. She's here now, helping me get things ready. We're having a cookout."

"That sounds nice. You're not cooking, are you? I'd like to come home to an intact kitchen."

She rolled her eyes. "Ha, ha. Funny guy. But no, I'm not cooking. You can relax."

His chuckle was contagious. "Are you girls going to watch the fireworks tonight?"

"That's the plan, as long as the weather holds. How about you? Any fireworks?"

"Yes, your mother and I made some sparks."

Her eyes widened. "Dad! Gross! I can't unhear that!"

He laughed and she relaxed to the sound of his voice. "Now, you want to tell me why you're calling?"

"Can't a girl just call her dad?"

"Of course. But what else is concerning you?"

Rachael chewed on her lip and debated what to say, how much to share. "It's been a rough couple of days. Gabe came back and said he can't be friends. I basically had to choose all or nothing with him."

"That's not a fair proposition."

At least he got it. "No. So I did what I had to do."

He was quiet. "He's gone?"

"Yes," she whispered.

He muttered something under his breath. "I'm sorry, Rachael. I know he meant a lot to you."

"And Rick is back in the picture." She stretched her palm out across the bed where her life had become tied to his.

"Olive's vet? Is that good?"

"Yes, but what if things are moving too fast?"

"Then take a step back."

He made it sound so simple. She leaned back on her arm and thought about Rick. About the future.

"I feel like things are right with Rick. But it doesn't feel easy. I can't make up my mind."

"You're confusing the two, honey. Right isn't always easy and easy isn't always right. Sometimes you have to trust yourself to make the choices that are right for the moment. Figure out what will keep things right. Change the things that are wrong. And trust yourself to learn from the wrong choices. That takes courage and more than a little bit of wisdom."

She thought of Marie's words. They sounded like they were cut from the same cloth. "How do you do it?"

"One decision at a time. One foot in front of the other, and just keep moving forward."

"Easier said than done, but I'll try. Thanks, Dad."

"You're welcome. And Rach? Your mother and I are both very proud of the young woman you've become. Any decision you make, good or bad, we are here for you. I love you, sweetheart."

"Love you, too."

She wiped the moisture from her face and mulled over his words. Courage and wisdom. She sure could use a little extra of each right about now.

41

"**K**nock, knock! Can I come in?" Kim poked her head around the bedroom door. Rachael waved her in and she plopped onto the bed. "Hussy, huh?"

"She told you?" Rachael asked.

"Classic Marie. She should write a book. I'd read every fucking word. Twice." She whistled. "I'd hate to see what that looks like without the makeup. It's not pretty now."

"I did what I could," Rachael shrugged, patting the concealer around her eye.

"Does Rick know?"

"No. But it will be easy enough to explain."

Her skeptical look spoke volumes. "Uh-huh. Sure. You don't think he'll wonder how it got there? Who did it?"

"All easily explained."

"And Gabe's involvement?"

Crap. "What are you doing here already?" Rachael hedged. "I didn't expect you until closer to sunset."

"I thought you said five?"

"I know what I said, but you're actually early? Are you feeling all right?"

"I do have a clock, you know."

"Oh?" Rachael asked, all innocence. "Did someone show you how to use it?"

Kim flipped her the bird then shifted on the bed. "Actually, I was coming up here to see if Owen and I can steal Carlie away after we eat. A bunch of our old high school friends are in town. Going to catch a few drinks."

"Are you asking me for permission?"

"Guess so. I don't want to leave you here alone. Especially if . . ."

"If what?"

"If things don't go so well," Kim said bluntly. "You haven't told him about Gabe. Don't think I didn't catch you skipping over my question."

Oh.

Quirking her lips, Rachael tilted her head. "Things are going to go, whether they go well or not. I'll be fine, Kim. But thank you for thinking of me. You guys go have fun."

"You're sure?"

"I'm sure. Now go pour me a glass of wine. I'll be down in a minute."

"'Kay. And Rach?"

"Hmm?"

"You look stunning. He's not going to be able to take his eyes off you."

Rachael blushed. "Thanks."

Kim nodded and slipped out of the room.

Rachael took a last look in the floor-length mirror. Her short denim skirt and red tank top hugged her figure. She pulled on a breezy white lace shrug and flip flops. Backyard cookout casual, but still sexy. She could work it. Even if she did have another freaking black eye. She played with her long curls and tried to figure out if she could hide the eye, then gave up. Why bother trying to hide it? If she had to deal with it, they could deal with it.

"Here goes," she whispered.

Now to see if he showed up.

Courage. Wisdom. Please, God. Let me make the right decisions, say the right things.

The clock edged past five, and still no sign of Rick. Rachael tried to not stress. She busied herself with straightening up the house, talking to the dogs, playing hostess to the girls and Owen, and obsessively *not* checking the time.

Owen and Kim were on the deck with Carlie. They took on the task of grilling the burgers. Rachael finished picking up in the kitchen and was kneeling on the floor, searching for a plastic bowl for the chips in a cabinet when she heard him arrive.

Trying not to drop the tower of dishes that housed the one she wanted, she glanced over her shoulder to see Rick lounging at the entrance to the kitchen. He looked simply delicious in his khaki cargo shorts and plain white t-shirt.

"Need help down there?" he asked.

"No, I'm good. I wasn't sure you would come."

"I wouldn't miss it. And I certainly wouldn't want to miss this view," he whistled appreciatively.

That's encouraging.

Time to get the first shock out of the way.

Taking a deep breath, Rachael shoved the extra dishes back in the cabinet and stood, turning fully toward him.

His whistle took a turn for the dramatic as he saw her puffy, colorful eye. "What happened?"

"It wasn't a door if that's what you're wondering," she joked.

Rick frowned and touched the tender skin around her eye, noting her wince in pain. "Good God, Rachael. I need to cover you in bubble wrap and get you a helmet. Now tell me what happened."

"Last night, after you left, Brent came over and tried to get in to see Carlie." His face darkened and she set her palm against his chest. "It's fine. He didn't get in." Rachael hesitated briefly. "Gabe showed up. He got rid of Brent."

Rick digested this, his face tight. "Gabe? He was here?"

She nodded slowly. "Yes, but he left."

"What happened?" His face was impassive, and she swallowed nervously.

"Can we sit down, please?" It was hard enough telling him this without the extra foot-and-a-half height difference. She wanted—no, she needed—to see his eyes as she explained what happened. He had to see the truth.

He stalked out to the living room and sat on the recliner. Rachael took a deep breath and settled on the edge of the sofa to face him. "Brent showed up, completely lit. He was a mess. I asked him to leave several times—I even threatened to call the cops. Gabe showed up then and went after Brent when he elbowed me in the face. Brent heard Carlie crying in here and went completely berserk. I don't even think he realized he hit me."

Rick's hands tightened into fists and his mouth flattened. "Go on."

"I came back in here to be with Carlie while Gabe beat the shit out of him."

"Good."

"Afterwards, he came in here and Carlie left to go calm down."

"It was just the two of you?"

"Yes, but nothing happened, Rick. I told Gabe nothing was ever going to happen between us. I told him I couldn't do this anymore. He left for good this time. He's gone, out of my life."

Rick rocked the recliner forward and leaned toward her over his knees, his hands steepled in front of him. "I believe you."

"You do?"

"Yes. I trust you. I'm upset that I wasn't the one here to protect you. But I believe you."

Thank God. "I was worried when you left last night without a word," she whispered.

"Sorry, baby. I was angry. But not at you."

"It felt like you were angry with me. You didn't text. Call. Nothing."

He shook his head and ran a hand through his hair. "I can see I need to work on my communication skills. I didn't know you were waiting to hear from me."

Rachael narrowed her eyes. "Rick, come on. You left without a word. You didn't think I would be worried?"

"I'm sorry. I'll try harder."

She stared in his eyes, seeing that he meant it.

"Rach? Burgers are ready!" Kim hollered.

"We'll be right there! Ready to eat?" she asked him.

He stood and pulled her up. In flip flops, their height difference was almost funny. He ran a hand down the back of her head and kissed her gently. "Now I'm ready."

329

42

———

Bringing the last of the dishes to the patio table, Rachael introduced Rick to Owen and the makeshift family conversation resumed. The air was heavy with hints of smoke from the bottle rockets and other Fourth of July explosives, and the distinctive odor of charred burgers.

"They're not *all* burnt," Owen pouted as Kim used the tongs to search through the platter of steaming meat.

"I suppose it depends on your definition of burnt. There are clearly different levels of char. Light burn, medium burn, and brittle black brick. Well done, handsome," Kim teased. "Remind me not to let you grill again. Ever."

Rick was walking around the yard with Carlie, talking and playing with the dogs. Rachael was tickled that they were making an effort to get to know each other. Carlie had her phone out, taking pictures of Olive and Martini. They began to return when Carlie's phone rang. "Movers," she said, nodding at Rick. "They want to confirm everything got delivered. They said they'd need to talk to you, too." They descended back into the yard, taking turns talking to the moving company.

When they rejoined the rest of the group a few minutes later, everyone loaded up their plates and sat on the deck. Olive and Martini settled quickly at Rick's feet, watching and hoping for further droppings.

"See this?" Rachael pouted. "He's already stolen my dogs!"

Carlie giggled and tossed a pinch of hamburger bun to each of them. "He's a clever one. He found the secret path to your heart, Rach—the dogs! Though I must warn you, Rick, don't you dare try to come between the furballs and Auntie Carlie!"

He saluted her with his bottle of beer. "No worries on that front."

A lone firework popped over the tree line and the dogs didn't even glance away from the food-dropping humans. One less reason to stress. Rachael smiled. Looking around the table, she counted so many blessings to be thankful for.

And she saw the scorched, untouched pile of meat. "Let me see what kind of leftovers are in the fridge," she stage-whispered before running into the kitchen.

Owen followed her, anxious to redeem himself with some form of edible entree. She handed him a covered dish of cold chicken and he floated out to the applause of the assembled. Rachael watched the group laughing and diving into the main course, then set to making more pink lemonade. She may not be a great cook, but she could mix powder and water.

"You coming back out?" Carlie asked from the doorway.

"In a minute." Rachael grinned, a giant mixing spoon at the ready. "Did you need something?"

Carlie glanced at their gathered friends over her shoulder then lowered her voice. "I wanted to tell you that I like him. I like you two together. A lot. Something about him and you together. It works. And I'm sorry I freaked out about it."

Giving the mixture one last swirl, Rachael left the spoon to dance in lazy circles around the pitcher and smiled at her sister's earnestness. "No need to apologize. He's pretty great, right?"

"He is. You're going to move in with him, right?"

"Yeah, I think so. Is that crazy?"

Carlie looked out the window over her shoulder and back at her sister. "You know something? I did think it was nuts. But now? I think it would be good for you. I can't tell you how happy it makes me to see you crazy in love. Finally."

Rachael hugged Carlie and swiped at her own eyes. "I cut up some onions earlier. Must be from that."

"Sure, sure, short stuff," Carlie went along, returning the hug. "You're back at the office this week, right?"

Rachael cleared her throat and nodded, grateful for the change in subject. "Yes, as long as Mom doesn't see my fresh prizefighter eye and decide to keep me away. My clients are thrilled to not have to deal with Larry anymore."

"Larry! God. I can't believe Mom would do that to you."

"It could be worse, I suppose." Carlie looked at her, waiting. "She could have hired Gina."

Her sister groaned. "Too soon, girl. Too soon."

Returning to the patio together, Rachael and Carlie stared in awe as more stray firecrackers lit up the sky. Owen raised his drink to the tree line. "Wait until it's dark out! No one can see them yet!"

They ate and drank, sharing stories from their childhoods, laughing about Kim and Carlie's college days, and talking about work and the latest movies and music. All in all, it was pretty darn perfect, considering the broken heart and black eye at the table.

After polishing off the desserts, Kim and Carlie offered to clean the kitchen, and Owen played with the dogs in the yard.

"He seems nice enough," Rick observed.

Rachael watched the carefree Owen laugh and zigzag across the lawn. "Yes, I just wish he was the right guy for her."

"What makes you think he isn't?"

"A hunch. Not to mention, they've broken up and gotten back together more often than soap opera characters."

Rick chuckled and sat back. "Time will tell."

It certainly would. A few months ago, this would never have been a worry. Live and let live. But now that she knew what it felt like to be in love and to want to commit to another person, her eyes were opened to the complex problems her sister and de facto sister faced. As her brain outlined ways to integrate all of her passions—Rick, the dogs, work, and her family—she was at peace and for the first time felt like everything was going the way it should. At least in her life.

When the girls came back out, they were carrying their handbags. "Ready?" Kim called to Owen.

Owen jogged up to them. "Thanks for having us over, Rach. Rick, nice to meet you. Take care of little half-pint here."

"I will," Rick responded, shaking his hand. "I look forward to catching your next show."

Rachael gave him a quick hug, then said goodbye to Carlie and Kim. "Be careful," she called as they ran out the door.

"Yes, Mom," Carlie called back, giggling.

Rachael smiled, glad to see her sister having fun and getting out.

"Wait!" Carlie called, reappearing in the doorway.

"What?" Rachael asked.

"You have to call me later."

"I do?"

"Yes."

"All right. You okay?"

Carlie nodded and ran back out the door.

Weirdness.

The sun was past its prime, promising a lovely sunset later, and they had the whole evening ahead of them.

"Another glass of wine?"

"Sounds perfect." She smiled, accepting the offering.

Sitting on the patio, they sipped and watched the sun start to kiss the horizon.

"Want to go for a walk?" Rick asked. "I've got about a pound of chicken and potatoes to work off."

She nodded, content to simply spend time together.

He took her hand and they left the dogs to play in the yard.

They walked to the end of the driveway and strolled down the wide, tree-lined street. The cicadas were calling and the streetlights were starting to flicker to life. They walked hand in hand, lazily roving the neighborhood and turning down a quiet side street.

A comfortable silence surrounded them, unbroken until they got about a block down the next street.

"Rachael, have you thought about what I asked?"

She nodded slowly. "I have."

They came to a stop and he stood in front of her, taking hold of both of her hands. "And?"

"I love you," she said simply, shrugging her shoulders as though that was all he needed to know.

Smiling broadly, he kissed her soft lips. "I love you too. But that's not your answer, is it?"

"It's the most important answer."

A crooked smile warmed his face. "This is true."

Rick continued walking and she stopped, frowning at the scene ahead of her. "Oh, that's sad."

"What?"

"There's that house."

The "for sale" sign had been changed to "sale pending." Rachael sighed. "It was silly anyways."

"Dreams are never silly, baby."

"This one was."

They crossed the street to look at the house that had so captivated her. The lights were on in the lower level.

"It looks empty," he said, walking up the driveway.

Her eyes widened and she gasped, trailing after him.

"Rick! What are you doing? We can't go up to someone else's house!"

Keeping a firm grip on her hand, Rick tugged Rachael along the path to the front door, peeking around the columns to see if anyone was inside. "If no one's here, who will know?"

"I'll know! And besides, they probably have one of those video doorbells. We'll be on everyone's social media, snooping in someone's house, stealing packages," she giggled. "America's most wanted!"

"Are you planning to steal something?"

"No," she scowled.

"I know. I'm teasing you." Rick laughed and dropped a kiss on top of her head. "Let's just pretend for a moment. Imagine someday we had a place like this. I'd come home to you each night."

"Or I'd come home to you," she amended.

He chuckled and wrapped an arm around her, looking at the front door. "Would we have a chair out here?"

"Hmm. Maybe a glider. White. That would be nice. Right there." She stepped forward and pointed to the wider part of the porch in front of the large double picture windows.

"And at Christmas, I'd string lights along these columns."

"And garland." Rachael smiled, picturing snow and colorful lights reflected off the white powder in the evening.

"Someday there would be kids, and a big yellow school bus stopping out here to pick them up."

No longer immune to that thought, she was carried away by imagining a pair of boys running down the street.

A little girl chasing after them with sparklers. Martini and Olive barking at their mischief. Toddlers running through the sprinklers in shorts and t-shirts, kids dressed up for trick-or-treating, a family building a snowman.

"That sounds wonderful," she said dreamily.

A brief burst of fireworks pushed the vision away. Blinking back to the present, she turned to see him holding his hand out, a flat box the size of a stack of business cards in his palm.

Confused, she met his eyes.

"I lost you once because I was a fool. And last night I worried I had lost you again. I can't keep wondering, worrying that I haven't made my intentions clear. I am lost without you, Rachael. You are the only thing I think about. When I wake up, when I go to work, when I eat, when I get home to my empty house. None of it matters without you. I love you. You have become my whole world. I know this is fast and I know you have worries, but I will be here for you. With you. I will be your partner. I will support you in whatever you want to do. Just promise me you'll share it with me."

Rick opened the box and a silver key winked in the light from the window.

Confusion and blankness merged; she couldn't give thought to what she was seeing. "What is this?"

He smiled as he picked up the key and unlocked the door, holding it open for her.

"Rick?"

He swept his arm toward the foyer and she walked in hesitantly, gaze brushing the bright floors, the creamy walls. The scents of floor and furniture polish mingled with the fresh clean air in the house. Lights were on throughout the first floor, but they were the only ones there.

Rick has a key to the house. THE house.

"When we walked through this house before, you fell in love. I saw it. I recognized it. And I wanted it for you. For Olive and Martini. For us, if you'll have me." Closing the door behind her, he turned her for a soft kiss, then took her hand, leading her around the staircase and through to the kitchen, where a bouquet of dark-red roses, greenery, and bursts of fresh baby's breath sat in an elegant crystal vase. A white velvet ring box sat before it.

Oh. My. God.

She couldn't breathe. Stunned, she peered up at him, speechless.

He crossed to the kitchen counter and looked into her eyes, her heart.

"I love you. You said you love romance novels, the grandiose gestures, the commitment. You said they don't exist. But they do. Between us. I'm giving this to you. We don't have to live here, but it's yours. I can wait. I can give you time. But say that you'll be mine?"

Tears slid down her face and she took a shaky breath, staring at him in wonder. Rick picked up the box and dropped to a knee before her, taking her hand in his.

"Rachael Eller, will you marry me?" He opened the box, displaying a perfect solitaire on a gold band.

"Rick," she gasped.

A flood of emotions rushed through her. She turned her head, surveying all that he had done. Rachael gazed into his eyes, noting the flickers of hope and nerves. Shaking, she held out her hand, and he slid the ring onto her finger. It was too big, but she didn't care.

"I know how important your family is to you. Charles and Carlie both gave me their blessing. Mary . . . well, she said it was up to you." He gave her his trademark crooked smile. "Will you? Please say you'll marry me," he said, grasping her hands in his.

"You talked to them?" she asked wonderingly.

Rick smirked. "It wasn't the moving company on the phone."

Closing her eyes, she took a deep breath and held it. She counted to ten, and with each number, each heartbeat, she saw another aspect of him that she loved more than the last. Rachael saw what led them here, saw them now, and saw their future together.

"Yes," Rachael whispered. "Yes to everything. To you, to this house, to our future. Yes, Rick. I want it all."

He stood and scooped her up, kissing her with all the passion she could dream of. And more.

It felt right.

LOOK OUT FOR BOOK 2

COMING 2022

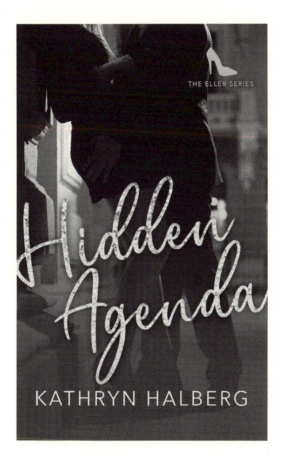

Thank you for reading *Animal Attraction*.

Please consider leaving a review so that other readers can find this title.

OTHER GENZ ROMANCES

All You Hold On To (Anderson Creek #1) by K.T. Egan
Escaping to the Country by E.A. Stripling
The *Internal Conflict* Series by E.A. Stripling
Take My Whole Life Too by Justine Ruff
The *Randolph Duology* by Catherine Edward

ABOUT THE AUTHOR

KATHRYN HALBERG is the contemporary romance author of Animal Attraction, the Eller Series #1, and the upcoming sequel Hidden Agenda, The Eller Series #2. She is a weaver of words to help you feel connected to the world around you. Often found with a large mug of coffee in one hand, her nose is perpetually buried in her laptop or smartphone, working round-the-clock in social media, reading, or writing. She holds a Bachelor of Science from Towson University in Baltimore, Maryland, and a Master of Business Administration from Wright State University in Dayton, Ohio. Kathryn resides in Ohio with her husband, their houseful of boys, and her lone female companion, an elderly dog named Chelsea Bell.

Connect with her: **KathrynHalberg.com**

facebook.com/KathrynHalberg

twitter.com/KathrynHalberg

instagram.com/KathrynHalberg